THE
COLORS
OF SNOW

THE
COLORS
OF SNOW

Kate Fenton

DOUBLEDAY

New York London Toronto Sydney Auckland

PUBLISHED BY DOUBLEDAY

a division of Bantam Doubleday Dell Publishing Group, Inc.
666 Fifth Avenue, New York, New York 10103

DOUBLEDAY and the portrayal of an anchor
with a dolphin are trademarks of Doubleday,
a division of Bantam Doubleday Dell
Publishing Group, Inc.

Library of Congress Cataloging-in-Publication Data

Fenton, Kate.
[Colours of snow]
The colors of snow / Kate Fenton.—1st ed. in the United States
of America.
p.   cm.
First published in Great Britain under the title: The colours of
snow.
I. Title.
PR6056.E54C65   1991   90-37979
823'.914—dc20   CIP

ISBN 0-385-41702-0

Printed in the United States of America

JULY 1991

FIRST EDITION IN THE UNITED STATES OF AMERICA

1   3   5   7   9   10   8   6   4   2

THE
COLORS
OF SNOW

OCTOBER

October had been a disappointing month so far. Damp, grey and withered.

I stood by the window scanning the road three floors below for Sebastian's van. A taxi was pulling up behind a 137 bus, and beyond them a lorry groaned as it hoisted a brimming skip on to its back. Where was the bastard?

This morning, the Common was disappearing into a dank mist beyond the first clump of trees. The leaves, in this dull light, were not gold and orange but dry, rusty brown. The grass, after a long and (for me) uncomfortably warm summer, was brittle and colourless as cheaply-bleached hair.

I suppose this is the appearance many people expect of October – dull, faded and tattered. For them, October signals the end of the summer just as winter portends the death of the old year. And it is undeniable that October is scattered with the evidence of time and decay: rotting fruits, desiccated foliage, balding flowerbeds.

For me though – illogically maybe, I grant you – October has always been a month of new beginnings, radiant with promise, quick with potential. Never more so than this particular October. The course of my life was set to change irrevocably any minute now . . .

I winced, suddenly breathless, and sat down at my drawing board.

Maybe my own feeling is something to do with the rhythm of academic terms. The new year for schools always begins in October. I had loathed school, but there was no denying that with each year, with each step up the hierarchy, it became more bearable. And after school the sweet pleasures of life were waiting to be discovered at college which opened its doors to me on a crisp October morning. I moved in with Sebastian in October. In October years later, I bought this bright and beautiful eyrie for myself. Sharp possessive pride in my home had barely dulled, even over the last three months when, occasionally, the flat had begun to take on the aspect of a prison.

Besides, it had amused me to reflect, when I was in danger of sliding, hippopotamus-like, into a muddy wallowing hole of self-pity, that I shared the decorative habits of old lags. My cell, in the time-honoured tradition, featured a generous acreage of naked and rampantly sexy flesh. Not magazine cut-outs for me, though, nor was the flesh female.

The wall behind my drawing board was hung with a single full-length acrylic of a nude man. He's lying down. His skin, warm in reflected firelight, is the beige-gold of thick honey. His hair is rumpled and damp with sweat after (and this was apparently obvious to the most casual viewer) prolonged and exhausting love-making. His eyes are closed as he dozes, but were he to open them you would see that they were of an indeterminate hazel shade, somewhere between gold and khaki. He has an immensely kind face.

This picture had both tormented and comforted me through the long dragging summer months. Now I was sorry I could not take it with me. When Christopher from the gallery had seen the painting he had been desperate to include it in the exhibition. Even though he accepted I would not sell it, he practically begged me on bended knee to lend it to the gallery for the duration. He said it was the best thing I'd ever done. But it could never go on public exhibition, and I could not fully explain to him why. Not without betraying too much. Christopher took serious offence and did not speak to me for a week.

The exhibition had opened for the private view last night. Cheap and well-chilled Sauvignon had been sipped from Christopher's elegant hired flutes, compliments fluttered like paper darts and a measle rash of red dots had begun to sprout before I left, as early as I decently could.

'Of course they're being nice. They're all frightened of what happens if you get upset,' Christopher had hissed in an undertone as he drifted past smiling. He had still not fully forgiven me for the male nude.

For myself, I had looked at the pictures — hazy quilted hills, walls pieced from a jigsaw of greys, mirror-calm waters, and people to match the strong silence of the landscape — and I wondered why I had not stuck to painting cities, my natural habitat. I could not imagine that these simple daubs could mean anything at all to this shiny clever crowd. I was embarrassed that I was responsible. It seemed like inviting Martians to appreciate cricket.

Sebastian had not come to the private view. Seb never went to private views. Not even under these circumstances. I had pretended I did not mind. I wasn't even sure whether I did mind or not. I had a suspicion he might be in the gallery this morning, this very minute, casting his cruelly appraising eye over Christopher's subtly spotlit walls. I told myself I didn't care what he thought, that I didn't even want to know.

All I wanted to know was where the hell he was. I walked again to the window. The road below was empty now. A black dog chased its tail round on the scrubby grass of the Common.

Don't panic. Mustn't panic. No need to panic.

Sebastian had installed his answering-machine two months ago. He had pretended it was for my benefit. How else could he justify the purchase of such a bourgeois toy? I had telephoned him an hour ago. Recorded a message with, I thought at the time, admirably understated hysteria. Perhaps I should have been less restrained. Surely, wherever he was, he must telephone home for messages soon?

In front of me, on the desk, was the catalogue of the exhibition.

WINTER IN YORKSHIRE

(Christopher had titled the exhibition, not me, but it seemed innocuous and was appropriate enough.)

Watercolours and acrylics by Frances Cleverdon.

The list of titles and prices was printed on silky-fine, dove-grey card. Christopher did that kind of thing with expensively good taste. The length of the prices inside demonstrated how he could afford to. Stuck on the front was a single photograph of the first painting in the exhibition.

I had not been able to muster the courage to tell Christopher that this painting was not for sale either. Ludicrous, isn't it? But after our last fracas, I simply didn't have the heart. So I had gone to the lengths of arranging for a stooge to buy FISHERMAN I as the first glasses of wine were being lifted from the trays. Rosie told me she had nearly expired with terror, nochalantly signing her name to a debt three times the size of her present overdraft. I reassured her that I would give her the money long before she ever need pay the gallery.

Buying my own picture. Some of the money would roll back to me, of course. It simply meant I would have to fork out Christopher's outrageous commission. Too bad. This painting was long promised to someone else.

Now this picture portrayed October as it should be. As, in my mind, October always is . . .

CHAPTER ONE

Imagine a great fat bear. He is gazing down at the glassy water which laps round his seven-league wellington boots. He appears bewildered. It is as if water were a substance new to him.

He wears a misshapen tweed hat which is eggcup-small on his magnificent ursine head. His sagging beige sweater must have stripped three sheep in the making. In one paw he holds a tube and I will swear – even at this distance – it is a tube of Smarties. Or rather, a tube which once held Smarties. Retrieving it from some fathoms-deep pocket in his breeches, Mr Bear has clumsily dislodged the cap. The bright pills have showered into the river, and that is why he is studying, puzzled and sorrowful, first the tube, then the tell-tale interlocking rings of ripples round his legs.

This is what I saw below me in the River Wrag on a gold and crimson October afternoon.

In my experience, the vital pivots on which one's life swivels tend to pass unrecognised at the time. The course of my life, anyway, has been governed less by profound decisions I have consciously weighed and pondered, than by absurdities. The fundamental turning points have crept up on me, camouflaged and innocent as a sheet of black ice. Suddenly, without touching the controls of the vehicle, you find you are facing in a different direction.

For instance, because I missed the train to my interview in Hull, I ended up at art college in London instead. Now, after days of ignoring the listless castings and wanderings up and down the bank of one or two other anglers, the fact that I happened to glance out of the window at the precise instant this huge and bear-like man dropped his sweeties, was to have an equally – if not more – profound impact on my life.

At the time, I burst out laughing. Closeted behind my sash windows, far above the river, I had no fear of injuring Mr Bear's feelings. Uncontrollable gusts folded me up like the cramp, and collapsed me with a bump on the meanly-padded holiday cottage sofa.

I don't know why the tableau struck me as so funny. Maybe it wasn't. Maybe, after eight days of solitude, my brain was softening. Anyone laughing alone in an empty house can easily begin to feel maniacal. Also, if you're as wretchedly despondent as I was, you might laugh at anything just to keep warding off the tears.

Only minutes earlier, sitting at my table with acre after blank creamy acre of virgin cartridge paper spread in front of me, I had decided this whole venture was mistaken. I had fallen prey, I realised bleakly, to the myth. Sebastian was right.

'You're off your head, Fanny,' he had said when I confided my plans. 'People think that just because the surroundings are beautiful, you'll automatically produce beautiful work. It's a myth. Beauty's in here ...' He did not indicate his eye (as in the beholder) or even his head, but tapped his chest. I think he meant the soul. From an Irish Catholic family, Sebastian is prone to referring to the soul even if his manner of living seems deliberately designed to imperil it. 'I like the country – you like the country, sure. To visit. But you're a city sparrow, not a country ... whatever bird lives out there. Anyway, you'll go out of your mind.'

I told myself he was only saying this because (secretly) he didn't want me to leave London. Ha bloody ha. I could be gone for a month before Seb noticed when the work fever was gripping him.

'And you won't have me around for advice,' he added. 'There's no way I can get up to Yorkshire in the next couple of months.'

'I don't want your advice,' I snapped. 'All you've told me for the last two years is that everything I've painted is crap. That kind of help I can do without.'

6

'If you can't take honesty you shouldn't come to me,' he replied distantly. There were times when I could see Sebastian with his thin, pale face and bright blue eyes as one of the early martyrs. Tied to the stake he would coolly disregard the smouldering faggots as he restated the immutable truth-as-he-saw-it.

Gerald at least said he would miss me very much. I was sure he would — in between the expenses-paid jaunts abroad, the twelve-hour working days in the City, and the wife and two kids in Hertfordshire.

'Where is this place anyway? I couldn't even see it on the map.'

'A valley running through the North Yorkshire Moors, Gerald. An old keeper's lodge four miles or so from the village. Sounds idyllic to me.'

'You do realise, Frances darling, that you'll be snowed up from now until Easter, of course?'

There spoke the dyed-in-the-wool southerner. Born near Manchester myself, I did not automatically pack skis and Winalot for the huskies. Even I, however, could not have anticipated this weather. The heat and sunshine had been smashing weather records daily.

Moreover, no artist could have asked for surroundings more beautiful than the Wrag Valley. The cottage I had rented for the winter months perched on a south-facing slope above a salmon river. For a week I had watched the moors toast under this extraordinary Indian summer from purple to brown. Swathes of bracken glowed more brilliantly on the hillsides than the polished copper jugs in the local pub. The last fat blackberries gleamed secretively in the bramble hedge round my wilderness of a garden, and the apples on the tree down by the river were small, warm from the sun and richly sweet as vintage port.

On arrival here, eight days ago, I had at once arranged the stout square table under the window of the sitting-room in order to benefit fully from the light and the panorama. A wad of folded reject sketches evened out disparities between flagged floor and table legs. Over the drunkenly slanted window-sill which, to pierce the cottage wall, was two feet deep, my steel toolbox scattered pencils and pastels, crayons and fine-tipped pens, brushes and rags — all the usual debris of a painter.

And in eight days, I had painted nothing.

I don't want to imply I'm the kind of wally who sits around brush poised, waiting for inspiration to drop out of the sky. I could have picked up a pencil, drawn any one of a hundred things — but there was nothing here asking to be drawn. Not by me, anyway. So that was why I was concluding Seb had been absolutely right. My milieu was houses not hills, streets not hedgerows, and streams of traffic — not of salmon-infested water.

Until I glanced up and saw that fisherman. I wasn't sure what attracted me to him — I had observed the odd fisherman down there before and been unmoved — but there was something in this particular scene which prompted me, once I had stopped laughing, to reach for my camera.

Already, outside, the sun was preparing to slot into the horizon like a fat gold coin. I seized the Polaroid (I had no less than three different cameras to play with these days) and hurried to the back door. But as I emerged into the warm afternoon, I saw that the bank below was empty. Not even a ripple crossed the glassy surface of the pool. Where was Mr Bear? It seemed impossible that such a mountain of flesh could vanish so suddenly and so completely. Then I spotted him. Hidden from me by a precariously leaning tree, he was wading slowly and steadily upstream, away from the lodge, a wake curling out from each solid, gumbooted leg.

'Don't go,' I called. 'Please. Not for a minute.'

He paused and looked round, evidently startled to see something resembling a black scarecrow leaping from tussock to tussock down the garden, brass earrings flapping. Working, I dress to please myself, not other people's aesthetic sensibilities.

I scrambled precipitously down the bank to the water's edge.

'I just wanted to take a couple of snapshots of you fishing,' I said. 'I'm so sorry. It's sort of research. For a painting . . .'

Mr Bear shrugged aimiably and began to stride back towards me.

'W-w-where would you like me?'

The voice was all wrong. Mr Bear should have communicated in gravelly Yorkshire grunts. This voice had the vowels and musical resonance of a Radio Three announcer, with the same paradoxical blend of assurance and terribly British diffidence. (*I wouldn't dream of invading your private sitting-room,* imply those mellifluous voices of the guardians of the cultural airwaves, *if it were not that I thought you might just care to hear the concert, live from the concert hall of Broadcasting House, etc., etc . . .*) The diffidence of the fisherman was emphasised by his slight stammer.

I smiled as winningly as I could. 'Just where you were. If you don't mind . . .'

He nodded, and applied himself to his line again. I snapped quickly and, while I waited for the picture to develop, studied the man. He was surprisingly young. Surprising to me, that is. I rather assumed fishing — like rose cultivation or bowling — was a hobby men didn't adopt until they were virtually drawing their pensions. This fisherman could not have been a great deal older than me. I was twenty-nine. Maybe somewhere in his early thirties — although his was one of those fresh and open, peculiarly English faces which remain schoolboyish for ever.

He fitted the landscape as naturally as the tree stump behind him — and was hardly less massive. His thatch of hair was as fair and crinkled as hay, and his face — focused on some point upstream with the kind of remoteness you find in Tibetan monks — shone gold in the dying sun. His rod slanted into the sky, serene as the bow of an Arab dhow. I barely glanced at the first snapshot in my haste to take a second before the light faded further.

I find bodies reveal an enormous amount about people. I don't mean naked bodies (or at least not in this instance) but simply the way people move and hold themselves. This is not a startlingly original reflection to offer. After all, ballet is surely nothing more than the art of communication through posture and gesture. When painting, however, I find the way people stand or sit tells me more than what they say.

When, as occasionally happens, someone actually poses for

me the words they speak tend to wash past my ears like the wireless — sometimes entertaining, sometimes tedious. Most people (not hardened professional models, of course) chatter fast and nervously while they are being painted. Their conversation, however, barely offers me the small change of their souls, compared with the stark strong truths I can see ringing out from their bodies.

The young owner of a chain of restaurants recently spent two long sessions describing to me every detail of his hugely successful business — how he had created it, how he ran it with his beautiful and talented wife, and how soon he was going to develop it along bolder and even grander lines. With what you might consider to be callous foresight, I presented my account almost before the varnish had dried. Every word he had spoken sparkled with confidence and *joie de vivre*. But the sharp angles of his shoulder blades, the awkward upward twist of his expensively shod foot, every line of his body in fact jangled with panic. Bleak, stark panic. I was paid a week before he went bust.

Even so, I am always being misled by preconceptions about bodies. Aren't we all? Thin people are nervy, fatties are jolly, handsome men are arrogant, beautiful women are bitches. Instinctively I had cast my woolly-clad giant as jolly. And because he was fishing — surely the most serene of all activities — in this most peaceful and luscious of landscapes, I awarded him peace of mind as well as happiness. A contented countryman at his leisure.

But as I pointed my camera and pressed the trigger for a second time, it occurred to me with a sense of shock — almost of outrage — that I was completely wrong. The distant expression, the slump of the woolly shoulders, the downward set of the mouth — these did not at all advertise repose and contentment. What I saw in my fishing bear was an intense melancholy.

I ripped the second snapshot from the camera and the plastic case which I was gripping between elbow and rib cage, slipped from its anchorage, bounced on the grass and fell into the water. I swore viciously.

The fisherman looked round, apparently startled by my language.

'Sorry,' I muttered.

He waded across and retrieved the case, shaking the water out of it before handing it to me.

'Got your pictures?'

'Yes. Thanks.'

'I'm f-flattered to be included,' he said with a polite smile, and raised one of his huge hands – a salute, a wave of farewell.

I wanted him to stay. I felt a powerful and quite irrational desire to keep him here and talk to him. Irrational because I had never been attracted by your mountainous outdoor sort of men. I preferred thin, dark, clever alley cats to shaggy lions.

Before I could think of a pretext, however, he was out of earshot. In fact he was wading so fast one might have thought he was anxious to escape.

Lamp Lodge was at the bottom of a metalled – but nevertheless deeply-rutted – lane which lurched down the side of the valley in a series of warped hairpin-bends. 'Heaven help me if there *is* snow,' I had muttered as I inched down on the day I arrived, with my foot wedged on the brake.

The lane did actually continue beyond the Lodge. It more or less followed the path of the river at a field or so's distance, but as no more than a rutted track. The hot dry autumn had solidified the surface into vicious ridges and gullies of dried mud, like a fossilised sea. In rain, I imagined it would be a squelching nightmare. Under neither set of conditions would I choose to risk the sensitive springs of my car. Such a lane was fit only for the cart-horses of automation, not racing thoroughbreds like my extravagant pet.

It had turned out, however, to be a shortcut into the village. The drive into Thornbeck – up Lamp Hill, over Thornbeck Top, past the Wheatsheaf pub and then down – I had clocked as four meandering miles. To walk to the village along the lane I estimated was barely a mile. I was surprised and oddly disappointed to find myself so close to other human habitation, but wondered why its muddy surface had never been metalled.

Mr Danby, the milkman, produced the most colourful answer. 'Corpse road,' he said.

11

'A what? You mean it's called Corpse Road?'

He shook his head. 'Lamp Lane — if it's got a name. But a historian bloke who took the Lodge last summer was telling me about it. That's what they built a lot of these green lanes for. From old farmhouses like. For transporting the coffins. I mean, I wouldn't like to get a coffin up Lamp Hill on the back of a cart, would you?' He lowered his voice. 'And nothing but the hearse ever passed along there.'

'You're making it up,' I said. 'There's tractors along here every day now, and I bet farm carts have been using it since — prehistory. You'll be telling me next a ghostly hearse trundles along at midnight.'

'If there's a ghost along here, it'll be the old Squire, nipping down the back way to visit one of his lady-loves,' said Mr Danby with lurid relish. 'A real character was old John Vaisey. Too mean to spend a groat on road surfaces round the Estate though, and that's why it's in the state it is. You wouldn't find cars coming down here nowadays.

'You do occasionally,' I said. 'At night. I've heard a car go past.'

Mr Danby looked at me sceptically. 'Likely it were up on t'top road.'

Maybe. I wasn't going to press it. The complete silence of the countryside is extraordinary after the unceasing buzz and hum of a city. A car revving a mile and a half away up the hill might sound as though it were barely outside my window. Certainly, during the day no cars passed. The odd tractor dragging any one of those fearsomely spiked instruments of torture you see rusting in farmyards was the only movement, plus daily packs of gaily-kagouled hikers.

The day after photographing Mr Bear, I followed a gang of them along Lamp Lane into the village. I had idled away the morning washing some clothes, and was looking for further excuses not to confront the accusing pile of paper, pencils and brushes.

After a little more than a mile, the lane divided. The left-hand fork veered sharply then forded a pathetically dried-up stream. Beside the ford, tall as skyscrapers in their waterless isolation, marched a line of neat stepping stones. I was not

12

tempted to cross because at the other side was a heavy gate labelled PRIVATE, THORNBECK MANOR.

I took the right-hand fork and emerged shortly in Thornbeck itself. This was a small village – one pub, one church and no shop other than the converted front room of one of the cottages which served, two and a half days a week, as a post office. Len also sold ice-cream to the hikers, excruciating plaster garden ornaments and a well-thumbed selection of greetings cards, distinguished by the length of the verse inside and the unlikely colours of the roses and bashful rabbits on the outside. I wondered afresh if anyone managed to survive in Thornbeck without a car. Man can hardly live by plaster gnomes and Mint Choc Chip ice-cream alone.

There was a handful of houses, maybe two dozen, of which every one I could see was stone built. Two hanging signs, Gothic black script on white board, advertised bed and breakfast. One even offered *en suite* facilities. I suspected in high season there might be more such signs. The village was postcard pretty.

In the angle between my muddy lane and the road, lurked – behind low but crenellated stone walls – an overgrown jungle of rhododendrons. I could believe that in spring they might be magnificent. For the rest of the year, their dense dark foliage struck me as claustrophobic and gloomy. Another heavy gate, black-painted iron and topped with dull gold spearheads, was propped open. A wooden sign dangling on wires at an uncertain angle from two of the spears announced that this was THORNBECK MANOR and a PRIVATE ROAD. The present squire (if in this democratic day and age there was such a being) seemed unpleasantly keen on marking out his terrain and hiding himself from the world.

PERSONS REQUIRING THE ESTATE OFFICE, the sign further directed, SHOULD CONTINUE BEYOND THE CHURCH AND TURN RIGHT. I did not continue beyond the church. I had visited the Estate Office – housed in what was undoubtedly once the village school – the day I arrived to collect the key to my cottage. Lamp Lodge actually belonged to the Thornbeck Estate.

In the village, in a desultory way, I took more photographs and bought the local paper and some postcards. They didn't look much like the valley around me. The re-touched grass in the photographs was traffic-light green and the sheep Persil white. The fields today were khaki-coloured and the sheep who scrambled out of my way on the walk home along the lane much the same colour as the dry-stone walls.

I made myself gather leaves as I walked, and berries and flowers. I picked dried grasses, and even retrieved a clump of fleece raked from a sheep by the barbs on a wire fence. At home I cut headlines from the paper, shuffled the postcards, scattered the natural harvest across the table and played with them listlessly. All the old tricks for triggering ideas. Zilch. I ended up reading the local news.

And when I looked out of the window, there was Mr Bear again. Just below the apple tree where the river nudged a weed-strewn bank of soggy turf and polished tree roots, he was casting his line.

I glanced at my watch, then at myself in the mirror. Never mind the shabby T-shirt, at least I looked healthier than when I arrived. Then my skin had been dungeon-pale and I was even skinnier than usual. I pulled the rubber band out of my hair and ruffled the only slightly dirty curls. This time I strolled down to the bank with predatory nonchalance.

'It's past five,' I said. 'Would you like a drink?'

'Well . . .'

There was a wedding-ring on his finger. Perhaps he thought I was making a pass at him. I could hardly say I had had my fill recently of married men. He was smiling − but in a polite, refusing kind of way.

'No doubt your wife is waiting for you,' I said gaily, keen to make clear that my invitation had been strictly above board, 'with dry clothes and a drier martini.' I laughed encouragingly.

No response. In fact, he looked away, but not enough to hide the spasm of pain which creased his big open face. He was shaking his head.

'N-n-no,' he said, so quietly I barely caught the word.

Oh Christ, I thought, has she just died? Or run off with the gardener?

'I've got a nice bottle of white chilling in the fridge,' I said

14

rapidly, 'and I thought it was a waste to open it for one person.' Worse and worse, I was underlining the anguish of living alone. I tried to turn it into a joke. 'I mean, drinking by oneself is positively sinful, isn't it?' Not that I had ever hesitated to do so. 'Actually, I've been staring at a table full of blank paper for more than a week and I think I might be going mad. Any minute.' Truth will out.

'You make it s-sound . . .' he said with an odd twist to his mouth which I triumphantly took to mean he was reconsidering, 'as though it's my d-d-duty to join you. Um, well . . . thank you.' Finding a point where the grassy bank dipped low to meet the river, he heaved himself out of the water.

'I'll go and open the bottle,' I said, leaving him to sort out his tackle and boots and follow me up the steeply sloping garden.

As I passed, I pulled an apple from the tree and bit into one rosy cheek. It was as sweet as I expected.

CHAPTER TWO

My visitor had to bend low to pass under the stone lintel of the kitchen door. He swept off his hat as he did so, and tucked it under his arm. The kitchen, like all the rooms except the bathroom, had a square casement window overlooking the valley. The furnishings were sparse and painted a lurid sky blue. There was a blessedly large fridge, however.

I handed him a misted glass. It contained – to be absolutely specific – Alsace Gewürztraminer 'Hugel' 1976. Once upon a time, before people started paying silly money for me to (as Seb described it) paint walls into doors and doors into walls, and before I met Gerald, wine used to come my way in three varieties: white, red and fizz. I swigged them all with indiscriminate joy. Now I furrowed my brow to read labels first, then swigged with exactly the same joy but trusted my shiny new credit cards to discriminate for me. The car had creaked all the way up the A1 under the weight of wine cases. Also, I'm ashamed to admit, delicatessen plunder. City dwellers, ignorant and suspicious as the Victorian pioneers conquering Africa, believe they cannot survive in the uncharted regions of the countryside without half of Waitrose in the boot.

I watched with interest as he swirled the wine in the glass, sniffed it with relish, and rolled a generous swig round in his mouth before swallowing. Mr Bear played the game seriously. Then he turned to me and smiled. The bottle in that instant became worthy of every penny of its startling price because the pleasure in his face chased away (at least temporarily) the dejection I was sure resided there otherwise. Concealed, maybe, but potent.

'B-b-bliss,' he said, and made an impressive stab at identifying what he was drinking. I find talents like that bizarre as water divining.

'You like wine.'

'L-love it,' he confided, with the air of one confessing to unmentionable vice, 'but I try and r-restrict myself to everyday plonk – not aristocrats like this. My wife, occasionally, used to buy me a c-case of Alsatian wine. I'm particularly fond of it . . .'

A gratuitously dragged-in reference to his partner, I thought, but noted the past tense and wondered afresh.

'Me too,' I said. 'I like Smarties as well.'

He coloured up as readily as a schoolboy. 'You were w-watching me yesterday.'

'Only in the pursuit of art. You looked so sad, standing helplessly as they cascaded into the water.'

'An elderly lady up at Peel Farm insists on tucking a tube into my hand whenever I call on her. As a seven year old I believe I confessed to a partiality for them,' he added. He was so polite, so formal. Kind to old ladies, and no doubt to every other frail species. A relic from another age. 'In her eyes, I d-daresay thirty-five scarcely constitutes more than schoolboy age.'

'And you – poor soul – have to eat them just to please her, I suppose.'

'I . . .' and for a moment he eyed me uncertainly, as though unused to being laughed at. 'I do like chocolate,' he admitted, grinning. 'In fact, I'm d-disastrously prone to all the sins of the flesh. As you can see.'

In the tiny cottage, he was even bigger than on the river bank. In his stockinged feet – and he was literally in his stockinged feet because he had discarded the green waders beside the step – he stood at least six and a half feet tall. My head barely topped his shoulder. He was not fat, so much as hugely solid. I wondered if my arms would meet behind his back were I to embrace him. I would not have minded finding out.

But he thrust a hand towards me.

'I'm sorry. I h-haven't introduced myself. I'm Ned Cowper, v-v-v . . .'

'Frankie Cleverdon,' I said, leaping into the breach – which is always a fatal temptation with stammerers. 'I've rented the Lodge for the winter.' His hand was warm and dry and engulfed mine which, I noticed with slight embarrassment, was grimy with newsprint.

'Oh, I know who you are,' he said.

'You do?'

'That is to say, Jack Calder in the Estate Office told me the Lodge had been let until February t-to an *artistic* young woman. From the *South*.'

'I was born in Manchester actually.'

'Worse. The wrong side of the P-pennines. But you live in London now.' This was not offered as a question but as a listing of known fact. 'And,' he continued, his forehead creasing with concentration, 'you prefer skimmed to ordinary milk, you have a Midland Bank account, and are partial to home grown vegetables.'

'Do you know my bra size too?' I exclaimed, and was rather touched because he blushed vividly again. Just like an over-grown schoolboy.

'S-s-some of the clichés about village life are true,' he said. 'One does tend to know what is going on.'

'So I see. Shall we take the wine outside and catch the last of the sun?'

Behind the Lodge ran a broad stone-flagged terrace. A peeling, green garden bench sunned itself between the two windows, and there was a comfortably wide, low wall marking the outer edge. Below, the river was already in shadows, but the terrace was still warm. Two geraniums, leggy and scarlet as roosters, sprung from pots on the wall, left by a previous tenant no doubt.

I perched on the wall between them, while my guest, treading carefully across the flagstones in his socks, lowered himself to the bench and leaned back gratefully against the sun-warmed cottage wall. He gave his maltreated hat an absent-minded shake and balanced it above his nose, closing his eyes. Surreptitiously, I picked up a pad and pencil. Quite automatically I had tucked this small sketch-book between wine bottle and glass on the tray I had carried out. Like a heroin addict with syringes, even when I hate what I do most virulently, I can rarely separate myself from the necessary hardware.

The evening light, slanting across the valley, was clear and gold as the wine we were drinking. For a while we did not speak, and there was only the soft murmuring of the river as I sketched. I thought a singularly companionable peace reigned between the dozing bear and me. I could not tell whether he was aware of the scratching of my pencil or not.

'I love Indian summer weather,' I observed after a while. 'Such an English light – warm and mellow and northern. You never get a light like this in July.'

He nodded, without opening his eyes. 'A day like today feels like a m-marvellous unexpected treat, doesn't it? One expects the s-sun in summer – even if in this part of the world recently that's been rather a vain expectation – but October? Glorious spells like this give one hope. Make one feel anything is p-possible.'

'Anything is possible,' I declared, more flippantly than grandiosely. Although that evening was one of the occasions, rare as roses on a football pitch, when I seemed to be watching my own hand sketch rather than actually consciously working at it. Perhaps tomorrow I would be inspired to pick up a brush and paint images bright and magical as this evening. My hand caught perfectly the tilt of the battered tweed hat. 'Anything is possible,' I repeated with muted, dogged determination, 'if only you set your mind to it.'

'Ah no,' said Ned Cowper softly, and I heard – or thought I heard – an undercurrent of bitterness, 'some things must not be possible . . .'

'What do you mean?'

He sat up abruptly. 'N-nothing,' he said. 'I'm talking nonsense. What on earth are you doing?'

'Only sketching you. Do you mind?'

His hat had tumbled to the terrace. He groped for it with one hand while gazing at me in alarm. 'I suppose not,' he said, but his voice was filled with foreboding.

'You can tear it up if you don't like it.'

It's perfectly safe to offer people that, I find. I have never met anyone with the courage to tear up an image of their own

19

face, however much they dislike it. 'Go back to sleep,' I said soothingly.

'I wasn't asleep.'

His chin was square and particularly smoothly shaven. He would smell, I decided, of soap with perhaps a whiff of potting sheds about the pullover. There would be no exotic colognes. In repose his mouth did not droop, but it tilted downwards. Resignation.

'Why are you so sad?'

The hat fell off again.

'G-good heavens, what an extraordinary question.'

'I'm sorry. Is it rude?'

'N-not rude, no . . .'

'I'm told I have a bad habit of interrogating people. I blame it all on portrait commissions. Some more wine?'

'I shouldn't.'

'Why not?'

I was standing over him, with the slim green bottle poised.

'B-but I haven't the will power to refuse. Why do portraits make you ask extraordinary questions?'

'I think sitters actually expect it of the painter. People bare their souls to their hairdresser you know. A portrait takes a hell of a lot longer than a cut and blow-dry and the subject tends to assume you need to understand their innermost thoughts in order to paint their outermost skin.'

'And do you?'

I filled my own glass, sat down and picked up my pencil again.

'Yes and no. If a portrait doesn't tell you anything about a person beyond the colours of their hair and eyes then it's an abject failure. But I find watching people can be more informative than listening to them.'

'You t-terrify me.'

'Why? Are you loaded with deep and dark secrets? Feel free to pour them out. I sometimes think it's like being a priest, this job. I maintain a thoroughly professional discretion.'

'Good God,' he said faintly – and then almost at once, 'Have you settled in here, at the Lodge?'

Diverting attention from himself. I wasn't fooled, but I told him, yes, I was settling in comfortably enough.

'And you're not t-troubled by the isolation?'

'Everybody seems to ask me that, almost with awe. Don't I mind living here *all alone*. As if the countryside is regularly combed by mad axe-men and sex maniacs. As a matter of fact I feel a great deal safer here at night than I do on Clapham Common.'

'So you are not nervous here? Not at all?'

I shook my head. 'Don't, please, begin to tell me why I should be. I prefer to sleep soundly with my illusions about rural England intact.'

'Human nature is much the same everywhere.'

'Too true,' I said. It's a chemical mystery, but alcohol operates on me much more powerfully when I'm excited. Depressed I can down a bottle of wine virtually without effect. That evening, with barely a glass and a half swallowed I felt recklessly merry. 'Your local paper's just like the *Sun*. Full of erring husbands and naughty vicars. Only unlike the *Sun* they don't give you enough of the juicy detail. Although I must say . . .'

'I beg your pardon?' Mr Bear sounded shocked and disapproving. I was disappointed in him.

'I happened to glance through the *Reporter* this afternoon.'

'Like everyone else in the valley I daresay,' he said, rather tersely, 'although I sometimes wonder why anyone bothers. We all get the news on the grapevine days before it appears in black and white.'

I smiled placatingly. 'Ah, but when it appears on paper everyone knows it must be true.'

' "I love a ballad in print, a-life, for then we are sure they are true . . ." '

'Shakespeare?'

'From *The Winter's Tale*. Do you know it?'

I shook my head. 'Someone once told me that with three quarters of all quotations it's a safe bet to guess Shakespeare.'

He laughed.

'I ought to be going,' he said uncertainly. But he did not stir.

'I haven't finished my sketch,' I said. 'Besides, I thought you were telling me how dangerous it was for a young woman to be alone here, at night.'

21

'I should think Wragdale is as safe as anywhere you could find,' he said, considering the matter. 'I virtually never lock my car, for example. No one does. The church is open all day every day. But there is a certain amount of crime. The river is heavily poached, for example.'

'You're not, by any chance, a poacher yourself?'

'P-p-perfectly legal, I promise. My brother-in-law holds the fishing rights. Besides, even he doesn't mind a local chap bagging the odd fish or two. It's the gangs who come down from Tyneside and string nets across the river which are the real menace. Not that I don't sympathise, even with them,' he added quietly. 'Times are hard and wild salmon c-commands the most immoral price. But they have been known to behave unpleasantly violently.'

'I'm not sure I like the idea of desperate gangs wandering through my garden.'

'I'm sure they wouldn't do you any harm,' he said. 'It's the water b-bailiffs they fall foul of. If, by the remotest chance, you should hear a noise down on the river bank, I should pull the covers over your head and ignore it.'

I had hoped he might suggest I telephone him.

'"Watch the wall, my darling, while the Gentlemen go by . . ."' I chanted, to show him I could quote things too.

'I fear they will leave no baccy or laces for you, however, my darling,' and when he said 'darling' it was as though a tingling electric shock touched the roots of my hair. 'Not even a fish. All these chaps leave,' he continued, rather breathlessly, 'are pieces of broken net to foul up the water.'

'Shame,' I said. I studied my pad. Mr Bear in my sketch was leaning against the wall, a tilted hat shielding his eyes from the sun, an exaggeratedly large glass of wine by his side, and an expression on his face of perfect contentment. I had quite deliberately relaxed his rather wide and straight mouth into a happier line. I wanted to make Mr Bear happy.

I sat for a moment with pencil circling like a plane waiting for permission to land on the paper. 'No. S'finished.'

'May I see?'

He dug in his pocket and produced a slender pair of gold half-moon glasses which perched on his nobly proportioned nose so comically I wished I could have included them in my picture. With unaccustomed shyness I thrust the notebook towards him. Usually I don't much care what anyone says about a picture – I can nearly always say worse myself – but I cared about Mr Bear's reaction. He took the pad and immediately burst out laughing – which pleased me very much.

'You're t-t-terribly clever,' he said.

I shook my head. 'Being able to catch a likeness is a knack,' I said. 'Some people happen to have it – like being able to sing in tune. It's what you do with it afterwards, how you employ the God-given knack, that matters. That's rather harder . . .'

'I should like to see s-something you've painted,' he said, but he was tucking away his spectacles again. 'One day.'

'Do you fish down here often?' I asked. Then recognised what I'd said and grimaced. Ned Cowper apparently did not notice the cliché.

'The season closes soon. On the last day of October. So one tends to gather one's final rosebuds – if you'll forgive an appallingly mixed metaphor.' He stood up. 'You must f-forgive me, too, for keeping you talking out here. The sun has gone and you're obviously f-f-freezing half way to pneumonia.'

'I'm quite warm,' I protested, springing to my feet. Excitement and alcohol are effective central heating. But it was true that, while Ned was packaged in wool and tweeds, I wore only thin cotton trousers and an even thinner T-shirt. 'Honestly, I'm not cold.'

'Of c-course you are,' he said, and to my amazement blushed and looked away. I glanced down and saw that my nipples were sticking through the T-shirt like small hard nuts.

He thrust out a huge paw again. Even when embarrassed, Mr Bear did not forget his manners.

'Heavenly wine,' he said. 'Th-thank you so much.'

'See you again,' I said. 'I hope . . .'

CHAPTER THREE

The next morning I was up with the birds and before the sun.

I woke with the glow of well-being I used to feel on birthday mornings in those days when birthdays promised an infinity of delights. At twenty-nine, birthdays are potent in a different way. At least partly responsible for my high spirits was the fact that for the first time in months I had not once, during the whole night's sleep, found myself plummeting into my recurrent nightmare.

In the most common version of this nightmare I would be imprisoned by white walls. Often they were defaced with vilely obscene graffiti – and I was terribly afraid I must have been responsible for the foul words and the sickening caricatures which I saw all round me. Then I would realise with horror that I was supposed to have painted these walls with a mural – but I could not for the life of me remember what was supposed to be depicted in that mural. All I knew was that it was vitally important the picture be finished before morning.

I dare say this may be a typical painter's nightmare. Every actor, after all, is haunted by dreams in which he enters a stage to discover he has no idea what play he's supposed to be performing.

Such dreams are potent because the terrors are only a hairsbreadth exaggeration of real life. An actor friend confided he had occasionally experienced genuine instants of total amnesia on stage – in the very middle of a play he had been performing for months – when nerves chased not just his lines but every coherent thought out of his head. However often he had played the part before, an audience could always terrify him afresh.

In the same way, white spaces, blank paper and empty walls have always possessed the capacity to panic me — because you can never be sure, even in the best and most confident of times, that you will be able to pull it off *this time*. This time you might not be able to conquer the space, impose your will on it. However many pictures I've painted before, this sheet of paper is virgin, entirely new — like a new audience. Nothing can be carried forward from last night's success. The whole process has got to be tackled afresh. On good days it's stimulating. On bad, the fear is paralysing.

It was a sympathetic teacher at art college who suggested that sticking together collages was a useful trick for easing one past the blank paper phobia. God bless Jonathan Blake. Precisely how these collages work is hard to explain though, because they rarely resemble the final work.

This morning I took my first mug of tea straight to the big table where I had scattered yesterday's gleanings. A collage had been the object of the rape of the hedgerows. Mind you, virtually anything can be included in one of these strange concoctions: not just leaves and flowers (until I journeyed up here, *rarely* leaves or flowers) but coloured paper, pebbles, bus tickets, magazine pictures, jewellery, sweets — and photographs. Thus the *paparazzi* collection of cameras. Photographs can be very useful. So are words, strangely. That's why I had taken scissors to the newspaper. A single black headline can be quite potent.

Described like that, the process begins to sound like the recipe for a magic spell. Sebastian had observed in the days when we shared a studio that I reminded him quite unpleasantly of a witch as I snipped and glued and muttered over one of my motley hybrids.

Now, I pulled a sheet of card towards me, and began to toy with patterns. Red and gold hawthorn leaves, feathery fronds of grass, a twig like a gnarled crocodile and a fat clump of fleece. Silver paper for water — but the silver was too synthetic, too Christmas-like. I spilled green ink over it. Not bad.

What did it achieve? Fixing an idea, I suppose you could call the process. Clever artists can concoct ideas in their brains, and simmer them there until ready to paint. I can't. I need to see colours and to feel textures. I need to play with them like a child arranging building bricks.

The finished collage is rarely beautiful. Quite often, like this one, it has a short life span. Already the leaves were losing their glorious blush. But eventually I reach a point when the arrangement conveys — something. That *something* lifts me over the blank paper hurdle, and, when I do come to start afresh on my spanking new board or canvas or sheet of paper, I have the jumble of collage beside me. And then, perhaps most bizarre of all, I may never even glance at the collage again.

Today's composition, however, was failing so far to say much. No whisper of the green, liquid peace of the river bank, no clunk of jumping fish and no sense of the particular soft haziness of a Yorkshire landscape which I supposed I should be striving for. I picked up one of my snapshots. With loving care I snipped round the image of Mr Bear as he fished, gazing with such sad intensity downstream. There is something very intimate in the act of cutting out a human figure. At eight-thirty in the morning, it can feel almost indecent.

A clink of bottles alerted me to Mr Danby peering through the window at my work.

I walked into the kitchen to meet him at the back door. Mr Danby was short, stout and sandy-haired with perhaps the most luminously pale blue eyes I had ever seen. A joke overheard in the pub suggested that a combination of red hair and blue eyes was held to be suspiciously common among children in the villages of Thornbeck and Langton-le-Moor. Perhaps people always make such insinuations about milkmen — particularly milkmen with seven children at home, and the blue eyes and merry insouciance of Mr Danby. He was also something of a philosopher.

'Now then . . .' he said, handing me one pint and a pot of yoghurt.

'Now then . . .' was the vernacular all-purpose expression; greeting, surprise or farewell — it served for the lot.

'Thank you, Mr Danby. Be a nice morning when the mist lifts.'

'That it will, Frankie. Funny old picture you're working on there. If you don't mind me saying.'

From the first day, I was Frankie — he was Mr Danby.

'It isn't actually a picture,' I answered resignedly. With good reason, I do my best to keep these monstrous stick-up jobs out of public view.

'Mind, I don't claim to understand Modern Art,' said Mr Danby, large-mindedly. 'These days, I dare say you can get a grant for that sort of thing? Ha ha . . .'

'From the Tate,' I agreed gaily. 'Ha ha . . .' How many times had I heard that particular quip?

I liked Mr Danby, however. On my first morning, he had demonstrated to me the trick which operated best the riddle of my wood-burning stove — a messy operation which had taken him the best part of half an hour. I had not made the mistake of offering payment. One lunchtime a couple of days later, however, I had insisted on buying him a pint of beer in the Wheatsheaf, when I chanced to call in for a box of matches. He had affected to be profoundly shocked by my forwardness, and there had been much ribbing from his cronies in the public bar about his liberated lady friend. Since then, however, few mornings passed without his offering me one or two reflections on local current affairs.

I wondered how, without being too obvious, I could introduce Ned Cowper into this morning's conversation. Questions, I had learned, could easily be regarded as offensive nosiness. Statements tended to be more productive. Thus:

'Fishing season's nearly over,' I remarked.

He shook his head gloomily. 'Bad year. There's been no decent rain to speak of, and we need water down t'river to see fish. Not worth getting your rod out.'

'Really?' I said, putting the milk in the fridge so that I was not looking directly into Mr Danby's clear blue eyes. 'There was one fisherman out yesterday, anyway. Ned Cowper.'

'Aaah now,' said Mr Danby and rich meaning coloured his tone, 'that's different.'

'I suppose it is,' I agreed without hesitation.

Mr Danby leaned his bulky haunches comfortably against the sink. 'They do say,' he observed sonorously, 'that fishing eases the troubled mind. In my opinion, Frankie, you have there a man looking not for salmon but for spiritual balm.'

Not for the first time I wondered if Mr Danby was a lay preacher in his spare hours.

'I thought he looked sad,' I agreed. Since I had evidence for this much at least, I ventured, 'Most people find it a miserable business, don't they, going home to an empty house when you're used to someone else being there?'

Mr Danby nodded. 'Poor lass,' he said soulfully. 'Poor little lass. And then there's the vicar of St Catherine's, too. That's the big parish only just over t'hill, you know, Langton-le-Moor. In the paper and all it was . . .'

I was taken aback by the change of subject, but recovered enough to say, 'So I read . . .' After my experience yesterday, I did not make the mistake of laughing. One man's juicy scandal is another's appalling tragedy after all, and I dare say this must have been the juiciest scandal to hit the Wrag valley for decades. The naughty vicar. The poor chap had been caught with several other men in – the inevitable cliché – a public lavatory. *In a compromising situation.* An' it please, M'Lud. I forget the name of the town – somewhere I didn't know, the other side of the Moors – but I remember the location all right. The Queen's Park Conveniences.

The *Northern Reporter* had found nothing to laugh at in this at all. I visualised some junior 'sub' stabbing a typewriter. Was he or she suppressing a grin, or were they as earnest and unworldly as their newspaper? At least one other man, the report continued stolidly, had escaped through a rear window, in which the police constable (in the pursuance, no doubt, of his duty and the fleeing gentleman) had got stuck. When I reached this Gilbert and Sullivanesque climax, I had roared and longed for Sebastian to share the joke.

'Bad business,' pronounced Mr Danby gravely.

'Must be awful for the poor man,' I agreed with fervency to atone for my irreverence yesterday.

'What about his sister, then? Looked after him for years. Poor lass.'

'Indeed.'

I wanted to turn the conversation back to the other woman-to-be-pitied, to Mrs Ned Cowper. But there seemed no tactful way of doing so. Mr Danby had described her as a poor lass too. Was she dead then? Ill?

'I'll be on t'road then, Frankie. Same again tomorrow?'
'Please.'
One pint of skim, one yoghurt and double information.

I finished the collage quickly. It half amused me, once Ned Cowper had been planted in the green-silver water, although I daresay the rest of the world would share Mr Danby's jaundiced view.

I could not bring myself, however, to begin a painting. I told myself that a gap between preparation and final product was necessary and helpful. Fibber. I cleaned my favourite brushes – although they were already perfectly soft and satiny – and sharpened pencils.

The weather, once the mists had melted from the valley floor, was even warmer than the previous day. At lunchtime, on impulse, I climbed into the car and drove all the way to York. Playing truant. There were some nice shops in York.

As a result, when the sun dipped towards the western end of the valley late that afternoon, I was sitting outside the back door, trying not to shiver as the breeze rippled through the flounces of an exquisitely flimsy skirt. An undeniably profligate purchase – in October – and unlike anything else I owned.

My wardrobe tended towards schizophrenia: drooping yards of dark sacks for painting in on the one hand and, on the other, a glittering cornucopia of creations for the pursuit of social life which (said Gerald snottily) might have dropped from the back door of a whorehouse. He had tried, without success, to educate me in classic good taste and correct brand names. Gerald was nothing if not correctly brand-named.

My suitcases travelling up here had bulged, additionally, with sweaters and thick socks, waterproofs and even thermal vests. Nothing, however, had suited today's purposes – or the weather. Hence the new skirt. Also an angora sweater, soft as a kitten's tummy, which slithered off the shoulder, as the designer, presumably, intended. I had kitted myself out, in other words, in what I trusted was an irresistible combination of sex and demureness to lure the strangely shy and elusive fishing bear into my lair.

I was pretending to read a book, and wore large sun-glasses

which I hoped would disguise my anxious surveillance of the river. I saw no fishermen, however, and was beginning to feel foolishly forlorn – a frilled, over-painted and discarded rag doll – when a voice stammered 'Hello' behind me.

I spun round to see Ned Cowper, delicious and solidly old-fashioned as a character from P.G. Wodehouse. The English Country Look has returned for men, of course. I had no doubt that for Ned Cowper, in his baggy corduroys and fair-isle pullover, it had never gone away. He was rounding the corner of the Lodge carrying a bottle. No waders today. Brogues.

'H-h-hardly worth trying for a fish this evening,' he said.

'Need some rain, don't we?' I observed wisely.

He was gazing at me earnestly. I stared back, wide-eyed as a cat – and more predatory.

'You look l-lovely,' he said suddenly. 'I mean – I'm sorry. P-p-pretty skirt.'

'Please don't apologize.'

'I owe you a b-b-bottle of wine,' he said, thrusting it towards me. 'New Zealand. Have you t-tried these people b-before? I think you m-m-might l-l-like it.' His stammer was much worse when he was nervous.

'Wonderful,' I cried, jumping to my feet. 'I'll get some glasses and a bottle opener.'

'I didn't mean to drink now,' he said hastily. 'P-p-present for you.'

'Can't you stay?' I could not hide the disappointment in my voice. I don't suppose I tried.

'It's not c-cold . . .' he protested unconvincingly.

It wasn't warm either. If you ask me that bottle hadn't been longer out of a fridge than it had taken him to walk here. The paper wrapped round it was soggy with condensation. Now, people don't chill bottles if they are delivering them purely as gifts.

'I'll fill the washing-up bowl with ice and water,' I said. 'That'll chill it in no time.'

'Well I d-don't know how to put this . . .' he began, then floundered, gazing down at me helplessly. I took ruthless advantage.

'One glass,' I said. 'What harm can there be in one glass of wine?'

CHAPTER FOUR

That evening set the pattern for several days.

In my memory they tend to swim together into one long and comfortable conversation. Sometimes, however, I remember Ned sitting on the bench, at other times on the wall; in one image he wears a shirt, in another a sweater, so I know there were several different evenings. He never ventured inside the house, however, or at least not until the last fishing day, the thirty-first of October, Hallowe'en. And after that everything changed.

The bottle of wine he brought that first evening was very good, I remember. He did not drink just one glass, of course, but shared most of the bottle with me. I also remember that, in my euphoria at having secured his company to drink it, I chattered fast and fatuously. My grandmother, had she been alive and present, would have been shaking her head, muttering glum prophecies about tears before nightfall. She would have been right.

We had been discussing something entirely innocuous – *The Archers*, I believe – when Ned asked why I had come to Yorkshire.

I needed to get away from London, I told him with more fluency than considered truth, because life was becoming too complicated in town. Too fast, too frenetic, too many parties, too many men . . .

'At least, I mean two men,' I said, aware belatedly of having dived headlong into mine-strewn waters. 'Not too many men. I wouldn't want you to think . . .' I did not know what I wanted Ned to think. Simultaneously I wanted him to know that I was (in important senses) unattached – but by no means unwanted. A *femme fatale*, I didn't mind figuring as, but not a tart. A single woman, but not a sex-starved spinster. 'Anyway, I couldn't choose between them.'

'Why not?' asked Ned.

The simplest questions are always the hardest.

'I don't know. Really.'

'P-perhaps you love them b-both equally?'

'Love . . .' I said with melodramatic contempt. Gerald once loved his wife — maybe he still did. I once loved Sebastian — maybe I still did. Sebastian loved his work. Gerald said he loved me. I certainly did not love Gerald. 'What is love?'

Ned smiled. 'I've s-s-spent half my l-life trying to work that out.'

'It's a bugger, isn't it?' I said, taking another swig of wine. 'It's easy enough at the beginning. There's nothing as wonderful as that first high. When you feel you could fly round the stars because you're so blissfully, mindlessly happy. But that doesn't last — and then where are you?'

Ned Cowper swirled the wine round in his glass contemplatively. He seemed embarrassed. I was not surprised. I realised, with discomfiture, I had been treating him to a description of my own incipient love-sick condition.

'Anyway,' I said switching course with brittle gaiety, 'out of one relationship I was getting an unremitting stream of insults about my crappy work, and from the other I was getting French underwear which didn't fit and criticism of my dress sense. And I thought that there has to be more to love than this.'

'Isn't love about p-putting in, rather than getting out?' said Ned.

'What a po-faced remark.'

'B-but true, surely?'

'You're hardly in a position to tell me what went wrong with two men you don't know the first thing about.'

'I'm s-sorry,' he said. But he did not sound sorry.

'I was half-joking anyway.'

'But you were asking what love was.'

'I wasn't asking for a sermon.'

'Hardly,' said Ned, smiling faintly.

'Anyway love's a combination of the two, I believe,' I said pompously. 'A balance between both. Giving and taking.'

'I daresay you're right,' said Ned – and it would have been all right if I had not then siezed the chance to divert and (I thought) lighten the conversation.

'Enough about me and my problems,' I declared with the subtle gaiety of a bulldozer. 'Let's talk about you.'

Ned flushed dull red. 'I'm s-sorry?'

'Don't say you haven't any interesting skeletons lurking in the emotional closet.'

'Not that I c-care to talk about.'

He wasn't even smiling.

'Only joking,' I began. 'I didn't mean . . .' I felt horribly snubbed. Already he was apologising too. Something incoherent about being surrounded by prying people – which wasn't exactly mollifying. 'N-not you, I mean,' he added. 'For heaven's sake. I'm just not g-good at t-talking about me. N-never have been.' He attempted a smile. A painful frozen grimace. 'You know, the c-classically inhibited Englishman. D-deathly boring anyway. I wouldn't inflict it on you.'

'Fine,' I said frigidly. 'What shall we talk about then? The weather?'

He left soon afterwards.

I was afraid he would never come again – but quite early the next afternoon his mountainous silhouette was reflected once more in the pool at the bottom of the garden. In miserable anxiety, I had been as unable to eat as I was to work. My immediate consolation, when Ned at last tramped up the grassy slope to the terrace, was that he looked quite as wretched as I felt.

'I t-talked like a p-p-prig yesterday,' he said with no word of greeting – and from then on, we were fine.

He stuck to the pretence of fishing, though. I say pretence because he never seemed to be in the least danger of catching anything. I liked to believe he was as anxious to walk up and join me as I was for him to do so. He never arrived again simply carrying a bottle of wine. He would only join me after the statutory hour or so flogging the water. Moreover, he never stayed with me longer than an hour. And he never again directly mentioned his wife. And you can bet your life I didn't ask directly about her. I had learned my lesson. No prying. For my own part, I was wary of mentioning Seb or Gerald, either.

Instead we talked about a great many other things. Ned was informative on country matters. In a single afternoon I remember he pointed out the location of a badger sett across the hillside and described to me both the wildly improbable life cycle of the eel and the (literally) colourful mechanics of impregnating sheep. I was relieved to learn that old-fashioned methods were still employed. No men in white coats with straws: the business was still left to a ram − only in this part of the world they called him a 'tup'. The poor old boy apparently had his undercarriage daubed with a dye beforehand, however, so the farmer could see afterwards which of the harem had received conjugal favours. I felt an absurd *frisson* (a little girl testing teacher with a rude question) asking Ned if a single fuck guaranteed pregnancy. But Ned's apparent prudishness was confined strictly to human behaviour. He discussed the mating habits of other species with unblushing candour.

He could be very funny. His description − almost a mime − of assisting a recalcitrant cow to calve enchanted me. The very idea of this giant playing midwife was a joke in itself. He had taken up farming, he told me, straight out of Oxford, with an excess of zeal and bungling ineptitude. But he had learned.

'Do you farm now?' I asked.

Even in my town-reared ignorance, I suspected that farmers might have more pressing demands on their time in October than casting for absent fish, drinking wine and discussing *The Archers*.

Ned's face was charmingly transparent. He glanced down, and shuffled his feet before replying cagily that he still enjoyed lambing time.

'Jim Rutherford says I'm as good as any shepherd with a tricky ewe,' he informed me, with pride.

So, what with one thing and another, I assumed Ned Cowper was that character out of novels (in my limited experience): the English Gentleman Farmer.

This assumption was reinforced when he mentioned that his home was the Dower House, in Thornbeck. On driving

34

through the village the next day, I looked eagerly for the Dower House. It turned out to be a Georgian delight, tucked away from the road on the other side of the Manor. Nestled amid massive chestnut trees, built from the creamy local stone, with tall windows and a prettily pillared porch, it was symmetrical and perfect as a doll's house.

That day I stuck conkers into a collage, and a scrap of Regency striped wallpaper, with lace doilies. By now, the sitting-room was festooned with collages in various stages of decay and construction. Ideas were flooding out, varied and dangerously precipitous as floating debris on a river in spate. But I had not started a single picture. I blamed it on my preoccupation with Mr Bear. When that was sorted out – one way or another – I told myself I would be able to paint. In the meantime, I walked, picked berries, read thrillers and dissected and evaluated the previous day's conversation.

These analyses were all the more absorbing because our conversations were so impersonal. Strangely impersonal from my point of view. My idea of an intimate conversation with a friend had been more in the nature of mutual soul barings on the psychiatrist's couch than cultural chatter on the chaise longue. Ned's conversation, however, was cast strictly in the old-fashioned drawing-room mould. Books, music, art, a lot about country life, a little about current affairs – I believed we even steered politely clear of religion and politics. In fact, in retrospect, I am sure we must have done. Of the former at any rate.

The scope, therefore, for my speculations afterwards was vast. I felt it was rather like solving a giant human crossword puzzle. I was piecing together a biography and character assessment from an assortment of literary, topical and musical clues, plus the few more direct facts he chanced to let fall.

I could only guess whether Ned's had been a happy childhood (I decided it had been), but a few concrete details emerged. He was an only child. One parent still living – mother in Cheltenham. And (I had a charming vision of a curly-headed infant Mozart) he had begun to play the piano at the age of four.

'Do you still play?' I asked.

Ned gazed down and flexed the square, brown fingers of his left hand. Almost as though he were wondering whether they would still perform their duties at a keyboard. 'I – um – well, yes and no really. Not the p-piano very much. I don't actually have an instrument these days.'

'There's a piano here,' I exclaimed. 'In the sitting-room where I work.' I sensed a ploy to lure him inside the building. I was beginning to resemble a voracious spider who waits, with patient cunning, to lure the bumbling fly eventually to set foot in her web.

'I know,' he said, grimacing. 'An ancient Broadwood which must be even more out of tune now than it was t-twenty years ago, and it was excruciating then. Do you know why it's here? The b-builders modernising the place before Roger p-put it up for holiday letting n-narrowed the far door so much, the damned piano won't fit through. Have to knock a wall down to get it out.'

'How do you know all this?' I asked.

'Roger Vaisey at the M-manor is a sort of c-cousin of mine you know.' I did not know. Although I suppose a connection between Dower House and Manor might have been deduced. 'My p-parents and I actually used to stay here for occasional holidays when I was a boy. In the shooting season mainly.'

'In Lamp Lodge?' I said, charmed by the notion of Ned living here, actually in my cottage.

He nodded.

'There is still a squire then?' I said. 'People only seem to talk about the Old Squire – which sounds too feudal for words.'

'John Vaisey died eight years ago,' said Ned with an expression I couldn't interpret. 'His son Roger is at the Manor now.'

'I decided that if anyone lived in Thornbeck Manor they must be wildly xenophobic,' I said, 'with all the keep out signs and the twenty-foot rhododendrons.'

'Ghastly, aren't they?' said Ned. 'But you're wrong. Roger's a f-fearfully gregarious type. Terribly good chap. And I don't say that just because he's my brother-in-law . . .'

'Your brother-in-law?'

'And c-cousin naturally,' said Ned, apparently unaware of my surprise. 'But more than that: Roger and I have

36

been f-friends for years. Through s-school and university.'

So (since Ned was an only child) Mrs Cowper, I deduced with avid swiftness, was or had been the Squire's sister. Ned's description of his own relationship to Roger Vaisey struck me as singular, however: the old-established friendship apparently carrying greater significance for him than the later, marriage-glued bond. Perhaps he was right, though. It's true that we cannot choose our relatives, only our friends.

I learned Ned had read classics at St Edmund Hall.

'You must be terribly clever,' I said.

'Roger was the clever one,' he replied quickly, 'even if he only took a third in the end. He read history at the House and never attended a single lecture to my knowledge. I was much better at c-cricket than Latin. They appreciated that sort of thing at Teddy Hall. Never worried too much about the brain capacity of a good spin bowler. In those days. Times have changed, of c-course. I hear they're all geniuses now.'

Did Ned have girlfriends at Oxford? I visualised him cycling along, wobbling, because he was hand-in-hand with a leggy Betjeman-esque girl whose flowing skirt was bundled over the handlebars of her own bicycle. Being a useful spin bowler was the most intimate revelation Ned made about Oxford, though. He simply did not talk about personal matters. And neither, after that early and disastrous argument, did I.

This was, I discovered with surprise, strangely liberating. The walls of one's own psyche, so often and intimately explored, can sometimes begin to resemble the walls of a prison. With Ned I had, perforce, to look through the window. I learned how passionately Ned felt about Bach and Renoir. I found myself trying to interest him in Dufy and Van Morrison. We both liked Dorothy Sayers, Ealing Comedies and Victorian Gothic architecture. I learned how much he loved France – wine, culture, language. I did not learn how much he loved his wife.

I put this in the past tense, loved, not just because I did not care to think of Ned loving another woman, but because, increasingly, I found myself believing Mrs Cowper was no longer on this earth. She was certainly not at the Dower House. I had deduced from any number of chance remarks that Ned was living there alone – he said something about cooking

37

his own meals, for instance. I could devise no immediate way of confirming my suspicions, however. I could not ask outright. His avoidance of mentioning his wife (I didn't even know her name!) was too marked to make it easy to introduce the subject. But I could not resist trying.

We were talking about the fishing. Ned – doggedly refusing to admit that Mr Danby and his fishing colleagues might be right in their gloomy assessment of the river – was wondering whether he was trying at the wrong time of day.

'I always used to get up before dawn to fish,' he remarked, 'when we first came to the Dower House.'

Cruelly, I leaped on the 'we'.

'Your wife must have loved that,' I said smiling. 'Being woken at daybreak by you lumbering out in your vast wellingtons.'

He started, and looked puzzled. Rather like a dog which has been undeservedly slapped.

'I don't think she minded,' he muttered uncomfortably, drained his glass and rose to leave. I did not try asking about his wife again.

Even more unfortunately, at about this time, my chief informant temporarily deserted me. Mr Danby's troublesome disc slipped again, which put lifting milk crates out of the question. Mrs Danby was friendly and efficient, but much too harrassed by combining her husband's business with her own home and seven children to enjoy a gossip. I am not sufficiently bold to drink in pubs alone, and one can hardly walk into a post office and ask outright, 'What's happened to Ned Cowper's wife, then?'

Soon I ceased to care. As our meetings began (in my eyes) to develop the reliability of habit, I felt perfectly justified in dismissing Mrs Cowper from my mind. Besides (although this was certainly not from my choice) no word or gesture passed between Ned and me that was not entirely proper.

In my frequently fevered imagination, however, I would detect currents of passion – invisible and devastating as radiation – swirling between our bodies as we sat, a prim four or five feet apart discussing the tourist industry or Monet, dog licences or the English landscape.

'You have no soul,' I declared hotly.

'I assure you I have.'

I had been describing, with purple lyricism, my morning's hike over the moors, and bemoaning the impossibility of catching on a brush the incandescent copper of bracken in the sun. Ned had only replied with perfect seriousness that bracken was a scourge and a menace, carcinogenic to sheep and impossibly expensive to eradicate.

'We towny children appreciate the countryside much more than you yokels,' I declared. Ned, I had learned, was reared in Gloucestershire.

'How's that?' he said grinning. I flattered myself that every day Mr Bear was growing a little happier.

'There's a great green pastoral streak running through all us urban northerners. Look at Delius. Look at D.H. Lawrence. We don't just look at the countryside, we feel it in our souls. On a day like today I see trees prematurely and poetically bare, and fields of gold. You country philistines see Dutch Elm Disease and a cash crop.'

'Ah, but you're an artist . . .'

'Yes,' I said, and suddenly the bubble of elation burst. 'Yes,' I repeated bleakly.

'I see now what b-brought you to paint in Yorkshire,' he went on mockingly. 'The craggy Lawrentian poetry of the northern landscape. None of your m-manicured southern molehills here.'

'No,' I said flatly. 'What brought me here was a newspaper advertisement for this cottage. The place I was looking for could have been in Wales, or Scotland or Cornwall – or almost anywhere. Anywhere remote.'

'Ah yes,' said Ned quietly, 'of course. You weren't c-coming to Yorkshire so much as escaping London.'

'That's right. I suppose.'

He looked at me speculatively. 'Running away from your complicated love l-life,' he said, to my astonishment. The most directly personal comment he had ever volunteered.

'Perhaps.'

'The c-conventional wisdom seems to be that people only really want to run away from themselves. Which of course they cannot easily do.'

'I was doing that in London,' I said. 'Losing myself in work. I didn't take a day off for ... months. I overdid it. I was getting very run-down, perpetual stupid infections.' Tonsilitis, cystitis, even athlete's foot. I had also been taking sleeping pills and hadn't had a proper period for over a year — but this was not a doctor's surgery.

There was a pause before he said neutrally, 'But you have come here to work.'

'To work on my own pictures,' I said. 'That's different. In London, I haven't recently painted many ... pictures as such.' In the last three years, precisely one. 'I tend to paint walls. Or doors, or ceilings —'

'Like Michelangelo,' suggested Ned, with a faint smile.

'— or murals round swimming pools, or anywhere really. You know, *trompe-l'oeil*, that sort of thing. Terribly fashionable these days. This agent, Magda, came to a small and rather tatty exhibition I had four years ago, and suggested I'd be good at murals. I thought, "Why not?" And since then I've been working solidly to commission. I'll paint anything as long as people are stupid enough to pay my outrageous fees.'

'Are you very expensive?'

'Amazingly,' I smiled bitterly, 'all thanks to Magda. She's done it all.'

Dragged me into the grown-up civilised world — according to Gerald.

Ruined me completely — according to Sebastian.

'But you're d-deserting this lucrative practice?'

'Temporarily.' I laughed and even in my own ears the sound was brittle and brassy. 'I hope people don't forget me. But I've had the most amazing offer of an exhibition. The Liszt Gallery — do you know them? Very classy outfit. Christopher Hamilton-Smythe. He wants about twenty paintings by next autumn. I daren't even think what he'll charge for a picture. When I've painted them ...'

Ned touched my hand gently. 'What's t-troubling you, sweetheart?'

It was the way he called me 'sweetheart' that pressed the trigger. Suddenly I was sobbing. 'I'm frightened I c-can't paint any longer ...' The relief of releasing the words was enormous.

Never, even to myself, had I framed the admission in actual words. Now I was almost babbling in the explosive recognition of the truth. 'I haven't done a painting of my own for two years . . .'

Ned held my hand steadily, and after a minute blotted my tears clumsily with a giant white handkerchief.

'You've just been t-telling me how much money you earn.'

'On commissions, yes. Murals. They're okay somehow. People generally know what they want. And it's a question of fitting work into a space, and matching their rotten colour schemes, and — it's just different.'

'You still had to p-paint them, though — and you obviously managed to do it.'

'But I didn't produce anything good,' I sobbed. 'Not what I mean by good anyhow. Not what Seb calls . . .' I retrieved a crumpled length of loo-roll from inside one sleeve — I couldn't despoil Ned's pristine linen — blew my nose vigorously, and concentrated on some slow breaths to calm the panicky clamour of thoughts. 'The things I was painting were technically okay,' I said carefully. 'What do I mean okay? Some of them were fine — whatever Sebastian bloody said. He just disapproves of anything which makes money. I wasn't ashamed of any of them — or hardly any. But I wasn't proud of a single one either. It's as if . . .' I paused to take another gulping breath '. . . not one of them said anything. Does that sound mad?'

Ned stared into his wineglass.

'I once read something by a painter — I forget who, someone quite eminent — who claimed that all artists paint the same things,' he said thoughtfully.

And even in my overwrought condition I thought how typical of Ned Cowper to channel this emotional outpouring safely into the third person. But I had underrated his perceptiveness.

'S-someone like me might say — with justice — that such-and-such an artist paints portraits, another landscapes. This one paints flowers, another still life. But no. He said that whatever might appear on the surface of their canvasses, all good artists are actually c-communicating the identical great preoccupations of mankind: life, death, l-l-love, pain, happiness . . .' Ned shrugged, tucked his tablecloth of a handkerchief back into his pocket.

'I don't set out to paint love,' I said, 'or death. Nothing as grand and mystical as that.'

'Love and death,' observed Ned, 'are surely the commonest of human experiences. C-commonplace even, in their way.'

I digested this.

'Seb's always going on about resonances,' I said. 'A piece of work must have *resonances* reaching beyond the surface appearance. But I always thought there was a touch of the Emperor's New Clothes about it. Only Sebastian bloody Ford can feel these resonances. I paint people and cats,' I added defiantly, taking a swig of wine. 'And houses and dustbins.'

Ned stayed comfortably silent. Somewhere in the valley an owl call fluted across the evening. I thought a bit more.

'But . . . well, yes. Maybe I understand what your artist meant. And even Seb. I do know that when I look at one of my paintings and see only a face, or a cat, a house or a dustbin — I feel I've failed. I'm looking for . . . something else. Although I can't say I know what.'

'There you are,' said Ned. 'I r-remember your telling me something like that about the portraits you've p-painted.'

'Did I? I don't remember.'

'I remember everything you say,' said Ned, and then looked conscience-stricken. 'W-w-we elephants, you know. Famous memories . . .'

'Thank you,' I said, boldly taking his hand for an instant and squeezing it.

'F-for what? You just needed to get it off your chest, that's all. We all have c-crises of confidence you know. No g-great matter at all.'

'I didn't intend to cry all over you in this boring way. But you're very comfortable to talk to. Do a lot of people say that to you?'

'N-no,' said Ned, evidently startled. 'At least, I hope they m-might think so, but no one actually . . . Anyway, you'll be all right now.'

This wasn't a question. He stated it quite matter of factly and I smiled cynically.

'How can you be so sure?'

'I'll p-p . . .' then, oddly, he flushed and bit his lip. 'How else am I ever g-going to see one of your p-paintings? You promised I could.' He stood up, placing his glass on the tray with his usual care. Behind him, a crescent moon shone coldly in the still light sky.

'Will you be here tomorrow?' I asked. It was the first time I had asked such a question.

'The last day of the f-fishing,' he said. 'W-wouldn't miss it for the world.'

CHAPTER FIVE

In the evenings, after Ned had left, I would sometimes light the stove in the sitting-room. The days were warm, but the evenings soon turned bitingly frosty. More often, like tonight, I retired early. Country hours. There was an enormous mahogany-framed bed squeezed between the eaves in my white-washed attic. I daresay, like the piano, it could only have been removed by demolishing the building. The mattress, however, was new — for which I was grateful. Old-fashioned feather mattresses can be drowning.

Reading a novel, lost under billowing acres of eiderdown, with half a dozen pillows propping me comfortably against the polished bedhead, I felt like Queen Elizabeth the First presiding over the State Bedchamber. It might be hard, I thought, to return to my workaday divan in the flat. I also thought that what this magnificent bed needed to complete it was another, much larger body, beside mine.

On the bedside cabinet (the drawers of which smelled nostalgically like all the bedroom furniture of mothballs and camphor) one of my three radios cocooned me from the owl-haunted hush outside, with a soothing wash of Radio Four. That night, as usual, I automatically switched the wireless off before the financial news. Even as background noise, I was choosy about programmes.

Only then did I hear the car outside. There was no skylight on the north side of the roof in my bedroom so, impulsively, I kicked away the eiderdown and hurried through to the other, smaller bedroom. I had to stand on a chair to peer through the tiny square window, but I could see headlights weaving and occasionally vanishing behind a bend as they progressed up

Lamp Hill. So much for Mr Danby. Either that car had driven all the way down the hill, only in order to turn round and retreat – which seemed unlikely – or it had cruised along the ravines and gullies of Lamp Lane beside my cottage.

What would anyone want in this lane at eleven o'clock at night? There were only fields, the Lodge – and the river.

I am not of a nervous disposition and did not seriously suppose I had observed salmon poachers about their business. However, even the suspicion that I might have done so intrigued rather than alarmed me. I snuggled back into bed – and watched the wall.

Early the next morning, I sat down determinedly at my table. Whether I did this out of an urge to please Ned, or whether I would have done so anyway, I cannot say.

At eight-thirty the telephone rang. The shrill bell startled me because I don't suppose the contraption had rung more than half a dozen times in two weeks. It had a real bell too, not an electronic trill. In fact, this telephone not only possessed a silver dial, it was old-fashioned enough to be moulded in that heavy black material which is cool and clammy in the hand as carved marble.

'Morning, my love.'

'Who's that?' Even as I tucked the receiver under my chin and spoke, I was squinting at the blank oblong of paper on the table.

'Darling, really . . .'

Who else, at precisely eight-thirty in the morning? Gerald had left the wife and kids in the rusk-war at home, to arrive in his bleakly glossy executive office exactly twenty-five minutes before the arrival of his bleakly glossy executive secretary. Frankie, part-time mistress and not at all glossy, had to be fitted neatly between the two worlds.

'I'm busy, Gerald. I've just started a picture.'

'When will you have time to talk? I need to talk, babe.'

'When I've finished the picture.'

'When will that be?'

People often ask how long it takes to complete a painting.

How long is a piece of string? Anything between a quarter of an hour and forever. My giant folder is stuffed with pictures I have never quite got round to completing but cannot (a mother with a delinquent child) bring myself to cast out because I feel sure there is promise concealed there somewhere.

On commissioned work, naturally, I can answer precisely how long a work will take. My agent battered that into me. For an average size mural — the size of a double doorway — allow approximately four weeks. Increase or decrease time allowance according to square footage and complexity of requirements.

The most expensive complication you could ask me for was my speciality: the inclusion of a portrait or portraits. Magda had seized on my knack for catching a likeness as the perfect sales gimmick. There was absolutely nothing, she declared with cynical certainty, that people liked looking at better than their own image. Give anyone a photograph album, and whose picture do they look for at once?

No man, she said, would be able to resist the promise of seeing himself (with flatteringly enhanced biceps) swinging across the Rousseau-esqe jungle on his own bathroom wall. Wouldn't a rich lady hotelier, she said, just adore to see herself foxtrotting in the arms of Fred Astaire through the glittering crowd, painted on the wall of her cocktail bar?

(In the background, of course. Nothing too ostentatious. Decking Madame lavishly in Wallis Simpson jewellery — it was just about the time of the big Windsor sale — was an afterthought of my own which went down particularly well.)

You name the fantasy, I bet I've painted it — from couples sunning themselves in ancient Pompeii along the wall of their swimming pool to children clutching the neck of Pegasus, as the horse springs from the battlements of a fairy-tale castle over the nursery mantelpiece.

Hurray for Magda, I guess. I could only marvel at the quantities of disposable income there proved to be washing around the home counties to pay for these self-indulgent creations.

Sebastian, sneeringly, called this paintings-by-the-yard. No matter that, in the four years immediately after leaving college, the sale of my paintings had barely lifted me into the income tax bracket. Half the time I couldn't even afford to frame the pictures to exhibit them in the grotty nearby Art Centre. I had waitressed and bar-maided to keep me (and him) in food. (And Ned Cowper dared to suggest I was a taker from relationships.) Meanwhile, Sebastian had continued to construct his huge, brooding edifices from scrap iron in the garage which for a long time was our shared studio. Rich in resonances no doubt, but bloody useless when it came to paying the bills. These days, I refused to listen.

Sebastian was my most trusted (if harshest) critic, but his obsession with sticking to his own cruelly difficult path could easily veer into bitter mockery of any other branch of art. His eye was perceptive, but his tongue was excoriating. Most of the time – even before I had supposedly sold out – he gave the impression he didn't think me fit to paint my own eye make-up, let alone to sell my daubs. Believing he actually rated my talent quite highly had been a perpetual act of faith for which I could rarely discern evidence.

Besides, by the time Magda walked into my little exhibition at the Art Centre, I had grown weary of communal living as well as of our draughty shared studio. It was all right for Seb, charging round with his blow torches. On my platform in the corner, my mittened hands would freeze to the brush. *La Bohème* without the songs. Sebastian and I both rented rooms in a damp Victorian cavern on the boundary of West Hampstead and Cricklewood. Five of us lived there, an arrangement which had drifted on from student days. As a student one can afford to wait half an hour for the bathroom or the telephone, and in those days I didn't mind finding my All Bran had been nicked again. Once Magda began to supply work however, when I was hurrying out at seven for a long day's graft, I began to find the old bohemian habits intolerable.

So, after a while, flush with the philistine gold, I ingratiated myself with bank manager and building society and bought my sunny, airy attic in Clapham. A year later, I had my car. Long and lean with black bodywork and white interior, it reminded me of an after-dinner mint. Sebastian's contempt for my materialism knew no bounds. It would have carried more weight if, after barely a month, he had not shamelessly tried to move in with me.

I refused point blank, but continued to see him from time to time. A taste of his own medicine. 'Attempted possession of partners,' I reminded him tartly, 'is even more bourgeois than possession of property.' Shortly after that, his sculptures started to find a market. His clothes remained equally crumpled and monochromatic, but were new. This jacket looked exactly like the old but actually smelled of leather instead of stinking of the paraffin which had fuelled the lethal studio stove. Mingling with the sweet leather-scent was often an elusive and expensive tang of female perfume. That, however, was nothing new.

Nonetheless, Seb's recently-acquired wealth did not sweeten his attitude to me. I told myself he was jealous because I still made more money than him, and that I could return to painting decent pictures whenever I chose.

It was about this time I met Gerald. He was a client – commissioning the decoration of the company dining-room. Not surprisingly, Gerald was the antithesis of everything Sebastian stood for. Gerald was an account director in an advertising agency. He wore immaculate suits, hand-made shirts, hair gel and mouth-watering aftershave. He showered me with attention, endearments and costly trifles in the most traditional way; and the sense of being a *mistress*, in the full-blown, naughty, old-fashioned sense of the word, added no end of a *frisson* to our relationship. For a while, anyway.

I just wished he would stop trying to improve me. Gerald's life was one long self-improvement drive. Under his influence I quite took to sensuous underwear (why not?) but I would not have my hair cut or give up chips. I liked the classy restaurants too – and the wine. He had certainly opened up a whole new world of delights here. I was duly grateful, and only sorry that he couldn't entirely share my pleasure. Wine, you see, was a game Gerald played (like all the many games in his complicated life) intensely seriously. My heart went out to him because he could not help but view bottles less as a delicious liquid to be consumed than as a fresh challenge to his hard-won expertise.

Anxiety to predict every last word on the label obscured the joys of the contents. Actually, this made him more likeable. Gerald, perfect, would have been unbearable.

He was also endearingly insecure about his painstakingly-concealed working-class origins and tiresomely miserable in his marriage. His wife, an ex-nurse turned earth mother, did not understand him. I was beginning to suspect this meant she did not particularly want to recast her personality every morning according to Gerald's latest improving plan.

This morning he told me again how much he needed my spiritual input into his life. Gerald's life was a dynamic flow chart of inputs and objectives. Fleetingly, I wished Ned could hear this exchange: Gerald too believed I was responsible for an input into the relationship. I did not merely take.

'I'm sorry,' I said firmly. 'Really Gerald, I can't talk about it now. I'm working.'

'I was going to come up to Yorkshire,' he said.

'I've tried to tell you. I'm busy. Up to my eyes.'

'After Christmas then,' he said, sounding hurt and huffy.

'For God's sake, that's years away. Not now, Gerald. Please . . .'

The conversation could not continue much longer. Gerald's secretary was due to arrive, and he was meticulous in keeping separate his working, family and sexual lives.

I suppose it was inevitable that, within minutes of my replacing the receiver, Sebastian telephoned. He was staying in the parental home of a wealthy girlfriend in Surrey, Felicity ffoulkes. I had met F-felicity a couple of times. Sebastian was completely frank about his many and varied affairs, and completely ruthless in abusing hospitality — as, for example, in making long-distance telephone calls at peak rates for no more urgent reason than to tell an erstwhile girlfriend she was throwing away her life and talents by burying herself in the sticks.

'I'm trying to work, Seb. I can't argue now.'

At least Sebastian would understand that. In one of his manic work-bouts he would go without sleep or food until his eyes glazed and he could not string a coherent sentence together. Gerald also worked hard but believed (as propounded

49

by his bible of efficient management and inter-personal communication) that time could always be found in the busiest
executive's day for important conversations.

'Okay,' said Sebastian. 'Any good?'

'I haven't started yet.'

'Need any help?'

'From Surrey?'

'I'll come up. If you like.'

'I'm sure F-felicity would love that.'

I was touched, though. Sebastian was promiscuous as a
tom-cat, but redeemed by a surprising, underlying loyalty to
old friends.

'You remember what I said, Fanny?'

'What?'

'Landscapes aren't your thing and they never will be.
People are. And I don't mean those crappy cartoons you've
been daubing over half the walls in London. No, shut up and
listen for once. Real people in some kind of real world they
really live and eat and sleep and fuck in — not schmaltzy rich
bitches farting around sub-Hollywood fairy-tale sets. Try and
remember that blue roof, will you? And get your finger out —
you've been gone nearly a month already.'

'Sebastian?'

But the phone line was dead.

That blue roof — I knew exactly what he was talking about:
ROOFSCAPE WITH WOMAN AND CAT was one of the few
paintings of mine Sebastian had seen fit to admire. In justice to
him, I should add, he was equally scathing about his own
work. ROOFSCAPE ... was a rather mournful acrylic I had
painted when Sebastian was away on a trip to Paris (getting
up to God-knew-what and I could only guess and seethe) and
I was alone in the Victorian cavern. Basically, it was no more
than the view from my room. A dark and slanting landscape
of rain-polished roofs under a cloudily Wagnerian night sky.
But one skylight was illuminated. In this window sat a woman
alone, a cat on her lap, and beside her a telephone which did
not ring. 'Cat in a wet bint's roof,' Seb had christened it.
Charming.

I went back to the table, thoughtfully.

And suddenly everything was clear. Instead of the trees, or the sun on the water, or the colour of the bracken behind, or the hazy Yorkshire hillside, I picked up my pencil – and swiftly drew Mr Bear.

CHAPTER SIX

Ned caught a fish.

I saw it happen, although for once I was not waiting for him outside. The clocks had gone back and days were fading by mid-afternoon. At a quarter to five with the light nearly gone, I was painting as if driven, determined to finish before he joined me. I was close to the end when a flicker of movement caught my eye. I looked down at the river to see a streak of silver hurtling out of the water and Ned twisting and turning frantically. Then fish and fisherman disappeared behind the overhanging sycamore, so I could not tell if he had secured his prey until some minutes later when I watched him tramp up the grass towards the Lodge.

I met him at the kitchen door. He was still wearing his wading boots with his rod over one shoulder. His face was flushed and split into a beaming grin.

'Hen salmon trout,' he said, raising one hand from which dangled the fish. 'Nothing very s-spectacular, I'm afraid. But it must be three pounds.'

'There are scales somewhere,' I said, opening one blue door, then another. I found the scales, and placed them on the sink. With some trepidation I took the fish from Ned as he waited, still booted, on the doorstep. The fish was surprisingly heavy – and slimy in the fingers. I nearly dropped it.

'C-c-careful. That stuff helps them s-slip through the water, you know.'

Poor thing. Its skin had a glorious sheen the like of which I had never seen on a fishmonger's slab. Blue as slate, but with the rich opalescence of mother-of-pearl. The eyes were dull, however, and the teeth alarmingly business-like. I balanced the creature across the flimsy plastic tray of the scales.

'Two pounds five ounces,' I pronounced. Then, seeing Ned's face fall, 'Or maybe six. Nearly two and a half pounds.'

'Ah well. Amazing p-piece of luck to catch anything at all. I never expected to, you know. Not with the water the w-way it's . . .' and then his voice tailed away as the implications of that confession struck both of us.

'Come inside,' I said. 'Too cold to drink outside. What shall I do with your prize? No, I know. I must photograph you with it.'

'N-nonsense,' said Ned, laughing. 'A tiddler like this?'

But I photographed him nonetheless, standing outside my kitchen door with the trout suspended by his side, exactly as though it had been a thirteen-stone shark. Against Ned's bulk, it could have been a domestic goldfish.

'And now what do you want me to do with it?' I called, as Ned stripped off his waterproofs outside.

'Eat it.'

'I couldn't,' I said. 'You caught it. It's yours.'

'I've eaten hundreds of salmon trout fresh from the Wrag. You d-deserve to try one. My p-present in return for all the splendid wine I've drunk.'

'I wouldn't have a clue what to do with it. It must be full of intestines and things.'

Ned stepped through the doorway in his stockinged feet. Over the previous week I had been given plenty of opportunity to admire his selection of socks. For a man of apparently simple tastes they were surprisingly luxurious. Today's were a clear cornflower blue and — I would swear — cashmere.

'I'll g-gut it for you,' he said. 'Got a sharp knife? And perhaps an apron.'

The strings of my apron barely met round his waist, and I took longer than necessary to tie them together.

With the speedy nonchalance of a surgeon, Ned slit the silver belly of the fish. I did not observe the rest of the process too closely.

'And what now?' I said, as he briskly rinsed his hands under the tap.

'P-personally I favour a mixture of baking and poaching,' he

53

said. 'Plenty of butter, lemon peel, parsley and seasoning inside the bird, then wrap it in foil.'

'You wouldn't like to do it, I suppose?'

I had spoken jokingly, expecting him to laugh off the suggestion, but he did not. Immediately, I pressed home my assault.

'There must be far too much for one person . . .'

'B-b-beverley has only left me cold meat in the fridge,' he remarked.

'Beverley?' I managed to say. Fortunately my breath deserted me before I reached, 'Your wife?'

'Sort of p-part-time housekeeper,' he said, sounding surprised, as he often did, that I didn't already know this. With magnificent lack of logic he told me little or nothing about himself and apparently expected me to know everything. 'Bev d-divides her days between the Manor and us.'

Relief at learning Beverley's innocent identity mingled with distaste at his use of the plural pronoun, 'us'. But then many a once-married person continues to speak of their household in the plural.

'And the f-fishing season finishes today,' he remarked — I thought irrelevantly. He glanced at his watch. 'I have to be home by ten.'

'It's barely six.'

'Shall I c-cook the whole meal?' he suggested shyly. 'That is — if you have a lemon. And perhaps potatoes — a l-little salad?'

'Please do,' I said, unable to believe my luck. 'Help yourself to everything you need.'

'And you can f-finish your painting. You were hard at w-work when I arrived.'

'Do you like cooking?'

'Love it.'

'If you really don't mind . . .' So saying, I closed, triumphantly, the back door.

The spider secures her fly.

In spite of everything that has happened since, the memory of that evening can still start tears in me. And yet nothing remarkable happened. Nothing extraordinary was said.

54

We were like children playing house. Play-acting an evening at home, with, I suppose, the roles reversed. Ned, wrapped in his apron, pottered from cupboard to sink to fridge, singing softly and (even to my uncritical ears) tunelessly. I switched on a brilliant spotlight at my desk and chatted through the open doorway.

'It's better, isn't it?' said Ned, some time later, as I padded into the kitchen to re-fill my glass. 'The b-block — whatever it was — it's gone?'

'Do you . . . want to see?'

'If I may.'

I shrugged gracelessly and stood back to let him walk through to the sitting-room.

I wanted him to see the picture — of course I did — but I was naggingly afraid that he would get it wrong. I feared that Ned, like so many kind-hearted people in their natural anxiety to reassure and hearten a painter, would scan the picture in one fast glance and immediately begin to spout superlatives. This triggers an absurd and uncheckable progression. You, the artist, then feel it necessary (in a kind of desperate honesty) to point out one or two obvious flaws. They must then shower the praise even more smotheringly, unstoppable as foam from a fire extinguisher. If you continue to argue, suddenly it appears that you are making an unpleasantly personal attack on this person's critical faculties.

So, as Ned looked at my painting, I could barely bring myself to enter the room. I watched him from the doorway, suppressing thoughts of all the things I did not want him to say. These included: *Is that me?*, *Lovely sky* . . ., *Aren't you a clever girl!* ugh — and, *You've done all this in just one day?* Or, I suppose alternatively, *But what did you do before lunch?*

'It's extraordinary,' said Ned at length. 'It's a p-perfect evocation of October. The Indian s-summer afternoon. Radiant warmth — b-but you know there's frost waiting to bite, underneath. It's a landscape — nearly all t-trees and, well, c-countryside but the f-focus of the whole thing seems to be that little figure, fishing down there. That is to say . . .' he smiled apologetically, 'me. And, somehow, he makes the whole picture about fishing. Sorry, I'm talking b-balderdash.'

'Oh no you're not,' I murmured.

'It j-just seems to sum up what's so heavenly about taking a r-rod down to the river.'

He fell silent again.

'So you think it's — okay?' Now, when Ned had displayed such enchanting perception, I was prepared to receive the most outrageously over-stuffed compliments. I was even hungry for them.

'Okay? It's a p-picture worth selling your house for.'

'I don't cost that much.'

'You t-told me you were exorbitantly expensive. Several t-times in fact.'

'You shall have it,' I declared.

Ned flushed red. 'No,' he said, horrified. 'B-believe me, I would b-b-buy it if I could afford it, but . . .'

'Please let me give it to you,' I said. 'I shall probably put it in the exhibition, so you can't have it for a long time. But Christopher will just have to accept that one of the paintings is not for sale. No, I insist. It was watching you spilling your Smarties that was the starting point, somehow. And now I know what I'm supposed to be doing. I know what I'm going to paint. I almost can't understand why I was being so stupid.'

'And what are you going to p-paint?'

'People, where they belong. That probably means nothing, or nothing remarkable. Particularly if you'd seen my earlier work, because it's only what I've always painted. Sebastian Ford, an old friend, reminded me. He helped.' I added conscientiously. 'I must send him a postcard.'

'Ah Sebastian,' said Ned with a faint enigmatic smile. 'I must look at my fish.'

'We once shared a studio,' I said, 'years ago.'

I followed Ned to the kitchen. He was bending down to lift a foil-shrouded tin out of the oven, but I could sense the hostility which the mention of Sebastian had provoked. This both flattered and irritated me. Since Ned had never made a bolder advance than, momentarily, to touch my hand, there was little enough justification for resenting discarded lovers. Well, kind of discarded.

The kitchen table was neatly laid with the mongrel collection of cutlery and plates, and decorated (endearingly) with a broken sprig of geranium blossom arranged in a sherry glass. This touch could not disguise, however, the utilitarian bleakness of chipped blue formica in an overlit kitchen. On impulse I found a large orange, selected a small sharp knife and began to carve. Ned busied himself silently.

'You must tell me where I must look for subjects,' I said after a while.

'S-sorry?' said Ned, placing a bowl of salad on the table, from which the garlic sang alluringly.

'What goes on round here. In darkest winter.'

'S-same as everywhere else, I dare say. Hunting, shooting.'

'You're not serious.'

Ned looked at me inquiringly.

'It's so clichéd,' I said. 'Huntin', shootin', fishin'. I thought that sort of thing was confined to detective novels and ducal estates. Not real life in a little village like Thornbeck.'

'It's the local industry,' said Ned. 'Big business in this p-part of the world.'

'How is that?'

'Do you know how much p-people are prepared to pay for a day p-potting pheasants? Or rather, grouse up on the moor? Grouse is the real rich man's sport.'

I shook my head.

'Anything from a thousand pounds. Each.'

'Isn't it cheaper to go and buy a couple at Sainbury's?'

'When you buy a brace of b-birds in the shop, they cost you a fraction of what they cost the landowner to put the p-poor little blighters in the sky. That's what I mean about big business. Harry G-godley over the next valley has a farm rearing pheasant p-poults; Roger buys them, charges a k-king's ransom for the shoots; Sue and Albert Brough up at the Wheatsheaf accommodate the parties, feed them, water them with vintage claret. And then there's the fishing, of course, which –'

'And do *you* shoot?' I asked quickly. 'And hunt?'

He seemed to flinch. 'N-no,' he said. 'I d-don't care for killing. And I know that's illogical, b-because I do fish. And the s-salmon is quite as magnificent a specimen of God's creation as any bird or fox.' He spoke with passionate anxiety.

'I'm not accusing you of anything,' I said. 'I was only asking.'

'It's been p-pointed out to me often how inconsistent my position is,' he said, turning away again and beginning to unwrap the foil from his baking tin. 'B-but there you are. The countryside in winter. "The red blood reigns in the winter's pale . . ."'

'Shakespeare?' I put down the orange, and rummaged in the cupboard under the stairs. I was sure I had seen there a box of stubby white candles.

'I w-wouldn't like you to think I'm f-frightfully literary,' said Ned, neatly depositing his fish, whole and perfect, on a large plate. 'It's the only play I can quote from. *The Winter's Tale*, you know. I – um – helped out with a local production. The Langton Players. And you know how it is, the words g-go round in the head like a tune for months.'

'Shakespeare? In the local Am. Dram.?'

'It struck me as a c-cultural advance on last year's offering,' said Ned, 'which was entitled *Bell Bottoms or Bust*.' He grinned as he drained the potatoes. 'Several of the l-local teenagers were studying the play for O-level. That's what gave them the idea.'

'And you took part? You don't strike me as a would-be thespian.'

'Um . . . a v-very small part. I say, what's that?'

I had cut the shell of the orange into a prettily crenellated lantern and stuck the candle inside.

'Hallowe'en lantern.'

'All Saints Eve.'

'If you will.' I switched off the glaring hundred-watts overhead, and the kitchen became a glamorous cavern of shadows, lit only by the quivering flame and strip-lamp over the cooker. 'Can we see enough?' Then, swiftly, in case Ned said no, continued, 'The fish looks terrific. What part did you play?'

'What?'

'In the play?'

'Oh,' Ned dissected neat slabs of pink trout on to each of our plates. '*The Winter's Tale* is n-notorious, you know, for a particular s-stage direction. Shakespeare wants to get rid of a character and obviously c-couldn't be bothered to work it into the plot. So suddenly, from nowhere, he simply says, "Exit pursued by a bear".' Ned's shy smile flickered in the candle light. 'I was the bear.'

I burst out laughing. 'Type-casting,' I said.

I knew Ned had said he had to leave before ten. What sort of engagement could he possibly have at ten o'clock at night? In this part of the world? Or was this towny arrogance? I hoped he might be persuadable.

In fact, our dinner ended sooner – and abruptly.

I bounced and glittered through the evening with the airy insouciance of a soap bubble. My first picture in two years was on one table, Ned was sitting at the other. Every so often, however, I would look up to find him staring at me with an expression I was hard put to interpret. Nothing as simple and welcome as lust. Anxiety perhaps – as though he was forever on the verge of framing some searing question. At first, I smiled inquiringly – but at once he would glance away, and begin to talk about food or something equally innocuous. He was a good cook, incidentally. I ate a lot. More than I had for months, but he fussed over me like my grandmother.

'You obviously d-don't eat enough,' he said.

'Don't you like thin women?' I murmured, glancing at him lasciviously under half-closed eyelids – only to watch him flush and flounder among half-finished sentences. Of course he ... that wasn't what he ... Somehow, by the time we were toying with cheese, he had steered the conversation back into safer waters. Shakespeare.

'Perhaps,' I said idly, 'I shall call my exhibition "A Winter's Tale".'

'Does it have to have a name? Is that usual?'

I shook my head, 'No more than a painting does. Less. But sometimes just thinking of a title helps to focus ideas in your head. Even if it never appears in the catalogue.'

'The t-title of the p-play is actually *The Winter's Tale*,' he said apologetically.

I pulled a face. 'No. I think it would have to be $\underline{A}$ ...'

'A pity Shakespeare d-didn't have the benefit of your advice,' he murmured. And then, after a pause for thought, 'There's a line in it, "A sad tale's best for winter . . ."'

'Oh no,' I said, pouncing on the idea with soft and lecherous emphasis. The novelty of this continued role-reversal struck me as slightly comical even at the time — although I was in dead earnest. I was playing sweet-persuading seducer to a man twice my size who was blushing like a virgin. 'I think this winter could be a wonderfully happy tale. For me, and . . .'

'It's a r-r-remarkably foolish play in many ways,' he said breathlessly. 'Let me lend you a c-copy. I'll —'

'Listen,' I said suddenly, abandoning my pursuit only temporarily because I heard again a car's engine in the road outside. I seized Ned's arm and dragged him to the window. Today, the car's lights were vanishing in the other direction, towards the village. 'Is it poachers?' I demanded excitedly, and not in the least seriously. The suggestion seemed to offer a promising pretext to cast myself into his arms, in a flutter of feminine panic.

'No,' said Ned, staring out into the darkness. 'No poacher worth his salt would bother to waste his nets in weather like this. I think you and I have eaten the only fish in the Wrag.' Then he turned back to me. 'I must go.'

'Go?' I repeated forlornly. 'We haven't finished the cheese.'

'F-frankie,' he said suddenly and urgently, putting one hand on my shoulder — but with no more pressure than a feather — 'this evening has b-been wonderful.'

'Hasn't it just?' I agreed blithely.

'I j-just wanted to say . . . that I'll remember it.'

'Perhaps again?'

He was already hauling on his absurdly huge boots and appeared not to hear. Outside, the weather was markedly colder.

He vanished into the clear Hallowe'en night without another word.

CHAPTER SEVEN

I found a postcard featuring the Fylingdales Early Warning System to send to Sebastian. The science-fiction incongruity of these monster white globes squatting on the moors would, I knew, appeal to him much more strongly than pretty views of the Wrag Valley.

Ta v. much, I wrote. *All love, Fanny Adams.*

With anyone else I might have been more effusive, but not Sebastian. His most lyrical outpourings to me that I could remember were his observations on one occasion that I smelled like a puppy, and on another that I interfered less with his work than any woman he'd ever met. He had never told me he loved me. And yet, in his way, I had believed he did — more than Gerald anyway. Gerald did not love. Gerald conducted on-going inter-personal experiences.

On impulse, I added a postscript — *Almost suspect incipient splash . . .*

When we were all students together, drinking cheap wine and smoking unmentionable substances late into the night, Seb and I (and Rosie and Lawrence and whoever else was living in Limberton Gardens at the time) took infinite, narcissistic pleasure in dissecting and defining the nature of our own and (though naturally with less fascination) other people's creativity. One can only blush, and excuse most of the high-minded twaddle we propounded on the grounds of youth and drunkenness.

One of our longest-running and most lovingly detailed conceits we called The Splash Theory. This pre-supposes all kinds of dodgy premises, not least that the act of creation (any sort of creation — musical, literary or artistic) is not an intellectual activity at all. In fact, it emanates not from the artist's conscious self, but from some mystical source which might be identified as (depending on your point of view) his subconscious, a pool of universal experience, or even God. Whatever the origin, the artist is himself not a creator, just a channel. Thus, Mozart could sit down and pen symphonies faster than other people could copy them out precisely because he was *not* consciously making them up as he went along. Ho hum.

Naming this, 'The Splash', came from children's painting books. Do you remember the sort, described as 'magic books', which contained at first glance only blank white pages? All the child had to do was slosh on clear water and, magically, a coloured picture would appear. This was our image for the perfect condition of artist as channel. He was no more than the innocent splash of water which made the pre-existing picture appear.

Nonsense, of course. Leaving genius out of the question (although as students we were avid detectives of elements of genius in ourselves and each other) any creative work is surely ninety per cent perspiration. At least. But that image of the magic paintbook stuck because, very, very infrequently – like the day I first met Ned when my hand had seemed to be sketching of its own accord – there are pictures which appear, and (if you can believe this) I've no idea how I painted them.

There are one or two in my folder like that which I have kept, not because they're bad, nor even because they're particularly good (although good enough to have sold). I've kept them simply because I do not know how I did them.

In the days immediately after my curtailed supper with Ned, I painted furiously fast. I would get up in the morning with no idea of what I was going to do, sit down amid the wash of sketches, notes and decaying collages, and by the next morning I would be genuinely naïvely amazed to see what I had accomplished. I started many paintings, finished none. I knew they could be finished later. In London if needs be. Here, I felt I was riding a flood tide of ideas precipitously as a surfer.

Fishermen, farmer and sheepdog, loggers with a vicious chain saw. Even Mr Danby, riding shot-gun on his milk-float.

Mr Danby, philosopher and milkman, was back on the round by this time — although a nephew had been commandeered to drive and assist him. In fact, Mr Danby confided, he was not so much recovered as unable to bear the house at half-term with seven children. His shy nephew drove and carried and counted money. Mr Danby's contribution to the round was purely social, although the presence of the nephew was a further irritating obstacle to extracting the information I was after. I tried a fresh tangent.

'Shooting parties in at the Manor soon,' I said, 'Or so I gather.'

'Oh aye,' said Mr Danby. 'It'll be a regular battle of the Somme down here by next week.'

'Do I have to lie on the floor?' I said smiling, but Mr Danby took my feeble sally literally.

'Very careful is Mr Vaisey about safety procedures,' he said. 'Well, he has to be, doesn't he, to be with all these city-types who don't know a shot-gun from a pea-shooter. Make the old Squire turn in his grave, it would. My word, there was a man with a gun. A legend from Hull to Newcastle in his day was the old Squire.'

'That would be Ned Cowper's father-in-law?' I suggested recklessly, because the patient nephew was standing at the end of the terrace, empty bottles tucked under his arm, watching us.

Mr Danby glanced at me rather oddly.

'Yes and no,' he said. 'After all, they didn't wed until the old man was underground. Well they couldn't, could they? Did you enjoy the fish?'

The question, uttered so innocently, almost deprived me of speech.

'The trout? Yes. Very much. How . . . how did you come to hear about that?'

'Only fish reported caught in the last week.' He smiled, his eyes transparent as a Mediterranean bay. 'Mr Cowper told our Beverley he'd dropped it in at the Lodge, here. Course he couldn't be expected to use it himself. Not all on his own at the Dower House.'

All on his own. All on his own.

'Of course not,' I said faintly.

'Right then lad, I'm coming. Same tomorrow, Frankie?'

On several mornings, absorbed in my work, I failed to notice Mr Danby's comings and goings at all. More irritatingly, I was not aware of Ned's solitary visit either.

The first I learned of this was the following morning when I looked on the front door mat. I had never opened the front door – in fact, it gave every impression of having rusted comfortably into place long before the last war – but the post and newspaper (both delivered by the good-natured postman) were pushed through it daily. Beneath a couple of letters and *The Independent* I found a slim yellow copy of *The Winter's Tale*. There was a flimsy scrap of paper tucked inside, labelled 'Notes' at the top, clearly torn from a diary. Ned's handwriting was as tiny and spiked as he himself was large and curved.

You looked so absorbed in your painting, I couldn't bear to interrupt. Here's the promised copy. Thank you again.

Yrs, Ned

I muttered some foul words and returned to work.

Ensconced in the mahogany couch that night, however, I glanced through the play, not without difficulty, because I had not encountered Shakespearian language on the page since I was a schoolgirl. Moreover, a mildly dyslexic schoolgirl. Even now, if I panic, words can begin to crawl round the page like a tin of demented grey maggots. Fortunately there was a summary of the story at the beginning of the book for simpletons like me. This frankly reassured the reader that many elements of the plot were ludicrous, not least the unfortunately abrupt introduction of the bear.

The abrupt introduction of a bear into my life had not been unfortunate in the least, I thought, happily. The flyleaf was inscribed, in a hand slightly larger and not quite as regular as his present fist: *Edward Charles Seymour Cowper, Charterhouse School, November 1967.*

I should not have given the book more than a cursory glance had it not been for the crabbed maze of pencilled notes in the margin. I soon realized these dated not from Ned's schooldays, but from the recent production. They were not the notes of a walk-on bear either. Some were stage directions, some were illegible, some personal memoranda . . . *Vital Camillo help Leontes down vestry steps*, read one. *Harry to double if poss., Too much talcum powder!, Piano as cottage, sideboard?, Ask Mrs M. about Perdita's décolletage.*

The notes sketched a picture of a production of awe-inspiring awfulness which had no doubt been enjoyed hugely by participants, if not by the audience. Even here, I was probably being ungenerous. I dare say Perdita's mum and dad beamed besottedly throughout at their pretty daughter with her daring cleavage (if Mrs M. had proved ineffectual).

What the notes showed was that Ned had actually directed the show. At the time I wondered, smiling, why on earth he should have chosen to burden himself with such an extraordinary task. In retrospect, I realise I was remarkably dim-witted.

As the weather grew sharply colder and darker a week stretched into ten days and Ned did not visit the Lodge again.

In the meantime, I had noticed in a field on the other side of Thornbeck Bridge that a monumental bonfire was under construction. On an impulse, on Guy Fawkes night I had driven into the village to watch the revels. Inevitably, I hoped Ned might be present − but he was not, although I noticed there were no lights showing in the windows of the Dower House. Mr Danby pointed out his children to me with insults (bursting with pride) as they cavorted with sparklers, their chubby faces glowing, Bruegel-esque, in the hot light of the fire. I ate two hot dogs, took some photographs, gathered some spent firework tubes and then went home. It had not been a wasted evening by any means. It was the starting point of another picture, although it was impossible to catch the startling brilliance of fireworks in flat paint.

As if God was playing fire-warden, the rain streamed from the skies soon after midnight that night to douse the ashes of the bonfire, and barely let up for several days. By November the twelfth − a Saturday, I seem to recall − I was haggard-eyed from painting, and there was still no sign of Ned.

In the early afternoon the rain eased up, and my picture got stuck. Recognizing that the more paint I ladled on, the more constipated the beast would look, I washed my brushes. Actually, I think I had known ever since I woke up that morning what I intended to do. Since the mountain had not chosen to walk my way . . .

I pulled on a waterproof coat, wellingtons and a shiny red sou'wester which I had bought on impulse in South Molton Street, judging it just the thing for Yorkshire tempests. Up here, I was painfully aware that it was as appropriate as a ballgown in a fish and chip shop, but it was the only gear I possessed to keep my head dry. Humming nonchalantly, I tucked the copy of the play into one pocket, and set off down Lamp Lane.

The mud in the lane was as thick and glossy as chocolate mousse, and the ford which had been a dry slab of concrete the last time I walked past, was now a slick, swift-flowing torrent of oily brown. The rain steadily intensified from a damp drizzle to a purposeful downpour.

With the red sou'wester pulled low over my eyes I marched up the shallow steps of the Dower House and rapped smartly with the shiny brass knocker. I stifled trepidation, reminding myself I was a twenty-nine-year-old woman returning a book to an acquaintance, not a love-sick teenager with a feeble excuse to visit the love-object.

The door opened.

'Hello?' said Ned inquiringly. 'C-can I help you?'

I tilted my face up so that he could see under the brim of the hat.

'G-good Lord! Frankie.' This was not the most warming of welcomes, but he did then step back, holding open the door for me. 'My poor girl, you must be soaked. C-come in.'

'Just called to return the play,' I said. 'You don't want me dripping all over your carpets.'

'Nonsense. Leave the waterproofs in the porch there.'

Through an open doorway, opposite, I saw a big walnut desk, comfortably cluttered with books. A brass reading lamp cast a pool of creamy light over a sheet of paper and a discarded pen. Ned had been writing. He did not lead me into that room, however, but opened an elegant pair of double doors on the other side of the hall.

The drawing-room into which I followed him was perfectly proportioned, exquisitely furnished – and as inappropriate to Ned as any room could possibly be.

The satin-sheened legs of a Hepplewhite sofa and chairs looked far too slender to support his substantial frame. There were knick-knacks arranged on dainty constructions which resembled (and may even have been) cake stands. Crystal smelling-salt bottles clustered on one, thimbles on another. There was a collection of jewelled hatpins stuck, 'amusingly' hedgehog-like, into a cork ball. Skittish bows were knotted over an anaemic trio of water colours – pictures which, at a glance, I dismissed as having more to do with good taste than good painting. There was a fine eighteenth-century portrait over the fireplace, however, after the style of Gainsborough, and I was far from criticising the room. It would be impossible to do so. Every subtle colour and texture, from the faded carpet to the extravagantly draped curtains, the drum-tight upholstery to the flirtatious assortment of cushions, was blended with the unerring eye of a master. Or rather a mistress. I could no more believe this was Ned's room than I would attribute silk cami-knickers to a navvy.

'I'm sorry, there's no f-fire,' said Ned distractedly.

'Please, it doesn't matter. I mustn't stay.'

He did not sit down. Neither did I. Then, out of the corner of my eye, I saw her.

The photograph was enclosed in a delicately-wrought silver frame on a side-table. It was one of those old-fashioned débutante portraits, with bare shoulders, clever lighting and a single string of pearls. She had very dark, possibly even black hair, streaming back from a hairline which dipped, heart-like, into a point over the centre of her wide, clear brow. She had dimpled cheeks and enormous eyes. She was even more exquisite than the room.

'Would you l-like some tea? You really shouldn't have bothered to t-tramp all this way in such ghastly weather –'

'I wanted to see you,' I blurted out, and then stopped, unnerved. 'I mean . . .' But I couldn't continue. I hoped Ned would rescue me, but he only stared out of the window, even more tongue-tied than me.

The clock on the mantelpiece cut across our frozen silence with a sweetly-tuned chime. Three o'clock.

'F-frankie, I should have . . .' began Ned helplessly. All I could hear in his voice was dismay. Guilt and dismay.

'I'll go,' I said, and even managed a rictus of a smile as I turned towards the door.

'No . . .' Ned nearly shouted.

'No what?' drawled a rich bass voice, and the drawing-room door was carelessly kicked open in front of me by a short, black-haired man who looked from Ned to me, raised his eyebrows enquiringly, then glanced back towards Ned again.

'I was just telling Frankie − she m-mustn't walk back to the Lodge in this shocking weather,' said Ned with admirable presence of mind.

'The Lodge?' repeated the newcomer, in exaggerated tones of surprise. 'Is this by any chance my winter tenant?'

'F-frankie, you haven't met my b-brother-in-law, I believe, Roger Vaisey. R-roger, this is Frances Cleverdon. Frankie and I m-met when I was fishing down in the L-lodge Pool.'

'So you said, but you might have been more explicit, Neddy,' said Roger Vaisey. 'I got the impression the artistic Miss Cleverdon was a fifty-year-old gorgon in tweeds, executing lurid watercolours of sunset over the heather.'

'Not from me you d-didn't,' said Ned. 'Just come from the pub?'

'Certainly,' said Roger Vaisey loudly. 'What else is a chap supposed to do on a day like this?' He turned back to me, and took my hand. 'But Frankie brings the sun out.'

My first conscious impression of Roger Vaisey was that he was a ham actor over-playing the part of amorous upper-class oaf. The hearty type who knows only one way to deal with women − or rather with *gels* − which is to flirt with lead-clichéd gallantry. However, feeling snubbed by Ned, I was ready to play the game. I blossomed into my most luscious smile and told him I was delighted to meet him at last.

'But why haven't we met before?' he said. 'Have you been avoiding me?' He leaned towards me confidentially and I caught the faint whiff of whisky. 'Has Edward warned you against me?'

'Why? Are you dangerous?'

'Fatal,' he said and smiled back wolfishly. The smile did not, as they say, reach his eyes. I had plenty of opportunity to admire his teeth, though, which were white, even and numerous as an American soap star's. In fact, analysed feature by feature, Roger Vaisey ought to have been attractive — if you go for the glowering Heathcliff type. He had a long face with dark, hooded eyes set under craggy black brows, a splendid aquiline nose and a chin any romantic novelist would describe as masterful. A blue shadow over chin and jowls, obviously ineradicable even after the closest shave, completed the image of brooding brute.

His hair was prematurely receding — I say prematurely, because I knew he was much the same age as Ned — but he was far from bald. The high hairline gave him a noble forehead, and dipped into a dramatic widow's peak in the centre. This peak was evidently a hereditary trait of the Vaiseys, I thought sourly. Exaggerated by his receding and slicked-back hair, the effect on him was rather reminiscent of Dracula.

No, I did not find him attractive. Roger Vaisey was too short. Don't misunderstand me — I'm not saying there's anything wrong with short men (except, maybe, their tendency to Napoleon complexes). After all, Roger Vaisey was much the same height as Sebastian, but Seb was perfectly proportioned at five foot seven — a slim boyish manikin — whereas Roger's head was too big and all his lack of height, if I may so express it, was concentrated in his stubby legs. He had the rugged face and powerful chest and shoulders of a towering giant, with only half the length of leg to match. In fact, with his long arms and barrel-shaped torso, he was more than a little ape-like.

'Haven't you been lonely at the Lodge?' he said. I glanced towards Ned to see him studying the carpet intently.

'I've been busy,' I said.

'But what about the long cold nights?' responded Roger grinning. He was like a terrier: sees rabbit, feels obliged to give chase but, if you ask me, he was propelled more by instinct than any particular interest in the prey. Any old rabbit would have had the same effect. I felt rather piqued. He followed up with a few conventional questions about my comfort at the Lodge, to which I replied equally conventionally.

'You're very slow in offering us tea, Ned,' he complained.

Ned and I spoke simultaneously — only Ned stumbled and stuttered while I replied crisply that I was here only to return a book and wanted to get back to my painting. And Ned had been writing when I arrived and I'd already held him up long enough.

'You workers make one feel such a drone,' Roger interrupted. 'And you can't paint in this weather, Frankie. The rain will wash the stuff off your brush.'

'I'm not planning to work out of doors.'

'You mean you don't paint tasteful sunsets over the heather?'

'No.'

'What else do lady *artistes* find to paint in North Yorkshire?'

'I am *not* a lady *artiste*.'

'Wild flowers?'

'Not bloody likely.'

For the first time Roger smiled as though he meant it. 'Maybe you arrange piles of nappies,' he continued, eyeing me speculatively, 'and collect grants from some lunatic left-wing quango?'

'She p-paints rather wonderfully actually,' interposed Ned, and added with a simple pride which touched me, 'I figure in one of her paintings m-myself, as a m-matter of fact. I trust I m-may have earned my place in posterity by featuring in a F-frances Cleverdon masterpiece.'

Roger looked at me again. 'Frances Cleverdon,' he repeated slowly, as though assimilating my name for the first time. 'Wasn't it you who did Margery Feverley's nursery? Little Red Riding Hood, with old George lurking behind a tree as the wolf? I told Margie that image of their father would probably scar her little brats' psyches for ever. Was that you?'

I nodded.

Roger laughed. 'George is so proud of it, you know. Pretends he's mortally insulted, but insists on marching every guest up to view the wall. By the third visit the novelty begins to wear off.'

'I'm sure it does,' I said heartily. 'I must go.'

'It's raining,' said Roger, unnecessarily. 'Do you often draw people as animals?'

'Only when drunk.'

Or when, like Georgie-Porgie Feverley, they creep up to the nursery while Margie's away to breathe stale cigar smoke and much-too-fresh suggestions into my ear.

'How do you make a face into an animal?'

'Quite often I just — see people as animals. As soon as I meet them.'

His cousin would forever be a bear for me. Sebastian was a thin and wily, solitary black alley cat. Gerald — poor Gerald — had always been a pig. Pink, perfectly-groomed and perfumed, but a pig. As a matter of fact, I'm fond of pigs, but I wouldn't expect Gerald to be flattered.

'What am I?' demanded Roger.

'A gorilla.'

Not only was his shape unmistakably simian, he gave the impression, like many balding men, of being hairy just about everywhere other than on his head. Thick black tufts speckled his wrists. He even possessed, I had noticed, the long, curving and curiously delicate hands of an ape.

'Gorilla?' exclaimed Roger, the black brows colliding sharply.

I had answered promptly and truthfully, but as my grandmother was wont to point out, honesty and good manners are *not* the same thing. What the hell. He'd been needling me about painting.

And in fact, almost at once, Roger grinned and roared with laughter. 'Rude girl,' he spluttered, visibly preening. 'This *artiste* is *certainly* no lady, Ned.' For a second I thought he might actually thump his chest with Tarzan cries. Now isn't that just men for you? Tickled pink to be cast as a skulking scavenging wolf, or a brainless hunk of brawny ape — but draw them (say) as a friendly civilised domesticated pig and they never speak to you again.

'I will run you home,' he said. 'I insist. Ned should be scribbling words of wisdom, so you and I can slip away irreverently — two renegades together, eh?' His laugh gurgled with renewed innuendo. 'Coming across later for a nightcap, Ned?' I glanced towards Ned too, but if I was hoping for some protest, some sign of jealousy, I was to be disappointed. He smiled, distantly and dismissively as the Pope over St Peter's Square.

'And you must come to the Manor, Frankie,' said Roger, helping me into my mackintosh and allowing his hands to rest on my shoulders longer than necessary. 'How about drinks on Saturday? We're eating up at the boozer — join us there too if you like. Maybe even Neddy might be persuaded to join us.'

'Thank you,' said Ned. 'Shooting p-parties are not quite my thing.' At last he looked at me. 'Goodbye, Frankie. I'm sorry — we d-didn't have a chance to talk. To discuss the play, that is.'

Roger swept me away before I could reply. His sports car was even longer, lower and leaner than mine and for the early part of the journey we talked cars.

'Useless beast up here in winter, really,' he said. 'I have a four-wheel drive job for when the going gets tough. Marvellous things. Just like a tank. Drinks the sauce like a tank too, of course. You're a funny girl,' he said abruptly, 'talking about fuel injection and electronic ignition.'

'I don't understand the mechanics. I just happen to like my car.'

'You will come on Saturday, won't you?' I was surprised less by the change of subject than by the apparent sincerity with which he spoke. As though he really wanted me to be there.

'Thank you,' I said.

'It can get lonely at the Manor these days,' he went on. 'My wife's left me, as you probably know.'

After Ned's reserve, such an unsolicited confidence was almost shocking. Roger was taking the bends down Lamp Hill at hair-raising speed.

'I didn't know that, no.'

'People will tell you it was because I wasn't faithful,' he said, glancing at me between gear changes. I wished he would keep his eyes on the road. 'We Vaiseys have an appalling reputation, you know. Goes back to the first Sir Roger de Vaisey who was supposed to have been a favourite of Queen Elizabeth the First — and no one suggests it was for his madrigal singing. Anyway, it's not true in my case. I was mad about Caro and none of us is perfect. Any man is going to kick over the traces once in a while. But — the upshot is that I'm a poor abandoned boy these days.'

We were drawing up outside the Lodge. I was rather stunned by the stream of disclosures, but summoned the presence of mind to say smartly, 'Like Ned, then. In the same boat, as it were.'

'Oh, we won't speak about my sister,' said Roger with what sounded more like contempt than grief. Ignoring my protests, he scrambled out of the car and strutted round to open my door. I thought he might be manoeuvring to embrace me, but he just clasped my hand briefly between his long thin fingers, 'Until Saturday,' he said, and roared off up the hill.

CHAPTER EIGHT

Thornbeck Manor surprised me. I suppose I had expected a building as poised and pleasing as the Dower House, but there could scarcely have been a greater contrast.

I drove cautiously round a curving gravel path which was illuminated, with eerie charm, by stolid cast iron lamp standards of the kind you see peering through the London fog in Sherlock Holmes films. A few chilly plumes of November mist floating across the night air added to the illusion. Then the rhododendrons gave way and I drew up in front of the house, choosing at random the central entrance — there were three doorways visible.

The Manor was a conglomeration of sprawling ivy-thicketed wings, not one of which matched another. Even though it was too dark to make out details of the architecture, the variously shaped and sized windows, illuminated here and there, dated from widely differing periods. To the right the windows were paned and Georgian, to the left gleamed a solidly Victorian bay, and in the central body of the house, immediately in front of me, the windows were tall and almost church-like.

This was undoubtedly the oldest section of the Manor, with a gnarled pair of doors which would not have looked amiss on a modest-sized cathedral. There were lights in the room behind. I approached warily, looking for a bell. Roger Vaisey, however, darted out of a side-door in the Victorian wing and hastened towards me.

I had bumped into Roger early that morning, as a matter of fact. He was coming out of the Estate Office as I had called in to pay my rent. He had barely appeared to recognize me, however, and even when he did, had muttered a greeting and continued on his way so hastily, I had wondered whether to come tonight. Only a puny hope that Ned might be here had propelled me out of the Lodge. But there could hardly have been a greater contrast between the surly Roger of this morning and the man greeting me now.

'It's my favourite lady *artiste*,' he bellowed, seizing my hand. 'Don't waste your time at that door. Only opened in the event of deaths and weddings. Mainly the former since we have more of a talent for dying than living in our family. Come inside, and get even colder. Quite impossible to keep these barracks warm, of course. Know what Bess once said? "The central heating here's about as much use as a hair-drier in an aircraft hangar."' He laughed noisily, dragging me behind him as he led the way through a series of connecting rooms. I gathered we were passing the kitchens. Between us surged a panting glossy black dog. 'The only woman who truly loves me,' he said. 'Juno. She keeps my bed warm at nights. And if anyone tells you I'm not to be found there very often, don't listen. Foul slander. You hear that, Harry? I'm strictly a one-woman man. Juno is all. Mind you, I may make an exception for this delicious girl. Frankie Cleverdon, Harry Pouncett. Let me take your coat, and then if you get cold, just call on me to warm you up. Drink?'

We had arrived in a hall which extended up into a splendidly beamed and vaulted roof. There was a gallery with doors leading off along one side, and the far wall was dominated by the mighty pair of doors I had approached minutes earlier. I could believe that they were rarely opened to people (or corpses) but they were by no means sealed to the weather. The wind sang audibly round them and set the skirts shivering on two women who were sipping their drinks nearby. Harry Pouncett, a red-nosed large man with Dickensian sideboards, sensibly led me towards the fire.

There were upwards of a dozen people scattered across the flagged floor, although only three were women. Prudently, they were swaddled in high-necks, long-sleeves, and flowing skirts — feminine dresses of the frilly sort which make me look like a boy in drag. I could appreciate that they were practical here though. My provocative angora tumbled to expose

75

quivering goose-bumps. I clutched it as high over my shoulders as it could be persuaded to stay. I shivered in spite of the fire, which was burning like a blast furnace in a fireplace the size of the Lodge bathroom.

'Amazing fire,' I murmured politely. 'You could burn a sofa there.'

'We may be reduced to that soon the way the Stock Market's going,' said Roger gaily, handing me a weighty tumbler of whisky. 'That'll put the colour back in your cheeks.'

'What was it your father used to say, Vaisey? Had to fell how many trees a year just to feed this roaring beast?'

'I forget,' said Roger. 'You know me and figures, old chap.'

'Of course in the old man's day . . .' said Harry Pouncett, and went on to tell some rambling anecdote about forestry practices in by-gone years. Another world. Old chap . . . I listened with half an ear and wondered how Roger changed the light-bulbs in the black wood and iron chandelier-affair which swung menacingly, like a prop from Macbeth, over the centre of the hall. You'd need to build scaffolding to get up there.

Out of the corner of my eye, I scanned the company. Ned was not here. I had not been sure whether he had turned down the invitation to drinks as well as that to dinner. In my own mind, I had decided that his appearance or otherwise would be a decisive indicator of his feelings for me. Of whether he had any feelings for me at all. If he did, he would not be able to resist turning up. And he had not turned up. The conversation around me progressed from timber to the business in hand.

'Of course, it was the keeper's job in those days. There was none of this buying-in of birds then, was there?' continued Harry Pouncett and paused, apparently expecting a reply. Roger, however, was gazing into the flames abstractedly and I floundered. When people around you are talking about a subject so foreign they could be conversing in ancient Chinese, there are only two options I find. Either nod aimiably and pretend you understand – or admit ignorance. I had let the conversation drift past me, smiling as the occasion seemed to require while I speculated as to Ned's whereabouts. Now, caught out, I had to opt for the alternative. Frankness.

'I'm afraid,' I said apologetically, 'I wouldn't know a pheasant from a Rhode Island Rooster. I was born and brought up in towns.'

'A dash of your city sophistication is what we need round here,' breathed Roger lecherously, close to my neck. He reeked of whisky.

Harry Pouncett, however, soon joined by three other guests, was politely anxious to enlighten my ignorance. They were all friendly, and flirtatious in a strictly-by-the-rules avuncular sort of way. In the warmth of flames and flattery I blossomed, and barely noticed my glass being refilled.

I could not help but notice, however, the frequency with which Roger's father was cited; in support of arguments, to illustrate a case and as the subject of anecdotes, some of them considerably more interesting than others.

'My ma used to say she locked her bedroom door when she stayed here,' confided a thin-nosed woman who seemed to be livelier than all the other guests put together. She was horsey-jawed but attractive and had surprised me by mentioning a son at university, because her skin was clear as a teenager's. 'Old John used to get a husband paralytic downstairs, you know,' she went on, 'then sneak upstairs and jump on the wife.'

'Nonsense, Suzy,' said her husband who looked twenty years older than her, laughing with unconvincing heartiness.

'John was a bit of an old so-and-so,' agreed another man. 'But what a genius on a horse . . .'

'I heard,' ventured the thin-nosed woman again giggling — I was beginning to like her, 'that he handled them both in much the same way. Women and horses, I mean. Very free with his whip!'

'Control yourself, Suzanna,' said her husband. 'Roger's over there . . .'

'How would you know anything about it?' she said, staring at him in slightly cross-eyed defiance. Roger's drinks were wickedly large. I intervened before her strong-minded spouse could utter the crushing rejoinder I could see he was framing.

'The old Squire sounds like a throwback to another century,' I said. 'The hard-riding, hard-drinking philanderer. Like a character out of a Regency Romance.'

Suzanna Worrall – for that was her name – winked at me.

'Absolutely,' agreed Harry Pouncett. 'You're absolutely right, my dear. Old John didn't belong in this century at all. Mind you, he drove his cars like a madman, too. There was that famous time he bet Lord Grosmont he could drive to London in four hours flat – long before the days of motorways of course . . .' and so on.

The next time Roger drifted by to refill my glass, I whispered, 'Don't you get sick of your father, sometimes?'

'What?' In his surprise he sloshed whisky over my hand, and then made a gallant pantomime of mopping it off with a huge silk handkerchief, much to the amusement of his guests who murmured chip-off-the-old-block comments.

When I retrieved my hand, however, Roger drew me aside to ask curiously. 'What did you mean? Sick of the old man?'

'I didn't intend to insult your parent,' I said, 'but my life is plagued, when I return to Manchester for family reunions, by elderly relatives telling me fondly how simply wonderful my Great Aunt Evelyn (who died young) was at drawing and painting, and how I obviously inherit my talent from her. The implication being that I can never be half as good. I wouldn't mind, but the preserved works of Great Aunt Evelyn are the most nauseatingly sentimental daubs of flowers and kittens and curly-haired children you ever saw.'

Roger burst out laughing. 'I like you, Frankie,' he said. 'Ned was right.'

About what, I wanted to ask.

'People tell me I'm very like him, however,' he went on. 'God rot his ugly mug. I can't claim to have inherited his good qualities because he didn't have any. There's a portrait of him over here – come and look. You can give me your frank professional opinion of it.'

Invitations like that chill me. I can toss off polite white lies about most things except painting. The words stick in my mouth like lumps of dry bread. I followed him across the room, framing non-committal strings of adjectives. In fact, I did not need to employ them.

'It's all black,' I protested. In the dim lighting of the hall, the heavy gilt frame enclosed at first glance little more than a gloomy square yard of dull emptiness.

'The colour of his soul,' said Roger. 'It's not entirely black, actually. Just scorched from the time he nearly burned the North Wing down. Roaring drunk, of course, but there was no irreparable damage. Our Victorian ancestors built to last, but this picture got fearfully smoked up. I never had it cleaned because I thought the darkness gave it rather an Old Master-ish sort of patina, wouldn't you agree? Here . . .' He picked up a heavy brass lamp from a nearby table and tilted it to direct a wan beam on the painting.

Peering out of the gloom was a long, heavy-jawed face which indeed showed more than a passing resemblance to Roger's. The only other clearly visible feature was a kind of scroll towards the bottom with a Gothic-lettered Latin inscription.

'What does that say?' I inquired, grateful to be excused passing judgement on the painting.

'Family motto of a sort,' said Roger, replacing the lamp on the table. 'Roughly translated it means something along the lines of: those of us lying in the gutter can still look at the stars. Very appropriate in this —'

'D-doesn't mean anything of the sort,' said a familiar voice behind me.

'Neddy, my dear fellow,' exclaimed Roger. 'I was just about to say I needed you to translate . . .'

'"*Vide meliora proboque, d-deteriora sequor*",' said Ned. 'Liter-ally, "I see the better way and approve it, but I follow the worse way."'

'There speaks the classical scholar, Frankie. It's still a highly appropriate motto for this family. Forsooth, the very story of our lives.'

'I w-would say it was a fair description of the human c-condition in general,' said Ned mildly, 'falling short of what we know we should do.'

'Ah, but we don't all recognise what is right, do we? Not according to you, my dear brother-in-law. Some of us, according to your reasoning, are incapable of recognising the better way and cannot therefore be blamed for choosing the wrong path.'

Ned stared at him in silence, frowning. Roger spoke without malice. This was evidently something they had argued at length before. I was amazed by Roger's articulateness after the quantity of whisky he had swallowed.

'Whereas I maintain,' he went on, 'that all us Vaiseys have twenty-twenty moral vision. If we turn left (as most of us invariably seem to do) we act from our own free and evil wills, quite deliberately knowing we're doing the wrong thing. We do not stumble in a kind of spiritual short-sightedness.'

'Is this the time for m-metaphysics, Roger?'

'Absolutely not,' said Roger with a sudden, brilliant smile and he clapped Ned's arm. 'Let me get you a drink, old man. I was only trying to explain the motto to Frankie. Bring her back to the fire. She needs keeping warm . . .'

To my annoyance, we were swept back into the general conversation and while Ned was monopolized by Harry Pouncett and another man, I found myself standing next to Suzanna Worrall who grinned conspiratorially at me over the rim of her glass. I grinned back.

'The Manor's so lonely these days,' said Roger, trotting back to join us. Poor man. He worked to maintain his raffish Casanova air, but his short-legged gait, with a giant cigar jutting from clenched teeth, was more reminiscent of Groucho Marx. 'Suzy here remembers what it was like when Caro was around, don't you, Suzy?'

'You should have behaved yourself better, Rog,' she said looking down her thin nose at him. 'I've no sympathy.'

'You have been introduced to Suzanna? Warned about her rather. Possessor of the most dangerous tongue in North Yorkshire.'

'You flatter me, my pet.'

'Look at this place, Frankie,' he said, waving an arm melodramatically. 'A man can't make a house comfortable. It needs a woman's touch.'

'Bollocks,' said Suzy hooting with laughter. 'The best decorators are always men, if you ask me. Philip Rowlant, who did my drawing-room last year, was an absolute poppet. Gay as a grig, of course . . .'

'Gay?' said Roger stiffly. 'I do wish people wouldn't murder the English language.'

'Piss off, Roger,' said Suzy. 'Out of the ark,' she added to me, when Roger had strutted away. 'This place is like a mausoleum, isn't it? Sorry . . .' She hiccuped. 'Bit plastered.'

'Don't apologise,' I said.

'Should've remembered. Bit of a sensitive issue round here at the moment.'

'What is?'

'The whole gay thing, of course. After that silly bugger from St Catherine's got caught with his trousers down.'

'Why should it concern Roger? I mean I know it's local . . .'

'That living's part of the Manor too, you know. Most of Langton-le-Moor lies within Roger's estate. And until the dust settles and they sort themselves out, poor old Ned is having to do double duties in Langton as well as —'

'Ned?' I said. 'What duties?'

'The services and what have you,' said Suzy, blinking unfocused eyes in my direction, like a sleepy owl. 'Haven't you met Roger's brother-in-law, Ned Cowper? He's an absolute poppet. Vicar of St Peter's.'

CHAPTER NINE

Of course, as soon as Suzy spoke, it was all so glaringly obvious.

Why the hell else would Ned have been producing the local amateurs in their play? Hadn't he muttered something about it being part of the job? At the time, I had thought he meant no more than a general duty to participate in village life. No wonder he had been stuffy about the meaning of love – and had not seen the funny side of the erring vicar. 'Dear God,' I thought (and started guiltily at my reflexible blasphemy), 'what else did I say?'

I glanced across the hall. Ned was stooping to catch the remark of a diminutive woman in red and laughing. It was like looking at a stranger. Why didn't he wear a dog collar?

And why, I thought with growing indignation, had he not told me what he did? More than that, he had quite clearly disguised his occupation. I remembered perfectly clearly asking him how he earned his living these days, and he had fobbed me off with some remark about the lambing season.

I could feel my cheeks burning bright under the combined influences of whisky and resentment. I had been deliberately misled.

'You will come and eat at the Wheatsheaf, won't you, Frankie?' called Roger, rejoining us. I noticed people were draining their glasses purposefully.

'I'm not sure I'm capable of getting myself anywhere,' I said distractedly, still glancing towards Ned. 'Not legally, in a car. Maybe you could give me a lift home?'

'Nonsense,' said Roger. 'Leave the car here by all means. We've two sober drivers and you can squash in with the other girls. I'll crouch in the boot, I don't mind. And then someone will run you home.'

'Do come,' said Suzy. 'It'll be dull as bog-water otherwise. I'm a lost soul without my chum Elizabeth.'

I could already see Ned shaking his head and smiling politely at the red-frocked dwarf, but I seemed to have no choice. Besides, I had drunk enough to prefer to remain in company – any company – than return to an empty cottage with no fire lit. I let Roger conduct me to the cloakroom where he thrust a surprisingly powerful arm round me and planted a wet kiss in the vicinity of my ear. It was aimed towards my mouth, but I turned away my face in time.

'Get off,' I said, struggling, and all the more indignant because I could see Ned's bulky silhouette in the doorway.

'Put her down, Rog,' said Suzy, who was following close behind us. 'Kick him where it hurts, darling, I would. You come and travel with us, Frankie, and we'll leave bloody Roger at the mercy of the Costley-Bannermans.'

She walked unsteadily towards the door. On a pretext of having dropped something, however, I managed to coincide with Ned in the corridor.

'I'm so sorry, *Reverend* Cowper,' I said, with tight-lipped emphasis.

'Oh God,' said Ned surprisingly. 'C-come in here,' he added and pulled me back into a dim ante-room, hung layers deep with green waterproofs and smelling of rubber like a school cloakroom.

The cool air, away from the blast of the fire, made my head swim dangerously. 'You deceived me,' I said. 'One hundred per cent deliberately. You let me think you were some sort of layabout farmer when all the time you were a . . .'

'P-priest,' said Ned. 'I know.' He hung his head like a schoolboy caught stealing the jam tarts. It would have been funny, except I felt cheated.

'I d-did farm for a while,' he added anxiously. 'They d-don't like to take you straight from university. They tell you to g-go off and get a bit of experience in the world first.'

'Well you've only yourself to blame if I said things that offended you,' I said stiffly. 'Christ knows what I . . . Oh *God*, I'm sorry . . . Oh . . .'

'D-don't apologise. It's me who should be sorry.'

'I'm afraid I don't know how to talk to vicars,' I said. 'It's not something I've gone in for a great deal since I was expelled from Sunday school.'

'Expelled? From *S-sunday school*?'

'For painting obscene cartoons of Miss Drinkwater.'

Ned gave a sharp crack of laughter. 'That's why I did it,' he said, and then remorsefully, 'Oh Frankie, you c-can't imagine what a relief it was n-not to be talked to as the — contents of a dog collar, but just as m-me. And I thought, if I told you, you wouldn't . . .'

'I don't believe in God, you know.'

I was quite drunk enough to feel it necessary to bring everything out into the open. Alcohol has always operated on me like a truth drug. I stared up at him defiantly.

'The s-stock answer is that it doesn't stop Him believing in you.'

'I didn't precisely *stop* believing. I just gave up church after I decided the cricket club boys were better looking than the youth club crowd.'

'Everyone has their own way of f-finding God,' said Ned, smiling faintly. 'Frankie, you needn't look so guilty.'

'I'm — not perfectly sober. But you should have told me. I might have been more polite.'

'Oh F-frankie, I am sorry. If you'd ever actually asked me directly, of c-course I'd have told you. Believe me.'

Suddenly there was a hush. The dining party, shouting noisy instructions at one another as to who was driving whom, had finally decanted themselves into the courtyard, and Ned and I were alone in the green, perfumed forest of waterproof coats.

'Well that's all right then,' I said unsteadily, 'I s'pose.'

In the hush I could hear my own heart beating. I wondered if Ned could too. He put his hands on my shoulders, and moved towards me, and my last thought as I closed my eyes automatically was that he might bloody well look a bit happier at the prospect of kissing me. I was happy. Nearly fainting with happiness. I had not felt so ecstastically light-headed since I was fourteen at the church youth club — when kissing was the most daring and exciting human activity imaginable. I could actually feel his breath against my lips when a door opened and a voice screeched from the next room.

'Where the hell are you, Frankie? The Costley-Bannermans have gone.'

'She's here, Suzy,' said Ned, his hands springing off my shoulders as abruptly as the released jaws of a trap. 'She c-c-c-couldn't find her . . . her . . .'

'. . . handbag,' I said helpfully, and, with a regretful but nevertheless conspiratorial smile, I ran out to scramble in the back of an over-crowded Range Rover.

I have suffered worse hangovers in my reprobate life, than I did in the dull grey light of the following morning. I have also had to suffer more embarrassing flashbacks of the previous evening's revels as memory has seeped back with the first cups of tea.

At least I had had the sense, once at the Wheatsheaf, to drink little more. But Roger's whiskies had been immorally strong and I was rattling with nerves and probably radiating sexual excitement like a bitch on heat.

Roger seemed to sense this, and insisted on placing me next to him. I had drunk enough to find his very public pursuit of me entertaining.

'And yet this morning you didn't want to know me,' I said owlishly at one point, waggling my finger.

'Was I sober?'

'I should hope so at a quarter past nine.'

'There you are then,' said Roger. 'I'm not worth knowing sober. Whereas now you're going to tell me I'm irresistible.'

Most of this struck me as one big performance for the benefit of the audience, rather than an actual attempt to seduce me. I noticed, with some awe, that his consumption of whisky did not slacken through the evening. He waved away offers of wine with self-righteous puritanism. ('It's the mixture rots the liver you know,' he whispered to me wisely. 'Stick to the grape or grain and you'll be all right.') With the quarter of my mind that was not absorbed in replaying the last ten seconds in the dim cloakroom, I exchanged banter with Roger and sympathised with Suzy as she grimaced at me from the duller end of the table where conversation seemed to be revolving dolefully round the condition of the Stock Market again.

Roger egged me on to perform my party piece — sketching animal caricatures of the company on his menu — which proves I must have been drunk. I enjoyed myself, however. So, to all appearances, did the others. Even the man I drew as a warthog.

I was impressed at ten the next morning when I walked into the courtyard of the Manor to collect my car, to see that all the Range Rovers had gone. The shooters were apparently about their business. Later, as I backed my car into the tumbledown outhouse which served the Lodge as a garage, I learned where. There seemed to be muffled pops exploding all around me.

In fact, over the course of the afternoon, I discovered the shape of the valley gave rise to misleading echoes. The guns were about a mile south of the Lodge, towards Langton.

The next day, they were closer. A line of mud-spattered four-wheel drive vehicles actually drove up Lamp Lane from the direction of the Manor and pulled up a couple of hundred yards away. I recognised several of the faces under the tweed hats as they climbed out of the cars and tramped up the field behind the Lodge. Retrievers and labradors, tails wagging furiously, wove in and out of the human figures like black and yellow fish. Roger, absurd in a belted tweed jacket with billowing plus fours, did not approach the Lodge, just raised a hand briefly in my direction as he strode up the hillside, stern and sober purpose advertised in every strutting step. Suzy, one of only two women as far as I could make out, was cutting a dashing figure in a bottle-green cloak. She waved at me, pointing expressively towards her head then her female companion and pulling a face. I thought she was indicating another hangover and waved back.

Automatically, I photographed them as they milled up the field. What caught my fancy were the colours. There were more hues of dull green and brown distributed between the twenty or so figures than I had believed existed. A million different tints in their waxed coats and tweed jackets, wellingtons and socks from olive to beige, khaki to grass, mustard to copper, fawn to chocolate. I observed that the people with whom I had dined were distinguished by the extreme shabbiness of their gear. I wondered if the unsagging smartness of some of the other jackets indicated the moneyed city-types of whom Mr Danby had spoken so scathingly. I scribbled a few sketches, then took refuge indoors from the cold, and drew a dog which looked undeniably more like a calf than a labrador. I have never been very good at dogs. Cats yes, dogs no.

Every so often there would be a burst of firing. Eventually, I threw the pencil down in disgust. I dare say my concentration would not have been so disrupted by the gunfire had my mind not been racing round like a caged hamster for two days with puzzles about Ned.

I was irritated with myself. This all-consuming infatuation was making an idiot of me. I had been so sure he would turn up yesterday I had worn a smart sweater. Since he had not, I was prepared to allow there might have been pressing parish business – in either of his parishes. But today? Our last parting had been a frustrating cliff-hanger of unresolved tensions and unanswered questions. I knew he must come.

Bang! Bang! Bang-bang!

As for his turning out to be a clergyman, well that, I had decided, was his affair, not mine. It would be unreasonable of me to regard Ned differently because of his profession. Did one describe it as a profession, or a vocation? Both maybe. If I were truthful I had to admit that one of the things which had appealed to me most strongly in Ned had been his gentle earnestness, the very difference between him and most men I knew. Perhaps, I reasoned hopefully, it was only his calling which had accounted for his tardiness in making a pass at me.

Bang! Bang-bang! Bang!

What was the C. of E. ruling, I wondered idly, on unmarried sex between two consenting adults? Was that fornication? (A word which had always struck me as being deliciously sinful.) Or was it only adulterous liaisons which were forbidden? My shaky recollection of the Ten Commandments suggested only adultery was specifically ruled out of court.

After another round of shots, I stalked through to the kitchen to make some coffee.

'Hurry up, Ned,' I breathed impatiently.

The situation could not be allowed to drag on much longer. I was not the weak-kneed wimpish sort of woman who would feel humiliated if she had to make a move herself to secure her man. I did not believe, I told myself, in the traditional feminine game of playing passive and unconcerned: a serenely floating duck who must appear to be doing nothing even if her little feet are paddling like fury under the surface. I was as prepared to play the blatant hunter as the simpering prey. If Ned failed to appear, I would telephone him. Any minute now.

And then I saw the pheasant. He — such glorious colouring could only belong to the male of the species — was frozen in magnificent immobility, between two geraniums on the wall outside the back door. I froze too. The plumage on his neck and head shone with the dark green gloss of wine bottles. His wary bead of an eye was set in a patch of startling scarlet. As I watched, he lifted one spiny foot cautiously and scratched under a tortoiseshell wing.

For the first time, it occurred to me with a sense of outrage that the gun-popping gang on the hillside was actually intent on killing this handsome creature. 'Stay here, baby,' I breathed, groping behind me for my camera. 'It's a healthier climate than you'll find on the hill.'

He caught sight of my movement, however, and with lazy nonchalance hopped off the wall into the sloping garden beyond. As quietly as I could, I opened the door and followed. To my delight, on the grass below, pecked two of his friends. The snapping of my camera shutter irritated them and they ran with astonishing speed, their long tails quivering like quill pens, to the far side of the garden, then stopped again. Again I pursued — and, round the corner of the Lodge, came face to face with Ned.

His exclamation alarmed the birds thoroughly and they charged off towards the river bank beyond the reach of my lens. At least it was not in the direction of the guns.

'Ned,' I said, 'I'm glad to see you. Come inside. I think we need to talk, don't we?'

'Yes,' he said uncertainly. 'Shall we stay out here, though? Keep an eye on what's going on?' Above us the camouflaged figures with dogs at heel progressed in line across the field. Distant shouts and whistles echoed down.

'Barbarous,' I declared. 'I've just been observing their quarry.'

'B-beautiful birds, aren't they?' agreed Ned. 'I only w-wish I could c-claim that I didn't like eating them. Then I wonder whether life isn't p-perhaps a jolly sight pleasanter for a pheasant, living out in the valley here, coddled from birth onwards, than the m-miserable existence of a supermarket shed-reared chicken. But maybe that's sophistry . . .'

'Ned, you were going to kiss me the other night. At the Manor . . .'

'Yes,' said Ned quietly. 'I'm very sorry, Frankie. I l-lost control of myself. Temporarily.'

'But I wanted you to kiss me.'

Ned's face was flushing to a dull puce.

'Thank you,' he said. 'I th-thought perhaps you did.'

I turned away to look at the river and stuffed my right hand under my left elbow because I saw it was trembling. 'I wanted rather more than that, in fact.'

The silence was excruciating. Then, shockingly, the guns exploded just as Ned began to speak.

'But you know, of course, I c-can't. Well, maybe you don't realise . . .'

'No, I don't,' I said frankly. 'Is sex against the law for clergymen?'

I never heard Ned's reply because at that moment the garage window next to us shattered in a tinkling shower of broken glass.

'Christ!' I said, spinning round dazedly. 'What the hell . . .?'

'Are you hurt?' said Ned.

I patted my hair, as though I expected splinters of glass to cascade to the ground, but there weren't any. The window was three feet or more away. The glass was silvered with a maze of cracks from a jagged hole at one side. Ned walked across and poked the remaining glass cautiously and another slice toppled with a crash into the garage.

'My car . . .' I began indignantly.

Ned leaned into the dark garage, carefully avoiding the last shards of glass, then withdrew, shaking his head reassuringly. 'Fine,' he said. 'M-miles clear. I just c-can't understand how . . .' His voice tailed off, and I noticed suddenly how pale he was. He was looking up the hill.

Two of the figures in green, both skirted, were tripping down the field immediately opposite us, pursued at a distance by the unmistakable tweed-suited shape of Roger. There were querulous and angry shouts echoing all over the hillside.

Suzanna Worrall was the first to reach us.

'Are you all right?' she demanded breathlessly. 'I might have known with Elizabeth. Mad as a hatter. Didn't I say as much to you, Frankie, when we were going up there earlier on?'

Behind her ran a tiny woman whose enviably curved shape was enhanced by the tailored hacking jacket. A saucily feathered hat tilted over one eye. The feather quivered as she threw her head back to stare up at Ned.

'Bloody hell,' she said. 'Did I nearly shoot my husband, then?'

CHAPTER TEN

She was not quite as beautiful as her photograph.

There were creases at the corners of her mouth, and between her eyebrows. But that was about it. Otherwise, with eyes wide as a fawn's, a nose so straight and delicately flared it should have been sculpted in marble by an Italian master, and a figure like an egg timer, she was perfect. In fact she reminded me of my best doll, a corseted Victorian maiden I had christened Jemima. Elizabeth Cowper was the porcelain doll to match the doll's house.

Roger arrived in her wake. His face was putty-coloured and twitching. I had never seen a man so physically possessed with rage. The nakedness of the emotion struck me as being even more obscene than the language he used — and that went way beyond anything I, even in my worst moments, would employ.

'But I am mad,' she said, apparently quite unperturbed and ignoring him to address her husband. 'Is Edward cross with me?'

Roger uttered something unprintable and turned to Ned. 'If I were you, Ned, I'd beat her,' he said, and tramped back to meet the others who were clustering by the hedge.

'Oh, he should, he should,' carolled Elizabeth, laughing merrily. 'But he won't. Will you, my poppet?'

I could hardly bring myself to look at Ned. He was stiff-faced as a waxwork.

'You s-seem to have behaved very f-foolishly,' he said quietly.

'What the fuck were you playing at, Bess?' demanded Suzy, looking at me and raising her eyebrows in an expression of helpless disbelief.

'But I saw a bird,' said Elizabeth, wide-eyed and guileless. 'Have you come to take me home in disgrace, Ned? But I promise you I saw a little hen just begging to be potted.'

Only after they had left, with Elizabeth clinging to her husband's arm, and I was sweeping up the scattered shards of glass, did I wonder, incredulously, whether the little hen could have been me.

Suzy abandoned the shoot to help me clear up. Unlike Elizabeth Cowper, she did not herself wield a gun, anyway, but merely watched the men.

'Bess always has been mad as a hatter. Charming, but off her little rocker. That's why she keeps buggering off to clinics for months on end. Costs a fortune – but she can afford it. Bess assures me that if you want to dry out for a few weeks, and lose a bit of weight into the bargain, they're more peaceful than health farms, with dishy psychiatrists instead of pouffy masseurs.'

Poor Mrs Cowper. Poor lady.

'Have a scotch,' I said, 'I think I need one.'

'I'm not surprised, nearly getting your head blasted off like that. Mind you, Bess's a terrific shot. I'm only amazed she didn't get the bird she was after.'

Maybe she damn nearly did.

I poured large glasses for us both, and swallowed half mine.

'Doesn't this make shooting a dangerous pastime,' I said, feeling my equilibrium restoring itself a bit, 'for innocent bystanders, if not for the participants?'

'Absolutely not,' said Suzy, shocked. 'They're fearfully hot on rules to keep everybody safe. That's why Rog was so enraged when Bess fell out of line and did that. I was surprised he didn't strangle her.'

'He looked as though he could.'

'Oh Rog has a foul temper, my dear. They all do – Bess too, although hers is more of the revenge-being-a-dish-best-eaten-cold variety. And there are all kinds of beastly stories about the old man beating a horse so badly it had to be put down. I don't know if it's true. John Vaisey was almost more my grandparent's generation than my parents'. Their mother was years younger than the old man.'

'What happened to her?'

'She ran off with a delectable boy to the Greek islands when her children were still at school. Lucky old her. But subsequently she managed to get herself killed in a car smash — or maybe it was on a motor bike come to think of it — which no doubt proves the wicked don't thrive after all. She wasn't as pretty as Elizabeth. But she had a wealthy papa, so what did looks matter?'

Since the worst was out, I resolved to extract every last agonising detail about Ned's wife. Suzy, as a self-professed connoisseur of gossip, needed no persuasion, few questions. She took a cigarette out of a gold case, lit it and comfortably settled back in her chair. Up on the hill, shooting resumed.

'When were they married? Let me think. Benedict was just leaving prep school, so it would be, what, seven years ago ... They'd known each other for ever, of course. Ned's some kind of distant cousin, and I know the Cowpers, *mère* and *père* often used to come up about this time of year. But the romance between Ned and Bess started, bizarrely enough ...' she knocked the ash off her cigarette, laughing, 'at the old man's funeral. I think Ned was barely more than a trainee at the time, deacon or curate or whatever you call the fledgling padres, but Roger summoned him in. He was desperately keen to have his childhood friend see the old man off.'

'What did their father die of?' I asked, as Suzy paused to take a swig of her whisky.

'Heart attack on the bog,' she said, laughing heartily. 'But he was well into his seventies. The priceless joke was that he couldn't stand Ned. Not always — they'd got on fine when Ned was a lad. Then he was always holding Ned up to Roger as a shining example because Ned could play cricket and soccer and so forth, and poor little Rog simply didn't have the running capacity in his pins. But when Ned got the God bug, that was it. Or maybe there was a breach earlier. I've a feeling there may have been a row ... Anyway, old John had no time for clergymen at all, not in the family that is. I remember at Bess's coming-out dance they nearly had a stand up row. Or at least John did. Dear old Ned just played least in sight. So you can imagine, his funeral address on the old Squire was a masterpiece of understated diplomacy.'

93

'I suppose it must have been,' I said dazedly. 'And that's where it all started? Ned . . . and Elizabeth?'

'They were wed within six months. Whirlwind romance with Roger the unlikely Cupid. He obligingly invited Ned here every weekend. They were absolutely head-over-heels, couldn't keep their hands off one another, and I suppose with Ned's job they couldn't shack up, so they got married. She was quite the most beautiful bride I've ever seen in my life, and at that time I seemed to be going to five weddings a week. In ivory wild silk with a veil which I think would have covered Twickenham. She quite took one's breath away.'

I could imagine. I smiled, nodding agreement, gritting my teeth.

'Then they went somewhere for a while – now, where the hell was it? Ned was a curate there. Near Birmingham, I think. Somewhere pretty ghastly anyhow. Well that didn't suit Bess at all, as you might imagine. So when, fortuitously, the living here fell vacant, it was obvious, wasn't it?'

'Can Roger actually choose the vicar?' I said marvelling. 'I had no idea church affairs were still so feudal. I would have thought that kind of thing went out with rotten boroughs and serfs.'

'Well I daresay he has to carry the churchwardens and what have you with him,' said Suzy fair-mindedly. 'But one way or another, he managed to swing St Peter's for Ned, and stop them amalgamating it with another parish – which in these deprived days probably required divine intervention. Our local chap has six churches under his wing, can you believe it? Anyway, Ned became vicar of Thornbeck. And then there was no question of them moving into the vicarage, which is a plain, rather draughty little place round the back of the churchyard. Bess had inherited the Dower House from her father – but no money strangely. Or maybe not strangely. Quite a lot of Yorkshiremen believe, like John Vaisey, that women are not to be trusted with money – although he always seemed to have a lot more time for Elizabeth than Roger. But he left her the Dower House and that was where she intended to live. Have you seen it? Heavenly, isn't it?'

I nodded. 'Like something out of a glossy magazine.'

'Oh, it's been featured in several, I assure you. Doing up the house occupied her for two or three years. It was only after that she began to turn seriously loopy. Does seem sad, doesn't it? So much going for her, with those looks, that glorious house – and darling Ned so completely potty about her. Isn't he adorable? Like a big cuddly Saint Bernard dog. I must say, if I had him waiting on my hearthrug of an evening I wouldn't be nearly as keen as Bess is to pine away in clinics for weeks at a time.'

'Neither would I,' I said bitterly.

'And after seven years of marriage too. Seeing them together is enough to turn anyone but Barbara Cartland queasy. Hardly takes his eyes off her.' She gave a brittle laugh. 'I suppose you could say that the eyes of *my* beloved husband never stray from me, but Alex is just counting my drinks. Maybe I should try Bess's clinic – although I can't see Alex forking out. Built in the John Vaisey mould, my husband.'

'How does Elizabeth afford it, if she wasn't left any money? Surely Ned can't earn a great deal?'

'Poor as the proverbial church mouse, my dear. No, Roger makes her an allowance, I gather – and it takes more than pinmoney to pay for Elizabeth's designer therapists. Lucky, lucky girl . . .'

'Generous of Roger.'

'Roger's – all right. Boring as hell sober, and an absolute wolf the rest of the time. But you've gathered that . . .'

Through the window on the north side of the kitchen a flicker of movement caught my eye, a yellow dog dashing past the fence.

'They're coming down,' said Suzy, stubbing out her cigarette hastily. 'I'm supposed to have given these vile things up. Don't let on, will you? Bye, angel.'

It now seemed to me vital I should see Ned. I was bitterly hurt – and, initially at least, I was angry. Misleading me about his occupation was a minor joke compared with conveniently forgetting his beautiful wife, just because she happened to be away for a few weeks.

And yet, had he actually deceived me? Throughout the night

and the next day, I laboured to recall details of our conversations. The longer and more painstakingly I did this, the more elusive became the enchantment of the sunny afternoons, and the more far-fetched my fond belief at the time that Ned had sought or found anything in them beyond a certain companionable amusement. Like pinned butterflies, the memories were dead and fading as fast as I identified and classified them.

First thing the following morning, a carpenter and glazier arrived to repair the window. So too did a cellophane-rustling armful of tightly budded long-stemmed crimson roses. For one breathless instant I believed they had been sent by Ned. But they came from the same source as the workmen – Roger. With abject apologies.

I was beginning to wonder if Ned had deceived me at all. I knew all along that he had never specifically told me his wife had died, nor that she had actually deserted him. Whenever the least hint of intimacy had threatened, he had leapt to distance himself. The more I thought about it, the less Ned figured as a cynical deceiver, the more like a bumbling innocent.

The most revealing – the only – comment I could remember his making was that his wife used to give him some wine or other. The 'used to' had seemed to place her in the past tense. Evidently, all I should have concluded was that his wife no longer presented him with Alsace Gewürztraminer.

The troubles of which Mr Danby had spoken were only that his wife needed psychiatric treatment of some sort. Perhaps, therefore, it was not surprising that Ned had been reluctant to talk about her. The words 'psychiatric illness' are still shame-ridden for some people, with the kind of stigma (if not worse) that used to attach to cancer. I wondered what form her illness took. She looked so well, so vibrant with life and health.

I also wondered if her illness inclined her to violence.

Burning hot shame thudded through me, however, when I recollected how flagrantly I had offered myself to Ned. It's one thing to behave with liberated frankness towards a man you believe is more or less unattached. When it comes to telling a happily married man, who has never laid a lustful finger on you, nor uttered a single word suggesting he wishes to, that you would like to get into bed with him – which was exactly what I had done – there is an unpleasant suspicion of having behaved like a whore.

This may seem illogical coming from a woman who cheerfully admits to a long affair with a married man. But Gerald had been embroiled with other women before me, and I did not seduce Gerald. Quite the contrary. Besides I had frequently (when bored) urged Gerald to return to his wife. I could no more imagine myself urging Ned to return to anyone other than me than I could see myself inviting thunderbolts to fall on my head.

So I did not want to see Ned in order to wheedle myself into his reluctant arms again. I wanted to explain. To tell him that I would never have behaved the way I did if I had known he was married. It was terribly important to me that Ned should think well of me. But how could I engineer a meeting? I could hardly telephone him at home.

Unintentionally, Mr Danby suggested the way.

His arrival that day, alone, was heralded by a lusty bass-baritone rendering of 'Oh, What a Beautiful Morning'. Since it was overcast, with a bitter east wind, I remarked on this, and complimented him on his vocal chords.

'Back's come right, today,' he said, with a beaming smile. 'I woke up this morning, four o'clock as usual, and thought, "Hey up, what's different?" No pain, that's what was different. I can't tell you, Frankie, what it does for a man's attitude to life. Mind, I always did like a good sing. No yoghurt, today? Mr Cowper told me time and again I could have turned professional if I'd been trained early enough –'

'Ned . . . Cowper?'

'A very fine musician is Mr Cowper. Of course, I don't take him at his word, and my family are chapel as you know, but I'm always pleased to be called upon to help out in the church concerts. Are you fond of the *Messiah*? "And I will sha-a-a-a-a-ake . . ."' and so he bellowed, his throat quivering as his mighty bass voice rumbled round my kitchen. The milk bottles shook too.

At the appropriate, flourishingly turned cadence, I applauded.

'I knew Mr Cowper played the piano,' I said. Even as I spoke, I despised myself for succumbing to the temptation to frame, on the shallowest of pretexts, his name. I expected Mr Danby to look at me suspiciously, divining at once my pathetic secret. Of course, he did not.

'When he can,' he said sombrely. 'Sad, very sad, about his own piano.'

I busied myself washing out an already clean bottle to return to him, hoping Mr Danby would continue. I had deduced that two contrary impulses were at perpetual war in his soul: his nonconformist conscience with his natural passion for gossip.

'Not that I blame her,' he said at length. 'My Audrey told me straight that she was only waiting for Aunty Ethel to die before she threw the old joanna out of our front room. Monstrosity, was what Audrey called it. Me, I always liked a good old-fashioned singsong round the piano at Christmas, but I couldn't argue. The room's a sight more comfortable these days.'

'And Mrs Cowper thought the same about the piano at the Dower House? She certainly did the most marvellous job decorating the house.'

'Well it wasn't the look of it, so much, not as I understand it,' said Mr Danby. 'I dare say in a house like that you could fit in half the Hallé Orchestra if you had a mind. No, it were the noise which played on her nerves. Poor lady. But she should've told him before she had it taken away.'

Poor lady . . . I felt a burning wave of indignation on behalf of Ned.

'But he's got his church organ. We raised a thousand pound two years back to have it restored proper. Beautiful it is now. Every week, after choir rehearsal's finished, you can hear him playing away for hours. Phantom of the Opera is what my Audrey calls him . . .' and Mr Danby laughed heartily.

CHAPTER ELEVEN

The church smelled like all country churches: of damp hymn-books, candle wax, polish, and air long-confined in stone. There was only one light, which shone over the organ console. I could see, reflected in the slanting mirror above, Ned's fair curls as he picked through the plangent maze of a Bach fugue. Otherwise, the church was empty.

I had laid my plans with care.

Nothing was easier than to ascertain that choir practice lasted from seven until eight-thirty on Thursday evenings. In the morning, I had telephoned Roger to ask if I could take up his proffered loan of a book of sporting prints.

'I could call round to collect it,' I suggested artlessly. 'Maybe this evening?'

'Not sure I'll be in,' said Roger, irritatingly. 'But I'll leave the book in the porch, off the kitchen. If that suits?'

'Perfectly.'

People locally, I had noticed, were almost unbelievably cavalier (by London standards) about leaving their doors unlocked and their precious possessions unprotected.

'Bye then.'

Roger sober, I had now learned, did tend to be brief to the point of brusqueness — but I could understand his surprise over my sudden desire to borrow his book. When he had first mentioned the prints my interest had been politely minimal.

Now, however, it enabled me to park my distinctive car innocently outside the Manor, and claim — should I meet anyone — that in calling to collect the book, I had been attracted by the light from the church. That casual curiosity alone had prompted me to lift the heavy iron latch and walk in. In fact, the village was dark and bleakly deserted and I met only a cat between car and church door which hissed at me warily. My intricate precautions began to feel overdone.

Churches have always unnerved me. I dare say they have the same effect on most people. Only those who are well in with the Divine (priests and such like), and those who absolutely couldn't give a toss (tourists whose own god inhabits differently-shaped houses), dare to raise their voice above a whisper in these echoing caverns of holiness. By the time I have progressed more than a few feet down any aisle, I am about as miserably aware of my sinful inadequacy as it is possible for mortal woman to be. A goat in a house reserved for sheep.

I shuffled down the scuffed carpet. St Peter's belonged to the gracefully simple era of Gothic architecture. It had retained old-fashioned carved pews like cattle pens, and the altar, stone pulpit and brass lectern were hung with embroideries which glinted in the dim light from the organ console. Like the hassocks and the carpet, they were comfortably frayed. New, they must have been pretty garish. The organ was tucked to one side, massive pipes like brass mill chimneys vanishing into the echoing darkness of the roof. Ned, absorbed in playing, was still unaware of my presence as I tiptoed round the choir stalls to stand directly behind him. A black robe, as well as his white collar, made him remote and untouchable in a way my Mr Bear in a woolly pullover could never be. Tentatively, I whispered his name. No response. I cleared my throat loudly, and tried again. 'Ned? . . . *Ned!*'

His hands fell on the keys in a squealing discord. I nearly turned and ran, but he spun round, swinging his legs over the polished bench and, to my surprise, caught my hands in his.

'Frankie, thank God,' he said fervently, 'I wanted to see you so much.'

His tone was not suggestive of love, however, let alone of lust. He sounded like a man at the end of his tether, strangled by torments of miserable anxiety.

'I'm so sorry,' he said, 'f-for what happened. M-my wife's behaviour . . .'

100

M-my wife ... The smarting flick of pain these words delivered was ludicrous. He was a married man. *His wife* ... Like silver paper on a filling. His shotgun-toting wife. I interrupted before he could tell me any more about his wife. 'No one was hurt,' I said. 'The window's repaired good as new. Better than new – the man even fixed the latch on the garage door as well, while he was there.'

Ned smiled perfunctorily, and let my hands drop.

'I want to apologise,' I said firmly – this noble little speech had been ringing round my head for twenty-four hours like a bitter nursery rhyme, 'for behaving as I did. I didn't realise – stupidly – that you were, as they say, a happily married man.'

Ned's head jerked up, and he stared at me. My last puny glimmering of hope was snuffed out at that moment. I had chosen my words deliberately. There had always been the chance he would sigh and murmur (as Gerald had once), 'I wouldn't say *happily*, precisely ...'

Not Ned. He could barely frame the words in his agitation. 'But I told you I was married,' he said. 'Oh, Frankie, b-believe me, I never meant to deceive you on that count. About my job, perhaps, which was f-foolish enough, but about my marriage ...'

'Maybe I *chose* to believe you weren't married,' I said. 'Anyway, if I had known, I just want to make it clear, I would not have thrown myself at you like a ...' I couldn't quite bring myself to frame the word 'whore' in holy surroundings, '... like a doxy.'

'Like a *what*?'

'Doxy,' I said firmly. 'Floozy. Loose woman.'

'How Shakespearian,' said Ned, with a ghost of a smile. '"The doxy over the Dale ..."'

'Exactly,' I said bitterly. The doxy over Wragdale, the loose lady at the Lodge. 'It may appear otherwise, but I am not in the habit of trespassing on other people's marriages.'

'I never thought you were.'

'Happy marriages, I mean. Gerald – was different. And I'm not making excuses for that ...'

'Why should you? To m-me of all people? Oh, Frankie ...'

Was he feeling sorry for me now? I can't bear being pitied – anything but pity. Secure in the warm citadel of domestic

101

bliss, the happy husband or wife, looks down on the lonely fugitives outside the gates.

'No point in being melodramatic about it,' I said briskly. 'Making a mountain out of a molehill. Stupid storm in a tea cup.' I cringed – how many more ancient saws would I trot out? – and finished weakly. 'Nothing happened, after all . . .'

'N-no,' said Ned with unnecessary forcefulness, 'nothing at all. No.'

His words echoed round the church – I heard a dozen no's whispering down at me from the roof. Then an uncomfortably resonant silence.

'I didn't mean to interrupt your playing. I – just wanted to apologise.

'Apologise to me? You've n-nothing to apologize for . . .'

'Well no, we've agreed all that, haven't we? Nothing. So we'll part friends still, I hope,' I said rapidly and then, with incongruous formality, stuck out my hand. He looked so perplexed, I was consumed with longing to throw my arms round him and hug him, reassure him that everything would be all right, that I would not blame him, nor embarrass him by pursuing him any further. I had thrust out my hand almost defensively.

Ned ignored it. 'Where's your car?' he said. 'You have d-driven down?'

'I've got to collect a book from the Manor. I've parked there.'

'I'll see you safely back to the car. It's a filthy night.' He began flipping switches and levers on the organ console, and a rasping sigh wheezed somewhere in the bowels of the machine. 'I'd like to invite you in for a d-drink, but I don't think . . .'

'Certainly not,' I said. Was he mad, or was I? The thought of sitting down in that too-perfect drawing-room with Ned and his wife – *drinks with the Cowpers* – was ghastly. Adam and Eve didn't entertain the snake to gin and tonics. 'And really, you needn't bother . . .'

But he insisted. So he walked beside me, in uneasy silence, through the dark churchyard, and down the road, his cassock flapping like the tattered wings of a crow. All I wanted was to cut myself adrift from this mortifying tangle and forget it. I walked faster, as though I might be able to escape that way.

102

In the grounds of the Manor, the lamp standards were unlit. The rhododendrons rustled and creaked in the cold wind and the house, with only a single light burning in an upstairs window, was sombre and desolate. Reluctantly, I found I was glad I was not alone.

'Roger promised to leave the book here,' I said, and opened the porch door, groping for a light switch. 'I . . . can't see a thing.'

'Over to the r-right,' said Ned, following hard behind me. 'Frankie, we c-can't . . .'

But I never learned what we c-couldn't because a black shape exploded from the darkness by my feet and hurtled into my legs. I staggered backwards, arms flailing, into Ned, who clasped me against him.

'What the hell . . .'

'Juno,' said Ned, and in that instant the inside door opened, with a flood of light, and Roger stood on the doorstep.

'Thought I heard you, Frankie,' he said and then, in tones of surprise – and unmistakable disapprobation, 'Ned?'

I jumped away from Ned.

'Your dog must have been lying inside the door,' I said. 'She ran out and sent me flying. Ned managed to catch me.'

'Ned could always catch anything,' said Roger with an unpleasant edge to his voice. 'Fingers like flypaper. I don't see Juno.'

I was furious to have been discovered even in this, very mildly compromising, situation when my behaviour had for once been blameless. If I were to be condemned, I would rather have savoured the pleasures of the crime first and be hung as a satisfied sheep than a frustrated lamb. I contrived to laugh carelessly. 'I'm afraid she rather alarmed me . . .'

At least Juno trotted back to us at that moment, pink tongue lolling out of the side of her mouth, panting noisily.

Roger's frown relaxed. 'I'm only sorry I wasn't here to catch you myself,' he said, sounding more his usual self. 'I must train this bird-brained hound to time her interventions better. Come in, come in. And you too, Neddy.'

I refused firmly. A single one of Roger's drinks was enough to render stronger-headed men than me unfit to drive, and I was certain Ned would refuse. I could hardly bear to part from him, finally, under such disagreeably messy circumstances. I hate loose ends. All I wanted, tonight, was to finish off the whole episode tidily. A few dignified last words in private and then I could climb into my car and drive away.

But even as I shook my head, I realised, to my exasperation, that Ned was accepting. Perhaps, unused as he undoubtedly was to scenes of extra-marital drama, he needed strong drink. It was too late to change my mind, however, and so Roger saw me to my car.

'You must come round for a quiet dinner soon,' he said. 'Make up a four, now that Bess is home.'

'Lovely,' I trilled, in that brightly hollow tone which acknowledges an invitation of this vague nature politely, but implies a mutual understanding that the event is unlikely ever to materialise. At the time, I resolved with gritted-teeth determination, that under no circumstances would it be allowed to happen.

I had better things to do in the coming weeks than study at close quarters, for a whole interminable evening, the spectacle of Ned mooning over his exquisite doll of a wife.

Sebastian had always said that work was the ultimate anaesthetic. Any pain, any hurt could be drowned if only one worked hard enough.

I tried — and, to an extent, it worked. For whole hours of the day I could shove futile speculations about Ned into some obscure corner-cupboard of the brain. As soon as I put the brushes down, however, the pain bounded back, almost as though it was invigorated by the rest.

Maybe the fallacy in the theory was that Sebastian had never cared much for anything beyond his work in the first place.

It ensured an impressive output of pictures, though. On any single day, I would seem to have five or six in various stages of development, and the piano was lost under discarded, decaying collages. I prefer having a lot of work under way all at once. Then if I get stuck on one painting, there's always another to occupy me. I don't have to pace up and down, worrying over the single precious offspring. Most problems of the painting sort are better solved by ignoring them, I find anyway, than by agonising. Given a few days' healthy neglect, the majority melt away of their own accord. A pity that emotional tangles don't respond to the same treatment.

As a result, I slept fitfully. And then, I awoke one night charged with an irrational certainty there was someone standing outside the cottage. The hands of my old-fashioned alarm clock glimmered pale green at a quarter to two.

More than once at night I had heard a car pass. I no longer bothered to get up and investigate this, however. Whatever it was up to clearly had nothing to do with me and I had seen when the shoot was here that the road was perfectly passable to any of the big four-wheel drive vehicles. But this was different. This was someone on foot in the lane below.

Ridiculous to be so sure, perhaps, because I had heard no more than what I thought was a cough. I lay still in the dark, straining my ears. But an old cottage creaks and whispers at night like an ancient sailing-ship. I was tempted to pull the covers over my head and go back to sleep, but that would be to give in to cowardice.

Instead, I went to the window in the other bedroom which overlooked the road. Not surprisingly, I saw nothing. I remained there, however, shivering in the darkness and watched a silky remnant of cloud flicker over the moon. And then, some distance away to the left of me, a pinprick of man-made light. Not a headlamp, not even a bicycle (as if a bicycle could negotiate that swamp) but almost certainly a torch beam. Not pointing in this direction, either, but weaving a zig-zag path towards the village.

It was a public right of way — why shouldn't someone choose to walk down there in the middle of the night? Perhaps they were exercising their dog. I should not have wasted a thought on it had I not been convinced, first, that they had stood outside the Lodge for some time, although I had no real evidence for this; and second, which I had good cause to believe, that they had deliberately not switched on their torch until they were some distance from the Lodge. As if they did not want to disturb me.

There was nothing I could do except, after that night, take extra care to ensure that every door and window was securely locked. There was even a bolt on the old-fashioned door enclosing the stairway, and for a while I locked that too.

CHAPTER TWELVE

My view over the valley was changed completely. The soft upholstery had been stripped away, exposing the bare framework of the country. In the late afternoons, a clump of dying elms on the skyline towards the west looked as though it had been etched in ink on the chilly wash of the sky. Here and there the artist had carelessly let fall a blot of a rook's nest.

I like the countryside in winter. It's strong and honest. Like a face with a good bone structure which is not reliant on the soft prettiness of youth but is even more splendid in withered old age, a fine landscape will improve when all its lines are starkly revealed.

Occasionally, however, I let myself look back to my first water-colour which glowed with the lush ripeness of autumn. The Indian summer weather which had blessed the last week of October seemed symbolic now. Not a real summer. Deceptively warm at the time, but destined to end abruptly in an icy frost.

It was hard to look objectively at this painting. The solid fisherman could never be just a piece of flat paint and paper, a figure in a landscape. I wondered whether I should stand by my promise to give Ned the picture. Not that I was reluctant to do so. If I could continue to work at my present pace – and carry it on in London afterwards – I would be able to offer Christopher more work than he could exhibit. I felt, fervently, that this picture belonged to Ned. But I feared it might be an embarrassment to him, not a pleasure. Evidence of an indiscretion that never was.

It would have been easier – I daresay for him as well as me – if I really could have excised him completely from my life. In London this would have been straightforward. In a community as tightly-confined as Thornbeck it was impossible to avoid meeting Ned occasionally – and Elizabeth Cowper, too.

The first time I met her – or rather the second – was in the post office. She was wearing precisely the kind of expensively understated clothes Gerald thinks are the cat's pyjamas. And exactly the kind I loathe. People I like make statements with what they wear. The object is to differentiate and define oneself, not melt into the uniformed ranks. And yet Elizabeth Cowper, with her fogey-ish cardigan, her white shirt, her plain skirt, and the silk scarf (shades of Her Majesty) knotted round her head, managed to radiate the immaculate self-contained chic I have only ever seen in French women. Moreover, with every garment entirely appropriate to the wife of a country parson, she could not have looked the part less. I, correspond-ingly, in baggy jeans and paint-stained pullover under the mac, felt clumsy and loutish.

She must have been entertaining Len behind the counter because he was still laughing wheezily when I walked in, shaking the rain off my coat, splashed thigh-deep with mud from the walk along Lamp Lane.

'It's Frankie, isn't it?' she exclaimed with calm cheerfulness. 'I'm Elizabeth Cowper. We didn't really get the chance to introduce ourselves what with one thing and another . . .'

Like you taking pot shots at my head?

'. . . and I've wanted so much to meet you. Suzy tells me you're terribly nice, and that I owe you an apology for giving you such a shock the other day. You will forgive me, won't you? Such a ridiculous trick to have played but I couldn't resist putting the wind up my fearfully respectable husband. I promise you faithfully, cross my heart . . .' and she did indeed cross her frail, pearly-nailed fingers across her pert bosom, '. . . there was no danger. I'm a terribly good shot. Aren't I, Len?' She raised her voice to address his question to him.

'You shouldn't go shooting out of turn, Mrs Cowper,' he said grumpily. 'Show a bit of the sense you were born with.'

'Wasn't born with any,' she shouted back cheerfully. 'You should know that, Len.' She turned back to me and lowered her voice again. 'Of course, I shouldn't have done it. Did my brother frighten you? I told him that the sight of him throwing a tantrum was more alarming than twenty loose cartridges. Didn't he go a funny colour? Do you know, for one awful moment I actually thought he might attack me. Ned was *terribly* cross too.' She rolled her eyes dramatically. 'Crosser than he's been for simply years. But he's so much more restrained than we are.' She smiled at me, seraphically. 'We Vaiseys have no self-control at all.'

'It's hereditary, is it?' I said, with a leaden attempt at humour. Little quicksilver women like Elizabeth Cowper make me feel as though I talk with size seven feet as well as walk on them.

'Oh God,' she exclaimed merrily, 'that's exactly the kind of thing Ned would say. And Roger would say . . .' and she lowered her voice to a comic gruffness, 'vice is bred in the bones, old man. No use pretending otherwise. Ho ho ho . . .'

I smiled perfunctorily. I did not much want to be entertained with the family anecdotes of Elizabeth Cowper. She would be telling me next how Ned liked his morning tea. I glanced round for Len, but he was studying a book of Post Office tables with an expression of total perplexity.

'And beastly Rog has banned me for the rest of the season. Father wouldn't have done that. He might have been cross but . . .' she sighed, and the beautiful eyes staring at me were all at once brimming with melancholy.

I didn't know what she expected me to say. I could hardly commiserate with her on the death of her parent seven years earlier.

'Anyway,' she said abruptly, 'Roger's banned me, so God knows what I'm going to do with myself. It's so un-be-liev-ably boring up here in winter, don't you find?'

'Well – I'm working.'

'Of course, you're a painter. How I wish I could do something clever like that. But no one taught us anything at my school except French conversation and Jane fucking Eyre.'

I found myself smiling. The language was so incongruous tripping off the cupid's bow lips. Len was less amused and walked out to busy himself noisily in the room behind the shop, evidently his kitchen. I heard an old-fashioned kettle whistle. Elizabeth Cowper chattered on regardless. 'I can't even cook. Half my friends seem to be making a packet with fancy balls of choux pastry for directors' drinks parties, but no one taught me even to boil an egg. I daresay it's the kind of thing one's mother should see to, but my mama waltzed off with a sun-tanned gigolo when I was twelve – did you know that?'

'Suzy mentioned –'

'Suzy filled you in on the sordid family gossip, did she? I'll bet. Suzanna Worrall eats lives and breathes scandal. I don't suppose she told you her husband's screwing his secretary three times a week? Pig of a man. Suzy's a poppet, though. I wish she'd come up more often. Amazing for her age, isn't she? She's forty-two, you know. I'm talking too much, as usual. It's your turn now. Confess, confess!' she cried, and she pointed an accusing finger at me.

Did she know? Know what? She couldn't seriously be expecting me to admit to lusting after her husband. Confess all, here in the village post office?

She burst into laughter. Her laughter rang out as readily and as musically as a peal of wind chimes.

'Didn't you play that at your school too? Confessions? Someone points at you and screams, "Confess!", and you have to say something interesting and scandalous. At once. Doesn't have to be true . . .'

'No – we didn't.'

'That's how I first heard the Facts of Life.' She leaned towards me conspiratorially. 'I thought they were making it up, of course. Too, too, utterly disgusting!'

I laughed, but glanced uneasily towards the back room where Len could be seen now carefully stirring sugar into a large blue mug.

'Deaf as a post,' she said. 'And what do you paint?'

I hate that question. I'm always inclined to answer stubbornly: pictures. But I murmured something meaningless about people and places.

'I don't suppose you'd like to paint me?'

'I – I rarely paint portraits as such, and besides . . .'

'Joking, joking. You'd be surprised how many painters have offered to do me,' she said, with another trilling laugh.

110

'I wouldn't,' I said honestly, 'I assure you.'

When all that three-quarters of sitters desire (in their heart of hearts) is a subtly realistic bending of the truth, to render them just a fraction more beautiful than life, the painter's problem with Elizabeth Cowper would be convincing anyone looking at the portrait afterwards that he had indeed represented his subject faithfully, and not been carried away by the lid of a chocolate box.

'I've been wondering though, seriously, whether I should commission a portrait,' she went on. 'There's a terribly good man near Harrogate. For the wall of Edward's bedroom. For his next birthday perhaps . . .'

A pinprick of resentment at her proprietorial use of Ned's full name (why should she not call her husband Edward if she chose?) was swamped by shamefully avid curiosity about their sleeping arrangements. Apparently the Cowpers had separate bedrooms. Resolutely, I smothered prurient speculation and was on the point of leaving the post office when I remembered that I had actually come to buy stamps.

'Five first-class?' said Len, returning to his post and tearing them out with care.

'You must come and see me one day,' said Elizabeth with breath-taking insouciance. 'When you're not too busy. I'd love to see you. You wouldn't believe how bored and lonely I am.'

'Thanks,' I said, 'how flattering.' This set her wind chime of a laugh tinkling again.

'I didn't mean that. I should adore to see you even if I had an engagement diary full as a telephone directory. Do you hunt?'

I shook my head. 'I can't even ride.'

'Well that's something at any rate. If you could ride as well as being incredibly sexy (that's according to my beast of a brother) and charming (according to my chum Suzy) and a brilliant artist (according to my husband) I might feel obliged to hate you. And when I hate, I'm completely unspeakable!'

And with that she was gone, leaving a whiff of mouth-watering scent behind her.

'Thank you,' said Len, taking my money. 'Don't take no notice of our Bess. All hot air.'

*

It would have been too obvious to have loathed Elizabeth Cowper on sight. I did not. She radiated a mixture of charm, gaiety and vulnerability which was impossible to withstand.

She reminded me, however, in manner not appearance, of an actress I had once painted. This woman cultivated a similar self-effacing, feather-headed charm. Having once secured the good opinion of her latest acquaintance, however, she would immediately abandon the effort to please and revert to type. Deborah was actually a likeable woman, but massively more egotistical and self-assured than first impressions would lead anyone to believe. It seemed to me that she cultivated the diffident veneer over her own, more abrasive personality in order to collect admirers — as compulsively as anyone else might collect stamps. Having once stuck them in the book, so to speak, she lost interest. The soft glow of charm was reserved for the next victim.

In fairness, I could not discern in Elizabeth Cowper the ruthlessly hungry ego which propelled Deborah, but I could not believe she was entirely the laughing *ingénue* she appeared either. I wondered afresh what form her so-called nervous problems took. Her fast and brittle stream of chatter suggested she was highly strung, but then so were half my friends — and very few thus far had required psychiatric treatment.

I did not, of course, take up her invitation to visit the Dower House. Masochism has never numbered among my vices. I turned down too several invitations to the Manor, on the grounds of pressure of work.

'Aren't you going out of your head, stuck there all on your own?' demanded Roger, when he telephoned. 'They'd have had to send the padded van for me weeks ago.'

Gerald asked much the same thing every time he telephoned — which was irregularly but always at eight-thirty in the morning, or six-fifteen at night. The greater part of his conversation glowed with sunshine and glamour like a travel brochure: the States, Barbados, Bangkok. It made me feel like a little grey hibernating animal — which was evidently how he saw me too.

'I'm quite content to be alone,' I assured him, time and again. 'I wouldn't be if this was for ever, obviously, but whilst I'm busy putting together an exhibition it's perfect. I can concentrate a million times better here than in the flat. Really, I don't feel the need of people at all.' Except one particular person – but that was inadmissible.

'If you're sure,' said Gerald, sounding offended. 'I've fixed the trip north for the last week in January. Filming an ad in Newcastle. I'm really looking forward to seeing you.'

'It'll be nice,' I agreed listlessly. Why not, after all? Gerald's rigorous diary would allow him to spend one scant night here at the most. Why shouldn't I have a man to stay, I thought defiantly? Ned wouldn't care – except probably to disapprove, in a sniffy, parson-ish kind of way, of the adulterous aspect.

'I could make either the Tuesday or the Friday. On the way up, or down . . .'

'Suit yourself. I don't go anywhere.'

'You don't sound very enthusiastic.'

'Don't I? Sorry. It seems such a long way off.'

'Much, much too long, baby,' said Gerald fervently, mis-understanding me. I'd only meant it was too early yet to worry about making arrangements. But nothing could ever be planned too early for Gerald. 'You will let me know if there's anything you want me to bring. Books, magazines . . .'

'There are bookshops in the north of England you know. What did you think we relied on? Missionaries?'

'Only asking.'

'And I'll take the coal out of the bath specially.'

'That's what I miss about you, Frances. Your sense of humour. I'll miss you in Korea.'

'Thanks,' I said ungraciously. 'Better get back to work.' I knew Gerald would have liked me to confide what I most missed about him, but I would have been hard put to answer. It would have been cheap to say the bottles of vintage champagne he was apt to bestow on me – and cruel to be honest. Which was to admit that I could think of nothing at all I missed about Gerald himself.

I returned to my table and, after a desultory search, con-cluded that my diary must be buried somewhere in the painting debris. By the time I found it, I had forgotten the likely date of Gerald's arrival. Never mind, I thought, I can check the next time he rings.

CHAPTER THIRTEEN

On a crisp morning in December, I climbed the hill to Thornbeck Top, to the Wheatsheaf. The landlord of the Wheatsheaf had suggested the expedition himself, as a matter of fact. Although Gerald might have gathered the impression – and I suppose I did not disabuse him – that I never saw another human soul, I was increasingly besieged with friendly invitations.

I've read accounts of those awesomely intrepid women travellers who cycle from Afghanistan to China with only a rucksack and a handful of dried biscuits. They all claim, I have noticed, that the most fearsomely-reputationed tribes are the very soul of kind hospitality when it comes to their treatment of a woman travelling alone. The Amazonian travellers say this is because the natives can only believe that a woman choosing to journey alone on a bicycle through their country must be stark staring bonkers. Thus, meals, puncture repairs, gifts, and advice are reputedly pressed upon the poor demented creature at every stage.

Whether or not this is actually true in Afghanistan, I can only say that it applied to me in North Yorkshire. Not that the country is inhabited by fearsome tribes, but a great many people locally quite clearly believed that voluntary incarceration in an isolated cottage, alone, through the winter for a (relatively) young single woman was the height of eccentricity. And the madder they obviously thought I was, the more correspondingly generous were their offers of company and food. I barely need ever have spent an evening alone, had I not wished to.

Also, I was inundated with advice on what I should and should not paint. I ought to walk up to the pub, Albert

Brough had suggested, to see the Wragdale Hunt meet. A sight not to be missed.

The frost was still shimmering in the shadows behind the hedge, but the sun was bright by the time I reached the top of the hill. There were horse-boxes strung along the road and far more people in dowdy green anoraks than in red jackets. I was rather disappointed.

In the carpark of the pub, however, the riders were turned out with perfectly tailored precision. I learned later that only the hunt bigwigs could sport the flashy red coats. It was easy to overlook the stomach-churning object of the exercise in the pageantry of the event. I stood warily on the low stone wall of a front garden to take photographs. Horses tossed their neatly knotted heads, snorted steam and skidded noisily on the cobbles. I was sharply aware of the tonnage of gleaming horse-flesh shifting and swaying inches away. I had forgotten how big horses were.

'Morning, Frankie!' shouted a voice. I had not even re-cognized Roger in the immaculate, straight-backed, red-coated rider. He was astride a prancing giant of an animal with a coat like a well-polished grand piano.

'You should always appear on horseback, Roger,' I said as he bent to drop a kiss somewhere above the top of my head. 'You look marvellous.'

'Is this the way to your heart then, you hard-hearted bitch?' he said laughing so loudly several other riders turned to look. 'Must I throw you over my pommel and abduct you at once? Such a pity to miss a good day's hunting —'

The exchange was cut short by another rider wheeling between us.

'No "antis" out today?' said the rider, gathering up the reins sharply and cursing her mount.

'Apparently not,' said Roger. 'Pity. The anti-blood sports crowd,' he added, for my benefit. 'Adds no end of a spice to the day. They enjoy it as much as we do.'

'How?' I said warily. 'I mean, what do they do?'

'Oh, they lay false trails to confuse the hounds. Doesn't work, of course. Easy, easy . . .' This last was addressed to his horse which had started nervously when he laughed.

Roger on horseback was a subtly different man. The height it lent him and his evident mastery of the animal inspired him with a confidence, and an air of authority he lacked on the ground. This should have improved him — he certainly looked magnificent mounted — but instead, obscurely, it made me uneasy. I had a sense of the man Roger might have been and was glad he was not. I preferred a lecherous dwarf to a mounted autocrat.

'Are you here for Christmas?' he demanded crisply.

I often wish my brain could invent politely non-commital lies faster than my mouth blurts out the truth.

'Yes,' I said — and added rather lamely, 'probably.'

'Only ten days away,' said Roger. 'Don't you know yet, my adorable nincompoop?'

This year it was my family's turn to gather at Aunty Dorothy's. Aunty Dorothy and I had disliked one other cordially since I, as a child, had been made to submit to kisses from her spikily moustached mouth — and then been graphically honest in describing my reasons for objecting. I knew perfectly well I was not going home. The most I could claim was that it had crossed my mind to investigate what Sebastian was planning for Christmas.

'I shall not send you an invitation,' Roger declared imperiously. He was performing as much for the benefit of the riders nearby as for me. Several raised their eyebrows in my direction and pulled faces, laughing. 'I shall follow the custom of the Palace and send a command. And if you dare to refuse I shall come and kidnap you. Thanks, Albert.'

The landlord, stepping nimbly between the shifting iron-clad feet and swishing tails, was handing round a tray of small glasses containing port or whisky. I chose port which tasted like cough medicine at that hour of the morning.

'Remember . . .' called Roger, over his shoulder as his horse plunged forwards.

'Image of his father, sometimes,' said Albert. He spoke in his customary dry and non-commital tone. I liked Albert. He was more soothingly philosophical than the most laid-back New York barman.

'What was the old Squire like?' I said. 'Really?'

'Really?' said Albert, glancing briefly round him. 'Well . . . people round here will often tell you that his wife, Margaret, was the only problem with old John. A young minx marrying a man old enough to be her father because she had ideas above her station – and then leading him a dance. And that's what made him such a bad-tempered old so-and-so. Which he could be. Sometimes . . .'

Albert paused to take an empty glass from another rider. 'Margaret's father was a well-to-do businessman – had a manufacturing plant up in Middlesbrough. There's always a certain snobbery about the Manor locally, and particularly in those days. Money talks anywhere now I dare say, but forty years back there was plenty of quiet sneering round here about *nouveau riche* types buying themselves in. Not from the local gentry, mind you. It was the folk in the villages. No one quicker to sneer about the new money than those who've never had money at all – old or new.

Somewhere behind us exploded a clamour of hounds' voices overlaid with a volley of shouted instructions.

'Anyway, Margaret Vaisey didn't fit the local picture of what the Lady of the Manor should be,' continued Albert imperturbably. 'Flighty, they said. Too much make-up. Flashy clothes. You might ask why she shouldn't wear pretty clothes. Her father gave her an allowance so's she could afford them – which was more than she would ever have got from old John. He was of the breed that gives Yorkshiremen a bad name . . .'

More horses spilled into the yard, and I waited impatiently while Albert handed round more tiny glasses.

'Anyway,' said Albert, 'to cut a long story short, I gave three cheers when I heard she'd cut loose.'

'You did?' I said, in some surprise. Part of the impassive bartender persona which Albert cultivated was that he was rarely, if ever, heard to disclose his own personal opinions. He specialized in playing the neutral sounding board to other people's.

'I think she was a better wife than she was given credit for. And if she laid on the war-paint a bit too thick now and then,' he said, giving away the last full glass on his tray, 'in my opinion it was because she had something to hide underneath the make-up. Coming, Caroline . . .'

'You mean – bruises?'

Albert smiled enigmatically, and he strode away to replenish his tray.

I climbed back on to the edge of the garden wall, camera in hand, and at that moment caught sight of Ned. There was a cluster of horses and riders between us and I doubted if he had seen me. He was not dressed for riding, but beside him Elizabeth, severely habited, was leading a handsome bay.

Apparently a mother in a ward full of screaming babies can pick out the faint note of her own beloved offspring. Even though I willed myself not to listen, across the crowded yard I could distinguish enough of Ned's urgently whispered exchange with his wife to hear that he was asking her to take care, to be sensible. His face was twisted with anxiety.

The perfect loving husband.

I couldn't hear Elizabeth's reply. I saw her laugh and persuade him to give her a leg up into the saddle. He tossed her up as though she were a feather pillow. There was a babble of yapping and howls as the hounds spilled across the green. Dogs up and down the village replied, excitedly. Horses and riders began to clatter towards the road. Ned followed his wife on foot.

'P-please,' he said, 'for your own sake, if not for m-mine . . .'

Elizabeth grinned and flicked her crop playfully towards him. When her horse had moved on, I saw with a certain fascinated horror that he was rubbing his knuckles and wincing. Roger evidently saw it too, because with that he kicked his horse into action sharply and veered over to Elizabeth, swearing at her in a harsh undertone.

'Be careful, Roger,' she said perfectly audibly. 'I'm watching you, little brother. I've an idea what your nasty little game is.'

Roger's face darkened and the effort of refraining from replying in kind was visibly enormous. He swung round in the saddle to address Ned. 'You make too many allowances,' he said angrily. 'I wouldn't let her get away with it. I'd beat her . . .' To my disgust, I found I was almost agreeing with him. Elizabeth Cowper behaved like a spoilt child.

Ned stared up at him. 'No, you wouldn't,' he said evenly. 'Would you, Roger?'

Roger held his gaze for a moment, then looked away and muttered something inaudible before clattering off into the thick of the riders.

Ned watched them depart. He had not even noticed me, although I raised a hand in greeting. I let it drop again.

'Devoted husband,' I remarked bad-temperedly to Albert. 'She takes her crop to him – and he just looks worried sick that she'll fall off and break her neck.'

'Weather seems to be turning,' said Albert with a bland smile. 'Dare say we might have a white Christmas this year.'

I took this to mean he was not prepared to gossip about the present generation at the Manor and felt suitably snubbed. After a moment's thought however he added quietly, 'He's a good man, Ned Cowper.' Then, more enigmatically, 'Bess Vaisey was always more her father's daughter than her mother's.'

Maybe that was it. A pretty little girl spoiled by a father whose wife had run off and left him, Elizabeth Cowper had acquired a taste for getting her own way and never learned it was not her inalienable right. Poor Ned.

The green anoraks, carrying weighty binoculars and vacuum flasks, were all piling into cars which were pulling off in pursuit of the riders. Apparently, following the proceedings from the warmth and comfort of a car was even more popular than doing so on horseback. I had no desire to see any more and, returning my glass to Albert with thanks, I turned to walk home.

A few hundred yards on, with a mixture of surprise and gratification I heard Ned calling my name.

'M-may I walk down the hill with you? I can cut through Lamp Lane then . . .'

I waited for him to catch up. As he did so I tried not to stare at the weal across his fingers but he caught the direction of my gaze and blushed.

'Horseplay,' he said briefly, and stuck the hand in his pocket.

'How are you?' We both said the same words simultaneously, and laughed. It defused the tension.

'Busy,' I said. 'And you?'

He nodded. 'I have t-two parishes to run at the m-moment, which actually means four. St Catherine's, Langton-le-Moor these days includes two smaller p-parishes up the valley and since St Catherine's has — well — lost its vicar recently . . .'

'Oh yes. I'm sorry. I think I was pretty tactless about, um, parish problems.'

Ned shrugged. 'Why not? I c-can see there must be comic aspects for an outsider. B-but here it's pure bloody tragedy.'

'Does he get thrown out of the Church?' I asked. 'De-frocked?'

Ned shook his head. 'Absolutely not,' he said. 'He can't c-come back here, though. I met the churchwardens yesterday and a stone wall is yielding in comparison with the Parochial Church Council. They have made their views clear to the B-bishop, who's a nice chap. But he's got no choice. Michael's actually in York at the moment, being given what they diplomatically term "counselling". Mainly comes in tranquilliser tubes, poor fellow. No, the Church isn't the problem. The Church can forgive — after all that's the Church's business. It's the local congregation.'

'In this day and age?'

'Someone c-came to me yesterday and asked if I would re-baptize their child. M-michael had already christened the baby, but they refused to accept this could be valid any longer. Someone else asked me if they could have contracted AIDS from the communion wine.' He laughed sadly. 'They're an unforgiving lot. Oh, not just here — you could f-find the same in a hundred country p-parishes, I dare say. A fine and popular parish priest slips once, fails after years of rigorous self-control to keep himself in check and . . . You know, there are times when the era of witch-hunts seems to be only minutes gone.'

'What made you go in for it?' I said. 'The priesthood, I mean?'

'I wish I c-could say I experienced a great and glorious call. I suppose I w-wanted to be useful about the place. You might ask why not b-become a social worker — and I did think about it. But they have to specialize, and I'm more a Jack of all trades. Not p-particularly brilliant at anything, but I can chat to p-people, and try to chip in a bit of help, and take choir practice to save Martha Berry, that's our organist you know, c-coming out at night and . . .'

'. . . and produce plays?'

He smiled. Nodded. 'Fund-raise, k-kiss babies, play piggy-in-the-middle on the Parish Council and ninety-three committees – even, sometimes, try to explain why God seems to have d-dumped us in this appalling mess. I'm n-not always very good at that either.'

There was real unhappiness in his voice. Was this Elizabeth's doing? Was she often cruel to her kind, bumbling husband?

'How b-boring I'm being, jawing on about my little problems,' he said, with transparently forced jollity. 'T-tell me about –'

'Ah don't,' I said impulsively. 'You don't have to pretend. Life's a sod sometimes. I don't know what makes you so unhappy. It's none of my business. But please don't feel obliged to act.'

'Don't you?' he said oddly, and then at once, 'Are you coming to the M-manor on Christmas Day? Roger tells me he's inviting you.'

'To what?'

'D-dinner, usually. Early dinner anyway. He assembles those of his f-friends who are without children, and w-want to avoid their own families. C-can be ghastly. Or it can be quite entertaining. We shall be there, of course. I h-hoped you might accept.'

'Well that settles it then,' I said, sternly smothering the hopes which were fluttering inside me, frenzied as a startled flock of pigeons. We had arrived outside the Lodge and I opened the garden gate. I knew without asking that Ned would not come in. 'I shall accept Roger's invitation, when it arrives.'

'Don't t-take Roger too seriously will you?' he said suddenly. 'He's a d-dear man, but . . . I wouldn't like you to b-be hurt.'

This bewildered me. Did he think I was in danger of believing Roger's absurd declarations of passion?

'I don't take him seriously at all,' I said, 'I promise.'

CHAPTER FOURTEEN

A picture of the hunt came easily.

In the centre was the diminutive and rotund figure of Albert with tray, dwarfed by the swaying mountains of glossy horse-flesh around him. The heads of the animals were not visible, nor were those of the riders. Only shiny booted legs and imperiously outstretched hands.

For some reason it struck me as seasonal – perhaps it was the knowledge that Albert was as much in demand as a local Father Christmas. Anyway, on impulse, I inked in one of the sketches, added a festive Tippex smattering of snow and had fifty copies run off on a trip to York. Printing melted away the smudges and the smears and left a shrunken, crisp, black and white drawing which I barely recognised. The paper smelled pleasantly of ink as I folded the pictures into envelopes and sent them off (late) as my Christmas card.

Gerald's card to me was (as always) the company issue. Flamboyant and cleverly ahead of the year's run-of-the-mill designs, it featured a shake-down snowstorm effect built into a window. The card was signed by him with my name inscribed on the envelope in his carefully italicised hand (his writing had been more of a leftward-sloping copperplate until he read what this revealed about his character) but the address had been added later by typewriter. Efficient old Gerald – no doubt sunning in some distant corner of the globe – had left a batch of cards behind to be dispatched with perfect timing by his secretary. I rated a Company card as the decorator of the Company dining-room. And, just in case glossy Melissa should peek inside, the message was suitably impersonal. He had merely inserted the word 'very' and underlined it before Happy New Year.

A cheering number of other cards forwarded from the flat joined those which arrived direct. Quite unreasonably, I loathe sending cards but love receiving them. I arranged them round my sitting-room with pleasure – those I wasn't immediately impelled to cut up into a collage. There's something so crisp and clean and colourful about certain Christmas cards which calls out for a pair of scissors ... Particularly when one is pondering a painting with a Christmas flavour. The only card I was not in the least tempted to deface was a quiet but expensively engraved silver star from the Dower House. The address was printed inside, which was as well because the scrawled 'Edward and Elizabeth' was barely legible.

Among them also was Roger's invitation. This did not take the form of a command. Roger's assertiveness diminished when he dismounted. He had written a formal letter, in a surprisingly neat and feminine hand with old-fashioned loops on the tall stemmed letters, begging me to join them for Christmas Dinner. *Dress for dinner, arrive for lunch* he had written, adding *3.30 for 7.00 pm* with several exclamation marks. I accepted.

Rather hurt, when Christmas Eve arrived though, I realised I had received nothing at all from Sebastian. No present, no card – not even a rotten telephone call. I tried to ring him a couple of times during the day, but there was no reply. He had said he was finally planning to quit the old shared house in Limberton Gardens. Maybe he had done so.

I found it strangely hard to spend Christmas Eve alone. Looked at logically, Christmas Eve should be no different from any other day – particularly in the countryside, where there are no shoppers rushing home with parcels tucked under their arms and no armies of carol singers on every corner. The birds in the garden were pecking at my toast crusts and going about the business of survival like any other day. The trees were not decorated. Sunset, although colourful, was not a special festive issue.

I suppose, like a teenager at home on a Saturday night, any solitary person is prone, at Christmas, to a lowering bout of 'outsider-itis'. It's almost impossible not to feel you're the loneliest and least-loved being left on earth. Even Radio Four ho-ho-hoed jovially through the day, full of people scurrying home to family firesides nibbling walnuts, to deck the tree and stuff the stockings. I was on the point of retiring, Scrooge-like, early to bed, when I had a better idea. I would attend the Christmas night service at St Peter's. Even the slackest of attenders are allowed to slip in at Christmas without God or his earthly minions taking offence.

There was a curious prickle of illicit excitement at the prospect of actually observing Ned at work. I also felt daring because I intended to walk to the village along Lamp Lane.

On another night recently, I had woken with the same irrational certainty that there was someone outside. This time I had seen no torch beam. I can only explain it as being akin to that feeling we have all had occasionally, in a dark and totally silent house – that someone else is there.

I reminded myself that, even if there had been someone outside, I had not the least grounds for believing they nurtured any designs on me. I was glad nonetheless of the stout bolt on the stairs.

On Christmas Eve, however, I armed myself with the flashlight from the car, and set off alone into the frosty darkness with impunity. And I enjoyed the walk along the ice-hardened lane. A bright moon almost made the torch superfluous. There's something about the very fact of Christmas Night which leads one to believe nothing untoward can happen. It must be a fallacy that thieves, muggers, rapists – and people who lurk outside isolated cottages in the middle of the night – recognize an unspoken armistice, but it's a pleasant one.

Curiously, Ned began his address with some observations on this very phenomenon. Maybe, given the season, this was not curious at all.

I had been afraid that I would be embarrassed to hear Ned preach. I couldn't help fearing he might be pompous, or unbearably overladen with story-book clichés I remembered from Sunday School (*I expect you're wondering, children, why I'm holding up this long pointy leaf?* – Because it's Palm Sunday, dimbo). I was also afraid he would stumble and stutter, or in some other way make a fool of himself in front of this packed congregation – the church was very crowded, with many people I knew by now, and even more I did not. The carols were belted out with sherry-scented gusto and a volume most churches only experience when *Songs of Praise* is being recorded. This Christmas congregation was, however, larger than usual because Ned made a particular point of welcoming the parishioners of St Catherine's, Langton-le-Moor who were, sadly, without their own priest this Christmas.

Roger, with some people the backs of whose heads I could not identify, occupied a forward pew. I did not join them. I had slipped into the Church, deliberately invisibly, at the back.

'It's an extraordinary phenomenon, the effect C-christmas has on people,' began Ned's address, unconsciously echoing my own thoughts. 'Even on p-people who probably never walk inside a Church.'

I sunk lower into the pew and studied my hymn-book, although I was sure he had not seen me.

'An image which has always haunted m-me is of the trenches of the First World War.' Ned paused and scanned the congregation. I began to think he was more of an actor than I had given him credit for. 'I know that at least two men here fought in those four and a half years of terrible, bloody carnage. One of them told me he thought he would never be able to believe in God again. Not after what he had seen on the Somme.

'Millions of troops waterlogged in holes not fit for rats, bedded down in filth and squalor amidst the bodies of their own dead – because there were corpses rotting unburied on both sides of no man's land. Eighteen-year-old soldiers who became old men in the space of a few weeks. There are families here who lost members in the mud of Ypres. At Passchendaele. Nearly every surname on the p-plaque in the porch is still familiar in our villages.'

The hush of the crowded church seemed to echo with generations of the same names stretching back over hundreds of years, hundreds of Christmas sermons, centuries of carols.

'And then, in the midst of this insane and dreadful blood-shed, it is Christmas Day. And for Christmas Day – by some unspoken and mutual consent between the two warring nations – the ghastly carousel of death is stopped for t-twenty-four hours. The guns fall silent.'

Ned smiled wonderingly.

'S-suddenly, one of the soldiers, a Tommy or a German lad, sticks his head above the trenches, and calls, "Happy Christmas!" – "Fröhliche Weihnachten!" – across the white frozen waste of no man's land. Minutes later, the men on both sides are scrambling up the trench walls, c-crawling under the barbed wire towards each other, not with bayonets at the ready, but with offers of cigarettes. Showing each other family photographs. Swapping the few w-words they know in each other's languages.'

Ned paused. He could afford to. He had his audience gripped. He studied his hands, clasped over the rim of the pulpit, before looking up again.

'Now, I've heard it said that this is a myth. That this fraternisation between the warring sides never happened. Worse, I've heard people claim behaviour like that merits a court martial. I do not believe that – and I do believe it happened.'

He spoke with passionate sincerity. I was moved. It seemed to me no one hearing him could fail to be affected.

'I think it's the most m-marvellous, the most miraculous image of Christmas that could ever be imagined. Men who had been reduced to a misery and suffering no human being should have to endure, were able to ignore the mean and base instinct which is in all of us, to lay the blame for their misfortunes on the obvious: the enemy. You m-might say they had every cause to hate. But on Christmas Day they could find forgiveness. Remember their c-common humanity.'

His voice dropped again, to an almost wistful reflectiveness, 'Christmas is, above all else, a time for love. Not just the cosy, easy love of those round our own firesides. Real love, Christ's love – the important sort of love – is difficult. Showing real love entails crossing the wire.' Ned stared very seriously round the church, and spoke very deliberately. 'It means embracing the person whom, not five minutes ago, you were treating as your enemy. As an outcast.'

Absorbed in the words, the physical music of the sound, I was slow to perceive that Ned was delivering something more specific than a generalised Christmas enjoinder to love and live at peace.

'N-none of us is perfect, so how can we be selfish and arrogant enought to d-demand perfection in others?'

Ripples of indignant whispers and shuffling alerted me.

'I hope we can all, each and everyone of us, find understanding in our hearts this Christmas – and with understanding must come forgiveness. And with f-forgiveness, love.'

Ned was, without question, having a go at his flock about their rejection of the erring vicar. I listened intrigued to the varied notes of protest and discomfiture in the murmuring about me.

'After all,' said Ned, lightening his voice abruptly, 'this Church is full of p-people who really know about love. I've been to two diamond wedding anniversaries this year – three golden, and I've lost count of the silvers. Now, anyone who has stayed married to the same p-person for anything over a quarter of a century knows a thing or t-two about love . . .'

There was a ripple of laughter. I was impressed. Ned's talent for preaching went beyond anything I could ever have imagined in him.

'I think they'd be the f-first to tell you that love – real love – isn't about fireworks, those crazy days when you feel you c-could fly round the stars because you're so happy . . .'

I heard these words in amazement. Ned was quoting *me*. Those were just the words I had used, such a long long time ago (it seemed now) as we had sat together in the sunshine on the terrace behind the Lodge. And then I began to wonder whether his second part of the sermon was entirely inspired by the unfortunate vicar of St Catherine's.

'. . . We might call that love, but of c-course it isn't. It's d-delightful and d-delicious and d-d-delirious and all those other words the American song-writer says, which are so hard to get a c-clumsy tongue like mine round . . .'

More laughter.

'. . . But real love is a much more serious b-business, isn't it? It t-takes working at when the p-person you're supposed to love maybe doesn't seem delightful at all. When, maybe at the moment you don't even like them very much . . .'

I watched the candles by the altar flicker in the draught. Could the rest of the congregation hear wretchedness in Ned's voice? Perhaps they thought it was unhappiness for his colleague.

'. . . On those days when you feel that, l-left to yourself, you would b-be happier never to see this person again; if then you c-can s-stick by them — until b-better times return, which they will, which they *m-must* . . .'

The emphasis was unmistakable. So, to my ears, was a dogged anguish.

'. . . then, that's love. That's what Christ meant by love.'

As the voices roared 'O Come, All Ye Faithful' around me, I sang too, but my thoughts were concentrated on Ned's sermon.

I was contemplating Ned in a new rôle. Instead of devoted husband, I wondered if what we had listened to was an unhappy man, trying desperately hard to love his wife.

Under other circumstances, I might have been elated, but at the time all I could feel was a kind of wondering pity.

CHAPTER FIFTEEN

I was sure Ned had not seen me in the packed church, and I hurried out ahead of the main crush in order to avoid him. None of the many things I would have liked to say to Ned could be uttered in a receiving line of formal handshakes on the way out of a service.

The bells were clanging gloriously across the frosty night as I slipped out of the churchyard, ringing in the season with every clamorous discord. I hummed a carol as I turned into Lamp Lane, thinking furiously. The one person I was fairly certain I had not seen in the congregation — although her height would make her easy to overlook — was Elizabeth Cowper. I wondered afresh how well-suited she was to the rôle of vicar's wife, if it suited her at all. Her bad language might make me laugh in the village post office, but it can scarcely have been what a congregation would expect from the clergyman's spouse. Perhaps they made affectionate allowances because she was also the Squire's sister, or maybe because of her illness.

I also wondered if Ned could have been talking about his wife's illness when he said that times *must* change. Unmistakably, the anguish in his voice had been personal. As though he was saying that however hard it was to love someone now, it must one day become less burdensome. Did he mean that he would find it easier to love Elizabeth again when she recovered? But from what? I had been unable to perceive in his wife anything beyond high spirits and the petulance of a spoiled child. Irritating but not an illness — and not curable by doctors. Poor Ned.

Having escaped the crowd, I was no longer in a hurry. The

night was cold, but I was warmly dressed and the moonlight glittered entrancingly on frosty twigs in the hedgerow and along the silvery tramlines of frozen mud in the lane. In the distance, the bells still pealed. I turned a corner and ahead of me Lamp Lane stretched like the highwayman's ribbon of moonlight. I've never been very successful painting moonlight, and I leaned on a stone wall, switched off my torch and contemplated the icy countryside, analysing where I went wrong.

My reverie was disturbed by a car-engine accelerating noisily along the lane towards me, from the direction of the village. I stood up hastily and switched my torch beam back on. The sudden glare of the headlights nearly blinded me as I pressed myself into the hedge to let the vehicle pass. I recognized Roger's Range Rover, and raised a hand in greeting. The vehicle squealed to a stop, and the interior lit up as Roger himself leaned over to open the passenger door.

'Frankie . . .?'

'What are you driving down here for, Roger? At this hour on a Christmas morning?'

'Coming in search of you, what else?' said Roger, but with rather less than his usual conviction.

'Did you see me in church? I rather thought I'd slipped in and out as silently as a ghost.'

'Nothing escapes me,' said Roger with a hollow laugh. 'I . . . thought you might like a lift home. Can't sit by and watch a young woman walk unchaperoned through the night.'

'That's very kind of you. But I was enjoying the walk, as a matter of fact. Truly.'

'But I'm much too lazy to walk with you, so come and give me a Christmas kiss, you desirable creature, and let me run you the rest of the way home.'

I hauled myself up into the passenger seat with some wariness. But Roger's salute on my cheek was chaste and bloodless as a maiden aunt's. The car was luxuriously warm and I flexed my cold toes inside my wellingtons, feeling the blood return.

'It was hardly worth your getting the car out,' I protested as Roger drew up outside my gate, almost immediately.

'Nonsense. The round trip up the hill and back barely takes ten minutes. Enjoy the service?'

'Well yes, as a visiting heathen, I did rather.'

Roger laughed, and I added shyly, 'I thought Ned was terribly good.'

'Oh he's a first class clergyman,' said Roger with unexpected passion. 'Tremendous.'

'Rather brave too, I thought, to tackle the congregation head on in that way.'

'What? Head on in what way?'

'Didn't you think he was reminding them of their Christian duty – towards the Vicar of St Catherine's?'

'Oh Christ!' said Roger violently. 'As far as I was concerned it was just the usual seasonal pep-talk. I've no time at all for that sort of perverted carry-on, I'm afraid.'

'Roger, I can't believe I'm hearing this. Today. And from you of all people.'

'What do you mean?' said Roger sulkily.

'I'll leave the sermons to your brother-in-law. I can only say that for someone who practically boasts that your extra-marital activities smashed up your marriage, I don't see what right you have to be intolerant of other people's sexual peccadilloes.'

'Be honest, Frankie. You must find it pretty disgusting.'

'Why should I? It may not be my own inclination. I don't enjoy shooting innocent birds either, or ripping foxes to bits. But I don't harangue you for doing it. And I feel bloody sorry for a man who has to resort to that kind of hole-and-corner . . .'

Roger let out a vulgar snigger which I ignored.

'. . . secretive, sordid kind of liaison in this supposedly enlightened age. I realise now it's bigots like you who must drive him to it.' My own passion took me by surprise. I must have been inspired by Ned's sermon. But you know how it is. The only thing I can't tolerate is intolerance . . .

'Well, well,' said Roger softly. 'I suppose you go in for bra-burning and bean-eating and banning bombs too?'

'I wear extremely expensive lingerie, I'm an unashamed carnivore and I don't personally own any atomic bombs. But on broad principle, yes, I'm prepared to defend all those things.'

'A champagne socialist,' sneered Roger.

'I'd swill the stuff for breakfast, given the chance. And precisely what's wrong with that?'

'Oh Frankie,' said Roger — astonishing me by taking my hand in the darkness and kissing it lightly. 'I wish I'd met you years ago. I'd have let you bath in champagne if you wanted to.'

Having neatly deprived me of words, he saw me to my door and, with a shouted reminder not to be late tomorrow, roared on up the hill.

Christmas is the time when a building like Thornbeck Manor comes into its own.

As I pulled up on the gravel drive, the crimson remnants of a winter sunset warmed the gloomy exterior to make it appear almost picturesque. Instead of condemning it as an ill-tempered muddle of styles, I could imagine someone describing the Manor fondly as a family house whose eccentric development over the centuries traced the interests and history of the family.

Inside, the hall was rustling with holly and berries, with armfuls of branches tucked round every picture. Even the giant stag's head over the fireplace was adorned with tinsel round the antlers. I noticed the two gleaming baubles, wittily suspended from his ears like the oversize earrings of a pantomime dame, and laughed.

'Bess's work, all the decorations,' said a stout man, discreetly parting the back flaps of his dinner jacket as he warmed his bottom in front of the roaring furnace of a fire. 'She's done a fine job, hasn't she?'

The high-vaulted panelled room, ablaze with scarlet ribbons and tall white candles, was dominated by a tinsel-covered, snow-spattered tree which was of scarcely less than Trafalgar Square dimensions. The scene could have been a magically animated painting from a Dickensian Christmas card. All that was needed to complete the illusion was the female revellers to be laced into crinolines and the men to be frock-coated and top-hatted, like the figures on a Quality Street box.

As it was, although most of the other women were again

billowing yards of jewel-coloured taffetas, I was defiantly underdressed in short and tight black velvet. My own Little Black Dress, and if it was littler than most, well too bad. It was my old reliable friend and I needed an old friend to face Christmas dinner with Mr and Mrs Cowper. So I had pinned up my hair and slipped with ankle-wrenching recklessness into my spikiest heels. A scrawny blackbird in an aviary of pretty parakeets.

'Oh, baby,' breathed Roger who crept up behind and wrapped his arms round me like a chimpanzee, 'how can I resist?'

'Easily,' I said, unpeeling his hands from my waist. 'Hello, Ned. Elizabeth.'

Roger's fulsome banter meant nothing. Ned's bashfully admiring glance made me feel as wanton as Cleopatra.

'Isn't it immoral, Ned?' demanded Roger. 'Tell this gorgeous Jezebel. Women shouldn't be allowed to flaunt themselves and lead us weak mortal men into the paths of temptation . . .'

'Hardly my style, R-rog, the hell-fire and damnation sermon . . .' Ned held my hand longer than necessary as we exchanged a formal handshake.

I was aware with a certain satisfaction that Elizabeth Cowper was eyeing me coldly. Her hand in mine was stiff and lifeless.

'You look beautiful too, sis,' added Roger genially. 'Fairy off the Christmas tree. Or maybe *in* the Christmas tree, on second thoughts.'

Elizabeth, a waif-waisted Scarlett O'Hara in dark green ruffles, really did look ethereally beautiful. She glanced at her brother venomously. He ignored her and swept me away.

'Now, who don't you know?'

There were to be sixteen of us at the table. Four faces I recognised from the shooting party, including, I noticed with pleasure, Suzanna and Alex Worrall. At least, I greeted Suzy with pleasure. Suzy told me their son was skiing in Italy, so they were spending Christmas here.

'I was stupid enough to think it would be a break from turkey fatigues for one year. Wrong again. Beverley's started the feast off, but yours truly will be supervising from now on.'

'I'll help . . .'

'I was hoping you'd say that. Roger seemed to think he could leave it to Bess. I tried to tell him that her most ambitious sortie into *haute cuisine* so far has been learning to operate a tin-opener, but he doesn't twig. Poor darling. He does indeed need a wife to sort him out . . .' And she stared at me with frank speculation.

'What's the quizzical look supposed to mean?'

'Nice house, or it could be,' she snorted with laughter, 'if you knocked it down and started again . . .'

'I promise I'm not nurturing ambitions to move into it. Not in a million years.'

'Pity. Roger buzzes round you like a wasp round a jam pot.'

'I don't think Roger has learned there's any way to talk to women other than breathing hot nothings down their neck. But if I turned round and invited him to go right ahead and have his wicked way, I bet he'd die of fright.'

She laughed cynically, then introduced me to a red-haired man with foul breath who was sporting a kilt and full biscuit-tin regalia, although his accent was purest Sloane Square. He was disappointed to learn I was not (as Roger had given him to understand) a portrait artist. He was looking for one. For his dog.

Across the room, Ned was being talked at earnestly by two women who gazed up at him adoringly. I caught his eye and smiled, but he made no attempt to detach himself. The hall was so big that individual conversational clumps were scattered across the flagged floor like islands across the Pacific. I wished I had learned the social adroitness to jettison a tedious conversation and swan gracefully towards more interesting prospects. But I had not. Elizabeth Cowper I could tell was an expert. Out of the corner of my eye, I watched her dart from one group to another like a humming-bird.

Suzy took pity on me after a while and swept me out of the clutches of the Scotsman. 'Divine dress, by the way,' she said. 'I forgive you only because it has put Bess's deliciously tip-tilted nose out of joint. Alex nearly had a coronary when you walked in. Don't expect any sympathy from me, though, if you turn blue with exposure in the course of the evening. Mind, I dare say you'd be in most danger from being crushed by the scrum to administer the kiss of life.'

'Suzy,' I said, watching Elizabeth with smiling skill detach herself immediately from the kilted bore, 'what form does Elizabeth's illness take?'

'Search me. I don't understand these medical terms anyway. I wouldn't know a psychosis from an Anadin. She's certainly up and down like a thermometer. You only have to spend a few hours with her to see that.'

'I rather got the impression she was down when I arrived.'

Suzy shuddered theatrically. 'But it won't last. The good thing is that the bad moods blow over as quickly as the good. I really don't know what's the matter with her. I believe there was a *bijou scandale* at school when things started – ah – disappearing from other girls' lockers. Or was that Roger? No, Roger's little school fracas was, I seem to recall, something to do with a letter . . .'

'Do you know everything, Suzy? You terrify me.'

'But I'm wonderfully kind-hearted. Anyway, ignore me on this. I may be wrong. It would hardly make sense, after all, because the old man lavished on her everything her avaricious little heart desired.'

'Her father? Albert, at the Wheatsheaf, described him as the quintessentially mean Yorkshireman.'

'So he was, my dear, so he was. Just look at him . . .'

We were standing close to the smoke-stained portrait Roger had shown to me on my last visit. In the glittering Christmas tree lights, the face was marginally more visible. The resemblance to Roger was marked, but this face was leaner and older, with grim channels scored between nose and mouth.

'Old John wouldn't give you the time of day, if he could help it. Used to pencil marks on his Scotch bottle when he had guests in the house. But his daughter seemed to be able to wheedle anything out of him. Unlike Roger.'

'Didn't Roger get on with his father? I don't remember getting that impression . . .'

'Roger has spent his life trying to live up to Papa – and failed. Poor little Roger coming top of his class for lessons – and all his father wanted to know was when he was going to play for the school team like cousin Ned. Now, was that the original row between . . .'

'Now then, girls,' said Roger jovially, interposing himself between us with a bottle, 'what's the gossip?'

'Only dragging the skeletons out of your family cupboard again, darling,' said Suzy smoothly. 'Trying to remember what the original bone of contention between Ned and your dear departed parent was.'

'Ned defending his little cousin, you mean?' said Roger laughing. 'Fat lot of good it did me at the time. Father gave me an extra whack for needing someone to defend me.'

Suzy raised her eyes. 'Such barbarous days. But I dare say a lot simpler. With our beloved offspring, Alex had to open annual rounds of pay negotiations for the pocket money. Fill up my glass, and I'll go and stick my nose in the Aga.'

'I'll come and help,' I said, lifting Roger's hand from my bottom.

Across the room, Elizabeth Cowper looked up sharply. 'I'll come too,' she said, 'I'm bored stiff here.'

CHAPTER SIXTEEN

'Frankie tells me she's not interested in marrying your brother,' announced Suzy, as she led us into the kitchen. 'Pity, isn't it? Is there anyone else hereabouts to amuse her?'

Elizabeth was walking in front of me, a full bottle of champagne tucked under her arm. Her expression, as she glanced back over her shoulder at me, was unnervingly knowing. Again, I felt a fluttering panic that she could read her husband's name emblazoned across my forehead.

The kitchen was cavernous, painted in ugly buttercup-yellow gloss and dominated by towering twin dressers stacked with blue and white pots.

'Could be much worse,' said Suzy, trying on an apron and lifting saucepan lids distastefully. 'At least Beverley's left everything ready.'

Elizabeth filled all our glasses, kicked off her shoes and settled herself into a large wooden rocking chair in the corner. 'I'm no use at this sort of thing,' she explained comfortably. 'So why don't you want to get married, Frankie? What are you – twenty-nine? Isn't it time you settled down? Started having babies?'

'You're pretty slow at that yourself, Bess,' observed Suzy, but Elizabeth ignored her.

'Doesn't the idea of marriage appeal?'

'I rather thought – it should happen in the reverse order. The man appealing to one first.'

'Less risky t'other way round,' advised Suzy with a cynical smile. 'Assess the potential benefits of the marriage first – house, social life, income – and then add the personal attraction of the husband as just another item on the list.'

'And hasn't a man appealed yet, Frankie?'

'I — suppose not,' I said uncertainly.

'Have you got a regular man?' inquired Suzy.

'Yes,' I said — and they both laughed, presumably because I exclaimed with with such eagerness. The interrogation was unsettling me.

'Well?' said Elizabeth, smiling now. 'Tell us more.'

'You've cheered up,' observed Suzy. 'Have you got a light?'

And they both lit cigarettes, giggling.

'Just like school behind the hockey pavilion,' said Elizabeth.

'Oh, was it the hockey pavilion in your day? It was the music room in mine.'

'All girls together. Swapping fags and secrets. We're boring, old married women now, but Frankie is going to reveal all — about the man she loves,' said Elizabeth. 'I wonder if we know him?'

I told myself I would not be needled.

'He's called Sebastian Ford,' I announced composedly. I had no intention of mentioning Gerald — that would be simply to advertise a predilection for other women's husbands. Seb was a brilliantly talented sculptor I had known since college days, I went on airily, but with whom I did not live. The construction of his mountainous compositions consumed tons of scrap iron and months of his life. Day and night for weeks on end. The edge of bitterness which unintentionally crept in here at least added verisimilitude.

'You don't see him for weeks on end?' marvelled Elizabeth. She was more avid for detail than a child with a fairy story. 'Do you get terribly frustrated? I mean . . .' she glanced towards Suzy, '. . . sexually?'

Ludicrous the way one harmless fib infallibly guides one straight into a bog of half-truths. Having implied Sebastian was the only man in my life I had to stick by my story.

'Not really,' I said uncertainly. 'That is to say . . .'

'Don't you like sex?' demanded Elizabeth.

'Yes,' I said indignantly, 'of course I do. Suzy, do you want the sprouts putting into here?'

'You must lead very independent lives, though,' said Elizabeth, staring at me intently, 'if he spends so much time working.'

138

'We do. Yes.'

Suddenly she smiled. 'Do the eventual reunions make up for it all? Does he lash you to one of his monstrous sculptures and rape you? Still filthy from his months of labour?'

'What a lurid imagination you have, Bess,' said Suzy. 'They must have been issuing D. H. Lawrence by the time you went to the old *alma mater*. We were strictly confined to Jane Austen. I'm sure your small talk must go down a bomb at the vicarage tea parties.'

'Oh, fuck them,' said Elizabeth. 'I gave those up after six weeks.'

'You're drinking too fast.'

'Certainly,' said Elizabeth. 'What else is there to do at Christmas? Come on. I want to hear more about sexy Sebastian.'

'You're becoming a bore, darling,' said Suzy. 'Now don't scowl. Have another cigarette and find some clean tea-towels for me, there's a love. All the Vaiseys drink like fish,' she added to me, as Elizabeth strolled out of the room. 'Colander's under there. And none of them can handle it. That was the real problem with Roger's marriage, you know . . .' She mimed a shaking glass in her hand. 'Caro was lucky if she got laid once in a month. I tried to tell her in a few years she might be counting it a blessing but —'

'Once a month?' Elizabeth laughed. Unheard, she had tottered back into the kitchen behind us. 'My dearest Suzanna, I haven't been screwed for a year. More.'

All at once, I felt I should not be here. Should not be listening to these cruelly intimate confidences. That it would be a betrayal of Ned just to hear any more.

Suzy, however, had spun round. 'You're drunk, Bess,' she said.

'Of course. But I'm telling the truth.'

'Which is?'

Elizabeth shrugged green ruffled shoulders. 'I think God inhibits him,' she whispered confidentially. 'He just can't seem to keep it up. Who cares, anyway?'

Suzy brushed the hair out of her eyes. All at once she looked older and troubled. 'Oh, Bess, I don't think you should be telling us this. In the cold light of sobriety you'll feel a heel. But don't worry, I'm sure Frankie, like me, will —'

'Nonsense!' Elizabeth smiled seraphically. 'My shrink tells me it's healthy to talk about it. Let it all hang out. Goodness, aren't you girls clever. Is it all ready? Let's go and summon the hungry hordes then.'

The dining-room was panelled in dark oak, with heavily leaded windows. Outside was only the sombre jungle of rhododendrons, so close to the house here that their waxy leaves tapped and scraped against the glass. Even the profusion of candles and crackers and other Christmas paraphernalia barely dented the impression that we were dining in an undertaker's parlour.

'It's Christmas, so I've arranged people exactly as I want,' said Roger. 'If you don't like it, you can move round after the pudding. Not before. And anyone who wants to smoke before then can go out and do it.' He had placed me on the right of his near-baronial throne at the head of the table and — to my great satisfaction — Ned opposite to me, on his left. Elizabeth, as nominal hostess, was stranded at the far end of the table. There was a hubbub of muttering and laughter as guests found Roger's arrangements to their liking or not. 'Just like his bloody father,' hissed Suzy, dropping her cigarettes back into her bag and stalking round to the other side of the table.

Roger and I pulled a cracker out of which tumbled a lurid green plastic ring.

'The fates are with me,' exclaimed Roger, seizing my left hand. 'Marry me, you adorable creature!'

'Thank you kindly, sir,' said I, fluttering my eyelashes and extending my wedding finger. 'And since we have a parson conveniently on the premises . . .'

But Ned did not hear me and Roger tightened his grasp on my hand. 'Do you mean it, Frankie?'

'Mean what?'

'That you'll marry me.'

'Roger! We're fooling around with a ring from a Christmas cracker.'

'I'd give you the most wonderful ring. Diamond, emerald whatever you wanted . . .'

I looked round, but Ned was now pulling a cracker with a hysterically giggling blonde woman next to him. No one was listening to what we were saying. It should have been a joke but Roger looked almost desperate. 'But, my darling, we hardly even know one another . . .' I whispered, simpering like the heroine of a B movie.

But Roger did not laugh. 'That's why I've got to secure you quickly,' he said and at last, to my relief, his face relaxed into a smile – but it was an oddly twisted expression. 'If you knew me better, you wouldn't hesitate to refuse.'

'For a self-confessed philanderer you're astonishingly keen to jump into lawful wedded matrimony again . . .'

'It's all an act, Frankie . . .'

'Roger, darling,' screeched the blonde next to Ned, 'just then you looked the very image of the old man!'

Roger smiled at her. 'More handsome, Rusty, tell me I'm more handsome . . .' And he left the table with a murmured excuse to open the lid of a spectacularly ugly mahogany casket, which turned out to contain not a corpse but the white wine. He fished out several slim brown bottles and strutted round the table, pouring, and pulling crackers with his guests.

'Did you know Johnny Vaisey?' said the blonde to me. She was middle-aged with triangles of eye-shadow which exactly matched the vivid turquoise of her dress. 'Wonderful man. If you look in the panelling over there, you can still see the holes he made one Christmas when he was trying to shoot a candle out. Drunk as a lord, of course, and the priceless thing is – the candle just went on burning!'

'Everything I've heard about Roger's father,' I said smiling politely, 'reinforces the picture of a complete nutcase.'

I heard a faint rumble of laughter from Ned.

'Ah, you never met him,' said Rusty, waggling a plump finger at me. 'You wouldn't talk like that if you had. Even in his sixties he was most fearfully attractive. Very tall and distinguished and a terrible ladies' man.' Her glance fluttered towards Roger as he poured wine at the end of the table. 'And son certainly takes after father in many respects, but, poor boy, Roger hasn't quite the same . . .'

'R-roger is ten times the man his father was,' interrupted Ned, with a vehemence which startled Rusty into offended silence. I waited until she began talking to the man on the other side of her.

'Everybody talks about Roger's father,' I said, 'and no two people say the same thing. How would you describe him?'

I suppose I knew the reply I expected: I had already formed my own picture of the late John Vaisey: a comic anachronism, an autocrat, a sporting boor, a groper of female flesh, a doting father (on his daughter anyway) and a bit of a maniac when he'd had too much to drink. Roger multiplied by ten. Ned's answer, therefore, took me by surprise.

'The man was a m-monster,' he said passionately. 'An out and out monster. I d-don't think I would ever use this word about any other human b-being I've ever met, but John Vaisey was . . . *evil*.'

'You look terribly serious, old chap,' said Roger, slipping back into his chair. 'Have some wine, and tuck into the smoked salmon.'

Four rooms and a twisting corridor between kitchen and dining-room ensured that the main course was less than tepid by the time it was distributed round the table. However, that same yawning acreage of sub-kitchens and pantries made life easy once the hot food was consumed. There was none of the frantic scrum of the average family in the average family kitchen. I was used to a tangle of my mother recycling the teaspoons, Grandad looking for his Rennies and the aunts getting into their pinnies for the main assault on the stacked battlements of washing-up. Here, after every course, Suzy imperiously directed her army of male minions to abandon cutlery and crockery anywhere in the empty echoing ante-rooms, then to shut the door and return to the table.

The party grew rowdier with every course. Streamers were cast over the chandelier and jokes from the crackers were shouted from one end of the table to the other. Alexander Worrall, surprisingly, leapt unsteadily to his feet, seized a sword from the wall and challenged the diner opposite to a duel. This was curtailed only because the other sword proved impossible to detach from its mount.

I should have enjoyed it, and indeed I laughed uproariously

at the riddles, tossed my streamers with abandon and did my best to act the part of the reveller. But all I could think about was Ned, sitting opposite me. Ned, who did not make love to his wife. Could not? Would not?

I picked at my food, trying to look as though I was eating. It was not that the food was inedible — although it was as appealing as dry turkey and wet vegetables usually are. Nectar and ambrosia would have choked me. Covertly I observed Ned — he hardly touched his plate either.

The fat blonde chattered busily to him, and I drank too quickly and flirted noisily with Roger. Every so often a foot brushed mine — and I knew it was Ned's. Whenever I allowed myself to glance in his direction, it seemed he was staring at me. Then he would look away, flushing.

I was sure other people must be aware of what was going on. That Ned and I must be making a public spectacle of ourselves. But the party roared on around the rest of the long table and we stared at one another, as though locked in a sealed capsule, foolishly unable to speak.

Barmy, I thought, and the next time Roger was out of earshot I gathered my wits together and pushed my untouched plate of pudding aside.

'I enjoyed your sermon last night,' I said with a glittering smile. 'Or is that the wrong word for sermons? Should I say I admired it? That too, anyway. Very much.'

'W-were you there?' said Ned, surprised. 'I d-didn't know.'

'You *quoted* me.'

'You didn't object, I hope? The words had stuck in my mind. I thought you p-put it so terribly well. Caught the feeling exactly . . .'

And then he stared at me in stricken silence.

CHAPTER SEVENTEEN

'Cat got your tongues?' said Roger, returning with a decanter.
'Frankie, dear one, you must try some of this delicious port at
once . . .'

And then I saw Elizabeth was following close behind her
brother. Her wobbly gait was evidence of the amount she had
drunk, but where other women might become shiny-faced and
dishevelled, she was merely glowing and becomingly ruffled.

'I'm going to sit at this end of the table now,' she informed
us. Then she turned to wave her glass towards the company
and roared in an astonishingly strident voice, 'All change
everybody – if you're getting bored like I am.'

'Whoopee!' shrieked Suzy, picking up her glass. 'I can go
and seduce Simon now and perhaps . . .?' she glanced at
Elizabeth and then Roger and gestured significantly with two
fingers to her lips.

'TheQueenGodBlessHerMajesty!' shouted Elizabeth. And
then, with a fair imitation of a boxing referee, 'Laydees and
gennulmen, we may now smoke . . .' Under any other circumstances, I could have found her very entertaining.

'Not near me I trust,' said the blonde stuffily, gathering her
handbag and getting to her feet.

'Good,' said Elizabeth, appropriating her chair and tucking
her hand round Ned's arm proprietorially. 'Well, darling, did
you enjoy your dinner? Have you been keeping an eye on this
dangerous woman? Has she been playing footsie under the
table with Roger?'

Ned smiled, but did not look at her.

'Drunk again, Bess?' said Roger amiably. 'Frankie, some
port.'

But I closed my hand over my glass. 'I have to drive home.'
I didn't dare to calculate how far over the limit I might be
already. I looked round hopefully for coffee – but Suzy was
draping her long body round the shoulders of Simon, a pretty
fair-haired young man who couldn't have been very much
older than her absent son. Simon was grinning in baffled besot-
tedness.

'Nonsense,' said Roger. Drink made him more bombastic
than ever. 'Don't be a spoilsport. You can stay here, for God's
sake – we've got more beds than I can count, but mine's the
warmest and the most comfortable ...' He laughed lewdly.
'And if you don't trust yourself with me and twelve chap-
erones, well then Bess would put you up at the Dower
House – wouldn't you, Bess?'

'I'm sure that's the last thing Frankie would want,' said Elizabeth.

'Frankie, please,' said Roger, 'you simply can't forego this.
It's some port the old man laid down. Taylor's '63. Ned says
it's the best bottle in the cellar. Tell her, Ned, tell her it's liquid
velvet ...'

'I'd love to taste it,' I said, 'but honestly, it would be crazy ...'

'I haven't drunk a great deal. I'll d-drive you home, if you
wish,' said Ned, with a bravado which took my breath away.
'In your car if you want, and then I'll walk back along the lane.
I could do with some fresh air.'

And, I thought dazedly, no one would wonder if he was
late in returning, if he was on foot ...

'Well spoken, that man,' said Roger, promptly filling my
glass to the brim. 'But you won't be going for ages yet – and
I promise, I could make you so much more comfortable here.'

Elizabeth was frowning ferociously as she leaned forward to
light her cigarette from one of the candles in the centre of the
table. 'My dear sober husband,' she said. 'So useful to have
about the place.'

Was she always so unpleasant to him? I felt a flicker of
annoyance that Ned never seemed to make any push to
defend himself. Helpless as a blundering cart-horse against the
guerilla onslaughts of a malevolent wasp.

'Be quiet, Bess,' said Roger, and jumped to his feet. 'Happy

Christmas!' he roared, and everyone raised their glasses blearily, murmuring seasonal messages.

'Absent friends,' said Elizabeth, smiling at me. 'Here's to Sebastian.'

'Sebastian?' said Roger, sitting down again. The difference in his height when he did so was barely discernible.

'The love of Frankie's life, didn't you know?'

Ned busied himself cracking a brazil nut.

'Tell me it's not true,' said Roger theatrically, clutching my hand against his chest.

'It's not true,' I said obediently, glancing round and laughing. Ned was staring intently down at the nutcrackers, squeezing them between his thick fingers.

'That's not what you said to us in the kitchen, is it, Suzy? Where's Suzy gone?' Elizabeth looked round impatiently. 'Oh God, got her claws into Simon. Cradle-snatcher. No, Frankie was telling us all about her interesting love life. But I have to tell you . . .' she leaned closer, and lowered her voice to a confidential whisper, '. . . she's quite used to long periods of absent . . . absinthe . . .' she giggled merrily. 'No, that's what you drink, isn't it? Going without it, I mean. Which is lucky, isn't it, considering? But I should warn you that she does like sex *very much indeed.*' And she rocked to and fro laughing helplessly.

'Christ!' The unlikely expletive was Ned's. 'T-trapped my thumb,' he added by way of explanation, holding up the nutcrackers.

Roger was staring at Elizabeth. 'Get out,' he said furiously. 'Get out, if you can't hold your drink.' His hand, gripping the edge of the table was shaking.

'It's all right, Roger,' I said, forcing myself to smile unconcernedly, 'Elizabeth was only joking.'

'No, I'm not,' she said indignantly. 'D-don't spoil the fun. Roger's just about to throw a tantrum.'

'This is a madhouse,' I said desperately.

'Of course it is,' agreed Elizabeth. 'No, Roger, don't growl at me like that. You look like a cross-eyed bulldog. Or do I mean terrier? I'm going, I'm going . . .' and she drifted out of the room, graceful as a ballerina, even when drunk.

'You m-must forgive my wife,' said Ned with painful formality. 'She has a very . . . highly-strung temperament. N-nerves . . .'

'Don't give me that bullshit again, Ned,' snarled Roger. 'You'd excuse a multiple murderer on the grounds his nanny wouldn't read him a bedtime story.'

'I don't think many multiple murderers were blessed with nannies,' I offered, in a feeble effort to divert Roger, who was still flushed and glowering. Ned's smile flickered gratefully in my direction but Roger took no notice.

'What you've got to accept, my dear sainted Ned, is that some people are just plain bad. Bred into the bone. All this liberal claptrap about environment and upbringing doesn't mean a thing. Look at dogs. Jock,' he shouted, hauling the Scotsman into our conversation, 'how do you produce a decent gundog? Is it the training? Is it hell. You choose a dam and a sire with the right temperament, don't you? Weed out the vices, breed the good points in. All in the breeding, isn't it? The best training in the world won't make a good dog out of a bad puppy.' The Scotsman who had not been given an opportunity to speak gaped blearily at him.

'Is that h-how you produced a lunatic like Juno?' asked Ned calmly.

'We're all the same, all the same stock. Look at the old man – and the whore. What can you expect? Only I don't make excuses for myself. I know what I am. Bess doesn't need a psychiatrist charging a fortune to pour mumbo-jumbo into her spoiled little head, she needs . . .'

'F-forgive me, Roger, but you really mustn't talk about my wife in those terms. No . . .' Roger had begun to protest again, but Ned held up his hand, 'I'm serious, R-roger. And you're embarrassing your guests.'

'Roger old man,' said Simon, who had temporarily slipped out of Suzy's clutches, 'did you say something about Havana cigars? My friend,' and he glanced lustfully back towards Suzy, 'is longing to try one.'

'Of course,' said Roger distractedly, standing up. 'Hold on . . .'

'And I think I must go,' I said.

'Go? Certainly not. You're not to move until I get back. Promise me now. We haven't even had the coffee yet.'

'I'm sorry,' said Ned to me quietly when Roger had hurried away. 'I d-don't quite understand what got into Elizabeth today.'

'You don't?' I said. Suddenly I was tired of play-acting. I glanced around to make sure we were being safely ignored by our neighbours before continuing softly, 'You don't think she might possibly have objected to the spectacle of her husband gazing across this table into the eyes of another woman for the last three hours?'

'Have I?' said Ned, flushing again. 'Sorry . . .'

He looked so troubled, so perplexed. I put my hand over his as it lay on the table, then almost at once snatched it away again as someone looked in our direction. 'Shall we stop this perpetual cycle of apologising to one another?' I whispered. 'I came to find you in the church that night to apologise, because I thought I'd behaved very badly. That I'd imagined all sorts of things that weren't true. Between, well, between you and me. Hush, please let me finish. And now today we sit here . . . Oh! Sorry, yes of course. Please do take the ashtray.' I waited until the woman had moved safely out of earshot again.

'Frankie, you must believe me. Whatever Roger says, Bess d-does have problems.'

'So do you, it seems.'

Ned's mouth twisted wryly. 'The p-poor child shouldn't have married a priest. P-people wouldn't condemn her so readily if she was the wife of a layman.'

'I'm not condemning her, Ned. I just don't understand quite what's going on. What happens next?' Then I was forced to smile and wave as a camera flashed from the other side of the table. 'We can't talk here,' I whispered urgently.

Ned stood up promptly.

'I'll t-take you home,' he said.

'I'll go and find my things.'

The hall was deserted and the fire had tumbled to a pile of glowing rubble. I found my handbag and, shivering, went in search of my coat. When I returned to the dining-room, the guests had scattered. A blast of music was drifting from another room, and someone was angrily demanding to be told the whereabouts of the *Radio Times*.

Ned stood by the head of the table where Roger and Elizabeth were once again locked in argument.

'Odd,' I said, walking to the table so that I could examine the contents of my bag more closely, 'I can't find my car keys . . .'

'Good Lord,' said Elizabeth, opening her eyes very wide. 'Does that mean Ned can't run you home after all? Have to stay for another little drinky. What a surprise.' She could not have sounded less surprised.

'Splendid,' said Roger loudly, ostentatiously turning his back on his sister. 'Where's your glass?'

'They're really not here,' I said, rummaging in the corners, but to no effect. 'I must have dropped them somewhere . . .' Or someone had removed them from my bag. But that was ridiculous, surely.

'They'll turn up, I dare say,' said Roger genially, still waving the port decanter at me.

'But not too soon, I dare say,' agreed Elizabeth mimicking his tone.

'For God's sake, woman . . .' snarled Roger.

'I'll go and have a look round,' I said, retreating from the threatening quarrel. The hall was no longer empty. The Scotsman was shoving logs on to the fire in a businesslike way, and Suzy, with a cigar clenched between her teeth, was embarking on a spirited tango with her pretty companion who was also providing the music in a breathy tenor voice. On one of the sofas, Alex snored.

'M-madhouse,' said Ned softly behind me. I had not realised he was following me.

I turned to look at him. 'I do want to go home,' I said. 'No one's going to mind if I borrow some wellies, are they? There are about a hundred pairs in that room where I left my coat.'

'You're not going to walk? I'll take you in our car, or one of Roger's.'

'I think I'd rather walk. I did last night.' I glanced up at him. 'Don't worry, I realise you can't get away. I'll just say goodbye to Roger and . . .'

'D-don't,' whispered Ned urgently. 'Don't say anything to

anybody. Let's slip away quietly now. They're all too drunk to notice.'

Suzy swept past us, in her partner's arms, beaming over one shoulder with unseeing eyes.

'Are you sure?' I said.

Ned took my hand and led me swiftly out of the hall.

CHAPTER EIGHTEEN

I woke early the next morning, wriggled carefully from under
the heavy arm which lay across my shoulders, and swung my
feet to the floor. Without waking the body which rumbled
and twitched with oddly syncopated snores in the middle of
the bed, I patted the eiderdown back into place. Pulling on a
dressing gown and knotting a sweater over that – the Lodge
was bitterly cold – I crept downstairs. I had not troubled to
lock the door on the staircase the night before.

There was barely a glimmer of pink behind the eastern dip
of the valley as I lit the lamp at my table. Cursing the cold,
but in too much of a hurry to light a fire, I selected a fresh
sheet of drawing paper. I would get moonlight right this time.
I knew I would. The essence of it, the secret, was that it was
cold.

Before now, I had been too romantic. I had seen night skies
as purple, drifting with dimpled clouds and touched with soft
violets. Result? They looked like stage sets. Overblown, Walt
Disney-ish. The truth of it was that moonlight was monochrome,
hard and cold as steel. I drew the Lodge exactly as I had seen
it last night. I needed no photographs, no sketches. Every
detail was, as they say, etched on the memory. As with
sulphuric acid.

We had not spoken until we were well clear of the Manor
grounds. I hopped from one stepping-stone to the next across
the ford, confident as a frog. Ned, more sensibly, waded
through the sluggish water, which splashed round his boots. I
suppressed a sharp urge to tell him to make less noise – in
case someone heard, in case someone came in pursuit.

Eventually the lights of the house vanished round a twist in the lane. Then, unable to contain my elation, I had looked up at the burly figure striding beside me, and laughed for sheer excitement.

'Of course, I m-mustn't be very long,' said Ned, dousing at once my fizzing fireworks of hope.

'Of course,' I echoed obediently. 'But no one even knows we've gone. Yet. Is . . . is Elizabeth very jealous?'

'I d-don't think she notices I exist half the time,' said Ned evenly.

The silence hovered between us as we walked swiftly down the lane. That's the terrible thing with married men. In fact, I suppose it's true of any lover, man or woman, married or unmarried, if they happen to have another partner lurking as the unseen ghost behind their shoulder. It's so very hard to judge what can legitimately be asked about that partner, what one can fairly expect to be told – and what merely sounds like undignified prying.

'Do you mean she doesn't love you?' I said eventually.

'I . . . No, I don't mean that. I think, in s-so far as she loves anybody, Elizabeth loves me. B-but perhaps, that's not very much.'

'Do you mind?'

Ned made a noise I couldn't interpret. He appeared to shrug, but I couldn't see his face.

Funny that, because I remember reflecting with astonishment how powerful the moonlight was. You never get to appreciate it in towns, of course. Over a city, the moon is just a white paper disc in the sky, its feeble rays blotted out in the busy orange glow. Here, I almost believed I could have read a book, so clear seemed the light.

'I thought,' I said, determined to drag all the misunderstandings out into the open once and for all, 'that you – weren't interested in me at all.' I was reassured by the harsh bark of disbelief which came from Ned, and continued more easily, 'I thought I'd imagined everything. After I met Elizabeth, that is. That you had simply been, well, enjoying my company I guess. In the most innocent way possible . . .'

'I t-told myself I was,' said Ned. 'Amazing the capacity for s-self-deception one has, isn't it?'

Ahead of us I could see the single light I had left burning in my sitting-room. I wished, bitterly, that I had had the foresight to light a fire. I had no intention of losing Ned this time, but visions danced in my head of us unlocking the back door and walking into the cold dark cottage. And then we would stand there, facing one other, shivering. The prospect of inviting him baldly to step upstairs to my warm bed was unnerving. Even more daunting was the prospect of attempting slow seduction in an ice-cold sitting-room.

Intentions would have to be prodded into words here and now. There was no option. At least then, by the time we reached the door, there could only be a feverish race up the stairs. The darkness, the fact that I couldn't see his face, made it marginally easier.

'So I wasn't making such a fool of myself,' I said doggedly, 'when I told you – I wanted you to make love to me?'

The dark figure beside me stopped dead.

'Frankie, my dearest darling,' whispered Ned, 'surely you know that I w-want you more than anything else in the world?'

Scraper-board is really the medium for night pictures, I reflected, trailing faint lines of frosty branches across the sky. Then you are working white on black, instead of the reverse. But as I laboured intricately over the rutted surface of the muddy lane, an iced-over puddle, fractured where Ned's heavy boot had trodden, I was not displeased with the effect. There were tiny icicles glittering on the gate. One had fallen off as I lifted the latch.

It was bright daylight outside now and a sleepy voice overhead called my name.

'Don't worry, I'm downstairs,' I shouted back. 'Don't get up. I'll bring tea in a minute. I just want to do a bit more work on a drawing . . .'

'I'm in your h-hands,' Ned had said quietly. 'I knew it that night in Roger's gunroom. If Suzanna hadn't interrupted, if we had . . . k-kissed, touched . . . then, well, I couldn't have stopped. Oh, I don't mean there among the boots and coats . . .'

'But you would have rushed me away and ravished me somewhere else?' I whispered enthusiastically.

I sensed more than heard Ned's laughter, it was so quiet. It was also sad.

'Who knows?' he said, and he spoke resignedly. 'And I know if I so much as touch you now, then I couldn't open the Lodge door, see you in and – l-leave. Not in a m-million years.'

'Good,' I said triumphantly, and took his hand. His fingers closed round mine tightly.

'Is it g-good?'

'Oh Ned, surely it is, please say it is? I want you so much I'm dizzy with lust. Please tell me you're coming in. Coming to bed . . .'

'I can't say no,' said Ned.

I dropped his hand.

'But you'd like to? Say no?'

'Frankie, I'm a p-priest.'

'Oh Christ.'

'I can't take adultery lightly . . .'

'Adultery,' I said. 'I knew we would get round to discussing adultery one day. It just seemed inevitable. Pretty high on the menu of possible sins I dare say, adultery?'

'If it was simply a question of that,' said Ned. 'D-don't you understand? If I once g-go to bed with you, I don't know if I could ever go back to Elizabeth. It's not simply a question of . . . a quick f-fuck and forgetting it. I love you. Don't you realise that, Frankie? I love you.'

There were tears on his face. I saw one glimmer for a second in the moonlight, and touched it with my fingertip.

'I . . . I . . . love you too,' I said in amazement.

Still he stood by the gate, frozen as a statue.

Gently, I put my arms round his neck and pulled his face down to mine.

The drawing was nearly all roughed in. A painting from it, which I might never even attempt, would take a lot more work – and there was still one vital element missing. *The* vital element. The tall, burly figure of a man, even bigger for being wrapped in a thick sheepskin coat. Like embracing an armadillo it was, hugging him in that coat. And a scarf — but that must not be drawn in too clearly. Because the figure is facing in the other direction, walking away . . .

'Fanny?' said the sleepy voice, at the top of the stairs. 'What happened to the tea?'

I put down my pencil. 'I'll make it now, love,' I called. 'Go back to bed before you catch pneumonia. Oh, and switch the immersion heater on as you pass, would you? Switch by the bedroom door. Did you hear?' I leaned back in my chair and raised my voice. 'Sebastian?'

The kiss was as muddled and as miraculous as it was bound to be. I nearly crawled inside Ned's thick jacket. He was crying, I could tell. I could taste his tears but I didn't care.

'Sweet, sweet darling love,' he was murmuring as he pressed soft hungry kisses all over my face — but he didn't sound happy. He sounded desperate. I refused to hear.

'Let's go inside,' I said, taking hold of his hand, tugging him towards the door. Then I heard it. Someone snoring.

'There's someone here,' I whispered.

Ned was two paces behind me. 'D-did you know there was a car in your garage?'

I stood still and shut my eyes. 'What sort of car?'

'A k-kind of van, it looks like . . .'

'White?' I said. 'Registration something-something N-A-B?'

'That's not yours, is it?'

I clenched my fists into tight balls of fury. I could hear it clearly now. Familiar, guttural, snoring . . .

'It belongs to a friend of mine,' I said. 'A friend who couldn't be bothered to send a Christmas card, and has apparently decided to bring his message of seasonal goodwill in person.'

'Ah,' said Ned.

'Sebastian Ford.'

There was only silence, punctuated by a rollicking snore from the garage.

'P-perhaps I had better go,' said Ned.

'You wanted to anyway. Didn't you?'

Silence.

'Didn't you?' I repeated.

'Frankie, I w-wanted to stay here, to m-make love to you more than . . .'

'. . . anything else in the whole world,' I said. 'Yes, so I gathered. Except returning to your wife like a good boy. Well, God certainly moves in mysterious ways and he's apparently stepped in to look after his own tonight. Though I can't say I would ever have cast Seb as an agent of the Lord.'

'I'm so s-sorry – I . . .'

'No apologising,' I said tightly. 'I thought we'd agreed that. No more sorries. Well, better hurry along. Otherwise someone might suspect you've been up to something.'

'You're c-crying, Frankie . . .'

'Of course I'm bloody crying. What do you expect? Go on. I'll go and wake the sleeping beauty.'

Ned walked slowly back to the gate. When he turned to look at me, I uttered the most bitterly shaming words of my existence. Hurt pride, of course, and being wrenched apart on the very threshold of success, had left a quickened mass of exposed nerve tissue.

'At least I suppose I won't have to face a cold bed after all,' I said.

Ned didn't reply. Just walked away with his shoulders drooping. That was what I drew now.

'Fucking amazing bed,' said Sebastian, his wiry form disposed, as always, straight down the centre of the mattress, and he tossed my novel to one side with an expression of disgust. 'Tragic to let it go to waste . . .' and he lifted the covers invitingly.

But I shook my head, handed him his tea and settled myself comfortably on top of the eiderdown.

'Sorry,' I said. 'I realize it must seem tough to have driven two hundred miles up here . . .'

'Two hundred and fifty-six.'

'. . . and then be turned down flat, but I don't want to at the moment, Seb. I can't.'

'And you don't want to talk about it.'

All this had been established last night. Seb, who had been planning to join yet another girlfriend in Glasgow for a long weekend including Hogmanay, had grown bored in the empty house on Christmas Eve. So on Christmas Day had decided (for the want of anything better to do) he might as well take in Yorkshire *en route* to Scotland.

His immediate explanation when I found him in his van, however, had been that he was suddenly overcome with concern for me, stranded in the wilderness over the festive season and had made this special journey purely for my benefit. When I had raised a cynical eyebrow at this story of self-sacrificing nobility, he had grinned but added (surprisingly), 'I've been missing you, Fanny.'

'Haven't slept like that for years,' he said now, yawning luxuriously and scratching one hairy armpit with the un-selfconscious earnestness of a chimpanzee.

'I'm amazed you could sleep at all. How long were you unconscious in the van for last night, waiting for me to get home?'

'Hours,' he said – and then when I looked disbelieving, 'About an hour. But I had to put away a bit of the Scotch I brought for you, just to ward off the cold.'

'Half a bottle by the look of it. You were lucky I got home at all. I was invited to stay at the Manor.'

'Oh, my dear . . .' said Sebastian, hooting with mocking laughter. 'I'm so sorry. Should you be down there now, spooning the devilled kidneys out of the silver salver? Thank you, Carmichael, fresh coffee for two would be simply spif-fing . . .'

'I don't think they'll have done the washing-up from yester-day by New Year,' I said, sipping my tea. 'It's a lunatic asylum without the central heating.'

'How the other half lives.'

'I could be joining them,' I said. 'The Lord of the Manor proposed marriage. To me.'

'You didn't accept, did you?'

I was touched. There was an unmistakable squeak of distress in his voice.

'It was a joke over a Christmas cracker. Although he almost

157

seemed inclined to pretend he meant it for one sticky minute. But we sort of laughed it off in the end.'

'Is that the man?'

'What man?'

'Fanny Cleverdon, I've known you for eleven years. The man who's bugging you at the moment.'

'Is it so obvious? No. God no, not Roger.'

'That stuffed shirt from Hobsons?'

'Gerald?' I shook my head impatiently. 'He hasn't telephoned for weeks.'

'Someone else. And you're not going to tell me.'

'Yup.'

'I could try and make you forget him . . .'

When he was gentle like this, and actually showing interest in me — instead of haranguing the world via me about his latest theory of space and time — Sebastian was at his most seductive. With his thatch of dark curls still ruffled from sleep, he looked like a lonely little boy in the middle of the vast bed. It would be easy to slip inside the covers beside him . . .

But I shook my head. We had spent the night side by side, chaste as Tristan and Isolde.

'Poor old Fanny. Fidelity always was your big stumbling block, wasn't it? When will you ever realise that real fidelity all happens up here?' He tapped his forehead with one grubby finger — Sebastian's nails were permanently engraved with metal filings and oil. 'A quick tumble between the sheets is neither here nor there. I've always kept faith with you . . .'

'Through a hundred other tumbled pairs of sheets . . .'

'No need to exaggerate. What I'm trying to tell you is that infidelity is a spiritual act, not physical. The real sin happens in the soul, not the loins.'

In that case, I thought, Ned was wasting his anguish. The sin was long committed.

'Father Ignatius always said it was short-sighted to concentrate on acts,' said Seb, grinning. 'Intentions were the dangerous things. Now you could argue that a quick fuck — without your heart in it so to speak — was the act without the intention.'

'I don't think that was what Father Ignatius had in mind.'

'How would a heretic like you know?'

'How would a sinner like you?'

'Ah,' said Sebastian, 'once a Catholic . . .'

I smiled sadly, shaking my head. 'I'd need to check the Church of England position.'

CHAPTER NINETEEN

The other thing I would not permit Sebastian to do was inspect my paintings.

Sebastian had always been my most valued critic, but in spite of this – or perhaps, because of it – I did not want him to see the work in progress. Even if he liked a piece of work, Seb's expression of enthusiasm rarely blossomed beyond a grudging nod, perhaps the odd astringent one-liner, appraising the technique. On the other hand, if he did not like it . . .

So, four days later, having divided his time about equally between eating, sleeping and roaming the hills, Sebastian resumed his journey to Scotland, pronouncing himself well rested and restored by his holiday. The countryside was a good thing, he said, *for limited periods* . . . In other words, *I* should be returning to London soon. What amazed and touched me was a sense that he so evidently felt the loss of me in London. I reminded him that my lease expired on the last day of February and he departed satisfied.

Fortunately he had been out walking at lunchtime on Boxing Day when Roger returned my car to me. I say fortunately because I knew Roger and he would loathe one another profoundly on sight, and even more deeply on further acquaintance.

Suzy had actually arrived first, driving Roger's Range Rover. 'That sadist volunteered me along to drive him back,' she said, in a voice half an octave deeper than usual. She was hidden behind a headscarf and saucer-sized dark glasses. 'I felt every rut along that goddamned cart track in the innermost recesses of my suffering being. Roger will be here shortly. He was driving your flashy little coach over the top road, of course. Is your hangover as bad as mine?'

'Actually I've been up since seven. Working. I don't feel too bad.'

'How disgusting.' Suzy capsized on to a kitchen chair, stuffing a pair of gauntlets into her pocket. 'What on earth did you do to offend the fair Gloriana?'

I jumped. 'Elizabeth? No idea. Nothing as far as I know. Coffee?'

Suzy winced. 'Fatal in my condition. Have you any lager?'

I poured out a chilled can which she sipped with little murmurs of gratitude.

'Is she . . . cross with me?' I said cautiously. 'You must have some idea why.'

'Well I can only guess . . .' began Suzy, and then stopped as she rummaged in her handbag for a cigarette packet. I wished I could see her eyes behind the pools of black. I was afraid she might be toying with me, like a cat with a mouse, waiting to spring some shocking revelation. But when she had lit her fag, and choked quietly over the first mouthful, she only said thoughtfully, 'Personally I would have imagined Elizabeth might be thrilled if you married Rog. She's always complaining about how lonely she is, and she never liked Caro.'

'But there's no question of me marrying Roger,' I said. 'It's not even a very funny joke any more. I can't imagine where the stupid thing started.'

'With Rog naturally. And Bess certainly seems to think so,' said Suzy. 'Why else would she be muttering darkly about scheming bitches? Who were threatening to invade her family home – and jeopardizing any hope of her future happiness. She was, you know. Late last night in the kitchen. Pissed out of her head, of course. Although how you or any other sister-in-law . . . yes, yes, I *know* you're not going to marry Roger in a month of Sundays – please don't *shout* at me, angel – but how *that* could spoil Elizabeth's fun is anybody's guess.'

Did Suzy know? Was she playing games? But the sunglasses flashed impassively.

'Sounds crazy,' I said brazenly.

'Maybe it is simply a touch of the old you-know-what,' said

161

Suzy, tapping her forehead with one elegantly manicured nail. 'Persecution complex or something. Never mind. I'm sure she'll get over it. She'll be all over you again next week. She took a hate against me last spring. It didn't endure.'

'Where were my car keys, by the way?' I said. 'They've obviously been found.'

'Were they lost?' said Suzy. 'I heard Roger and Bess arguing over them. Something about the drive.'

'They disappeared from my bag yesterday. Yes, I know that sounds unlikely, but I'm sure they did.' I rearranged the mugs on a shelf before continuing, 'Suzy, you don't suppose Elizabeth would have taken them? You did say there was some problem with stealing at school . . .'

'Well hardly,' said Suzy. 'I mean, what the hell use is a set of car keys to anyone? Now, if it had been that divine little motor itself, I might have considered stealing it personally . . .'

'I'm serious, Suzy. Someone removed the keys, I'd swear it.'

'What on earth for?'

I put the kettle on, observing her out of the corner of my eye.

'You don't suppose,' I said with studied casualness, 'she might not have wanted her husband to drive me home? Ned had offered to drive me back here, you know.'

Suzy shook her head decisively, then gave a little groan of anguish and clutched her temples. 'Ned? I've never seen Elizabeth betray the eensiest weensiest flicker of wifely jealousy.'

'Perhaps . . . he's never given her cause.'

'I'm very sure he hasn't. Darling Neddy would no more be unfaithful than . . . well, my pickled brain isn't up to thinking of sufficiently unlikely contingencies, but he just wouldn't. He's a model husband. I've told her about a million times how lucky she is.'

'Isn't she just?' I muttered, forgetting to sound casual, and Suzy lifted her glasses to peer at me with uncomfortably penetrating interest. Luckily Roger tapped on the window at that moment, and I opened the door for him.

'You snuck away – if snuck is the past tense of sneak – like a thief in the night! Without a word. Kiss me, you ungrateful baggage, for restoring your car to you intact.'

'How can you bear to make so much noise at this hour of the morning, Roger?' said Suzy.

'Still drunk,' said Roger promptly, and turned to me. 'Your keys, ma'am.'

'Where were they found, Rog?' said Suzy with sudden sharply focused curiosity. 'I saw you and Bess arguing over them.'

'Oh, in the drive. Bess ... picked them up.' He sounded distinctly uncomfortable and Suzy glanced at me, raising her eyebrows quizzically, and then back at Roger. 'Silly really,' he went on, 'but we were all under the influence, weren't we? And all's well that ends well. Etcetera, etcetera . . .'

'And who am I to talk about eccentric behaviour?' said Suzy, her gaze flickering towards me again. 'Or immoral intentions, come to that. Not that I was capable of carrying mine through. However, I prefer not to be reminded of anything I got up to after the pudding.'

'You were dancing the most spectacular tango when I left . . .'

She shuddered theatrically and turned away. 'Thank you. No more. I say . . .' In turning, her eyes had alighted on the other kitchen chair, over the back of which was draped a sagging, heavily-studded, and unmistakably masculine, black leather jacket. 'Do we have visitors, Frankie?' and she looked round, as though expecting someone to jump from a cupboard, as in farce.

'Sebastian,' I said promptly.

'*The* Sebastian?' exclaimed Suzy. 'Here, now?'

'Walking up on the moors, as far as I know. Wearing my pullover.'

'Well, well. And Bess *would* have it that there was something fishy about Sebastian. She was convinced you weren't telling the truth, you know — that's why she asked so many questions. Said so to me as we left the kitchen.'

Not so crazy at all.

'He exists, all right,' I said. 'He arrived as a surprise while I was carousing with you lot yesterday.'

'How sweet,' purred Suzy.

'How appalling,' said Roger. 'Heartless minx.'

163

'And is he staying long?'

I shook my head. 'Three, maybe four days. He's on his way to join his gir – some friends in Scotland.'

'Ah,' drawled Suzy, 'of course, you said you were used to leading . . . very independent existences.'

'Do you?' said Roger. 'Tell me the worst. Are you going to marry him?'

I couldn't, simply couldn't, tell such a sweeping lie, even though it would have been the most effective way of throwing Suzy off the scent. There was no question now that she was eyeing me speculatively. I shook my head.

'Why not?' said Roger. 'Do you love him?'

That was easier. 'Yes,' I said. 'Yes, I do as a matter of fact.'

I could argue that I loved a number of people after all: parents, sister, several friends to a greater or less degree, Sebastian . . . Then I wondered if this conversation would be relayed to Ned. Oh, poor Ned. Leaving here last night, believing I had jumped straight into bed with another man.

'Seb and I have what you might call a very open relationship,' I said now with defiant honesty. If Suzy suspected – well, what the hell? Ned and I hadn't done anything. One sodding kiss. 'We do tend to go our own separate ways quite a lot.'

'Sexually?' asked Roger.

'Is this an inquisition?'

'We're friends, aren't we? You can ask me anything you like – who did I sleep with last night? Answer: Juno. Who's the most precious woman in my life? Answer: Juno. Who's –'

'Where do you sneak out to late at night?' demanded Suzy, turning her inquisitive gaze on Roger now. 'Down this very back lane, so a little bird tells me, out of sight of the village, in the wee small hours?'

Was it Roger? The car I had heard? I stared at him, and to my astonishment saw him flush and glare with real venom at Suzy.

'It wouldn't be,' said Suzy cruelly slowly, 'anything to do with a certain long-haired fox-hunting lady whose husband spends long periods in Saudi Arabia, and whose name I won't mention, but whose initials are –'

'I'm not in the kiss and tell business, Suzy,' interrupted Roger. He smiled. 'Besides, John Hardinge — when he is at home — is two foot taller than me with a fiendish temper.'

'Randy bastard,' said Suzy amiably. 'I hope Caro screwed you for a lot of money.'

'She did, my dearest Suzanna. I promise you she did.'

'And my guess is,' Suzy went on, 'that Frankie and her leather-jacketed sculptor lead very separate existences indeed.' She smiled at me alarmingly wisely. 'So marvellously civilised these modern relationships,' she added. 'I wish I could interest Alex in that kind of arrangement.'

'From what I hear,' said Roger studying his finger-nails, 'Alex operates along those lines anyway.'

Suzy burst into sour laughter. 'Bess,' she said with angry certainty. 'I once, in a moment of weakness and distress, confided Alexander's beastly little philanderings to her, in the strictest confidence . . . Your sister is a prize cow, Rog.'

'Would I deny it? She should have been strangled at birth.'

'She positively deserves someone to come along and snaffle her adorable husband,' said Suzy — and smiled at me. 'Come along, Roger. Too much scandal too early in the day plays havoc with the digestion. You can drive me home.'

'Back to one bottle as usual is it today?' said Mr Danby. 'Your friend from London gone I see.'

'Oh, yes. Seb left yesterday afternoon.'

'Always nice to have a bit of company at Christmas. You look a bit off-colour, Frankie. Anything the matter? Not bad news I hope.'

I was holding an envelope and sheet of paper in my hand. The post had arrived minutes before Mr Danby rounded the corner.

'No.' I said, stuffing the letter under the newspaper on the table behind me. 'Sorry. Lost in thought. Please, one bottle. And maybe a small cream.'

'Manor's quiet again. Back to two bottles since yesterday. Quite a party on Christmas Day, according to our Beverley.'

I nodded distractedly.

'Now don't work too hard,' advised Mr Danby, as he took two empty bottles from beside me.

I had forgotten to hand them to him, and I smiled apologetically.

'You need a bit of fresh air to put the colour in your cheeks,' he said. 'You look quite pale.'

As soon as he had gone, I retrieved the letter which had been my only post this morning. A cheap pale blue envelope – postmarked York. But that meant nothing. York was fifty miles away, and as far as I could gather everything posted between here and there was postmarked York. There was one flimsy sheet of paper, which matched the envelope, with words carefully printed in capital letters.

I think that was what shocked me – the neatness of the printing. I had always imagined poison pen letters would be scrawled and backward sloping in green ink. Or glued together from fragments of newspaper. Not this. Whoever had printed this had used the guide-page of bold black lines underneath, because not just the bottoms, but the tops of the letters were aligned too:

I KNOW WHAT YOU'RE UP TO. KEEP YOUR WHORE'S HANDS OFF THE VICAR. DO YOU WANT TO RUIN HIS LIFE? HE DOESN'T REALLY WANT YOU ANYWAY.

DON'T YOU GET FRIGHTENED LATE AT NIGHT DOWN THERE? I WOULD IF I WERE YOU.

It never seriously occurred to me that the sender could be anyone other than Elizabeth Cowper. Therefore, I told myself that it would be foolish to be frightened by this piece of childish spite. That I ought to feel sorry for her, that she was sick. That the worst I could fear from her was public embarrassment if she chose to make a fuss. She was hardly going to come round here late at night and attack me. Now if the writer had been someone else, a man even, well then . . .

If I had not been so certain as to the identity of the sender, I would have sought out the local policeman without hesitation. Under the circumstances, I had no desire to advertise the accusations contained in this letter to the neighbourhood police.

I got into the habit of performing a ritual tour of doors and windows at night worthy of the Tower of London.

I wondered whether I should tell Ned. I wondered whether I would ever get the opportunity to tell Ned – this, and a great many other things.

CHAPTER TWENTY

In the week that followed the arrival of that vile letter, I began to find the evenings unpleasantly long and dark. For the first time, I wished the Lodge were not quite so far from any other human habitation. Ironically, after so steadfastly refusing invitations and offers of hospitality during the previous two months, now, when I would have jumped at any invitation, I was offered none. I suppose many people batten down the hatches after Christmas, and quietly slump in front of their own televisions for a recovery period. The kind souls who had so pressingly invited me to join them before Christmas had probably finally convinced themselves I preferred my own eccentric company.

I could have gone up to the Wheatsheaf of course, and been fairly sure of meeting someone I knew. Occasionally, at lunchtime, I did so. But I was nervous of leaving the Lodge alone at night. The leaving didn't worry me. It was the prospect of returning to the empty building alone. So I saw in the New Year in solitary grandeur in my mahogany bed with a mug of cocoa on the bedside chest of drawers.

I suppose I did not really expect to hear from Ned, but even Roger did not telephone. I began to fear that Suzy had confided her suspicions to him, and that he was outraged at my supposed interference in his sister's marriage. Although I had never detected even the most tepid of affection between brother and sister – in my company they had only ever quarrelled ferociously – I supposed wearily that the old blood and water clichés were true. Roger struck me as exactly the type to take umbrage at a supposed slight on the family honour. Particularly when he had made such an absurd song and dance over pursuing me himself. And all for something which had never happened.

DON'T YOU GET FRIGHTENED LATE AT NIGHT DOWN THERE?

Answer: Yes, I did now.

So I painted. I painted so hard I lost track of the days and kept going as long as Radio Four was there to smother the sounds of the night outside. The music stations were no good. Recorded music was too impersonal, too lonely. I needed human, talking voices for company. I even learned to be grateful for the abstruse dissertations on gilts and blue-chips. Then I hurried to bed with the shipping forecast, telling myself I was a neurotic fool and that, if there was anything to be frightened of, I should have gone to the police in the first place.

When the evening came that I finally heard the gate creak — the unmistakable squeal of the hinge on my garden gate opening — I was almost relieved. It confirmed I hadn't been worrying about nothing. That I had been right to lock and bolt the doors so meticulously. Right not to get in the car and drive to the pub.

I was also terrified. The blood was thundering in my head and for a moment I actually couldn't move with fright. And it was so early. Barely nine o'clock. I was still working downstairs. I had not even drawn the curtains.

I waited. If there were footsteps, I didn't hear them. If it was an innocent caller, they would knock on the door, wouldn't they? Or stuff a circular through the letter box.

There was no knock at the door, no circular rattling through the letter box. I could swear, although I did not turn my head, that a face flickered at the window behind me. The window facing north towards the road. I was still sitting at my table. In front of me was a nearly finished painting of Mr Harrison with his pigs.

And then, moving slowly — if they *were* watching me, I didn't want to panic them, didn't want them to smash the window, oh Jesus — I reached the telephone. And dialled the first number which occurred to me — Roger's. It was scrawled on the cover of the directory. He could speed up the lane from the Manor in the Range Rover. Whatever grudge he might be nursing against me at the moment, surely he'd love the chance to play knight errant.

Outside, there was only silence. And at the other end, the telephone rang and rang. Unanswered.

Boldly, I forced myself to look directly at the window. A black square of nothingness. I got up, drew the curtains. Then I opened the telephone directory and found the Cs. If *she* answered well then I would know it wasn't her outside. In which case it was someone else — *oh, my God* — but at least she could hardly object to my telephoning for help . . .

But the phone was answered instantly, almost before it began to ring, 'Edward Cowper. Hello?'

'Ned? Oh, Ned . . .' I whispered hoarsely.

'F-frankie! What on earth's the matter? Are — are you hurt? Tell me.'

'I'm fine. No, I'm not fine. Ned, you'll think I'm being very stupid but — is Elizabeth there?'

'Over at the M-manor, I think. Why?'

No she wasn't. There was no answer from the Manor.

'I'm afraid that . . . Look, once or twice since I've been here I've suspected there's been someone hanging around outside, late at night. I don't know who, or why. I've never seen them. Then, recently, I got an anonymous letter. And . . . I'm frightened they're here now. Outside.'

'Oh God,' said Ned. But he didn't sound surprised. There was a dull, dead note of recognition in his voice, as though he knew at once what to expect. 'Look, Frankie, don't worry. P-please don't worry. I p-promise you there's nothing to worry about. At least — there's someone there *now* you say? Are you sure?'

'I saw a face — at the window.'

'If you c-could get a look at them — maybe see who it is. But don't, for heaven's sake, d-darling please, do anything reckless. And don't worry. I'm c-coming now.'

After I had put the phone down, I crept upstairs. To the small bedroom, with the window overlooking the road. There was enough moonlight to see by, once my eyes adjusted. And I spotted the figure at once. A shadow by the hedge. So much for Ned's reassurances. And it was a man. He was wearing a cap. I dodged away from the window, heart hammering uncontrollably again. I should have taken the letter to the police. I was stupid to have assumed so automatically it came from Elizabeth Cowper.

As soon as I saw the headlights flickering over the crest of the hill — it never occurred to me that this could be anything other than Ned's car — I ran downstairs. The figure was still standing outside in the lane. Occasionally he — it was certainly he — had paced up and down a few steps. He was actually smoking. I had seen a glowing pin-point of red.

Now, hearing the car engine coming closer, I picked up a torch, unlocked the back door and inched my way tentatively along the back of the terrace. Once I could be quite sure Ned was up there on the lane, maybe I might just be able to catch a glimpse of the man. Shine the torch on him. I wasn't taking foolish risks, I told myself stoutly, well, nothing *too* foolish anyway. The man was round the other side of the house, the other side of the garden wall. And it was better to do something, anything, than simply wait, a quivering wretch behind locked doors, for the stranger to melt off silently into the darkness. If I were to continue living here until the end of my leave, I *needed* to know who was out there. A dark faceless figure terrifies twenty times more powerfully than a recognizable human being — someone with a name, a face, a Marks and Spencer pullover and pebble spectacles. My thumb was pressed ready against the torch switch as I rounded the corner of the building. I waited for the car to turn into the lane, brake. I would walk up the path and —

Something blundered into me, and two hands grabbed my waist.

I shrieked and turned on the torch.

'Be quiet!' hissed a female voice shrilly. 'Oh Christ, now you've blown it. What the hell are you doing walking round here in the dark like that?'

Elizabeth Cowper.

In the lane, the car door opened, and I heard Ned shout.

'What am *I* doing?' I said to her in amazement. 'What the hell are *you* doing? Ned! I'm down here . . . We're both down here.'

'Ned?' said Elizabeth incredulously. 'Ned?' Then she raised her eyes to heaven, and turned to shout towards the lane. 'Come and join the party, my angel. Anyone got a light for my cigarette?'

But it was not Ned who appeared at the gate first, it was, of all people, Roger who started down the path, then recognized his sister and stopped dead.

'Elizabeth?' he said. 'What in God's name are you doing here?'

'We're all asking one another that,' said Elizabeth. 'You have got a light, haven't you? Thanks. I thought I saw you light a cigar.'

'Saw me? You've been *watching* me?'

'What I can't work out is how my husband comes to be here . . .'

Ned was following Roger down the path.

'F-frankie telephoned me,' he said. 'She heard someone walking around outside the cottage and, h-hardly surprisingly when you think about it, she was f-frightened.'

'I'm sorry,' I said, 'I seem to have created the most ludicrous situation. Look, this is crazy. Had we better go inside?'

'You were frightened?' said Roger. 'Oh my poor girl . . .' He sounded genuinely upset. 'I'm a beast. I should be shot.'

'Come on,' said Elizabeth impatiently, 'I'm frozen half way to fucking death.'

By the time we reached the sitting-room, brother and sister were snarling at one another. I searched for whisky and glasses only to find I'd mislaid the bottle. The effect of relief flooding in over hard-knotted terror seemed to be a temporary dislocation of the brain.

Ned followed me into the kitchen with a preoccupied frown. 'I can't b-bear to think of you being frightened here, all alone,' he whispered to me as Roger and Elizabeth continued to quarrel. 'Honestly, I'm sure there's nothing to be f-frightened of. B-before Christmas, when you heard someone outside — w-well, that was probably me.'

'You?' I stared at him blankly. It was like reaching the last mirror in a house of mirrors when, after laughing un-comfortably at one grotesque distortion after another, you wonder if this is funny too — or if it's the truth. 'You, Ned?'

'Hush,' he said warily. Roger was watching us through the open door.

I handed Ned his glass and hurried back into the other room with the whisky bottle.

'And so you saw me in the lane and sent for Ned, did you?' said Roger chattily.

'I phoned the Manor first,' I said, 'but you weren't there.'

'Because he was here already,' said Elizabeth sourly, 'doing what, one wonders.'

'I was coming to see Frankie as a matter of fact,' said Roger. 'Then I looked through the window and saw her painting away − and, well, I didn't have the heart to disturb her.'

So he had walked up and down in the lane outside, smoking a cigar? But I was not about to cross-question him. I would not have been particularly surprised by a visit from Roger, after all. In fact, I would have been glad to see him. But Elizabeth? Her brother was there before me.

'And what about you, Bess?' he said nastily. 'Were you coming to see Frankie as well?'

'Yes, Elizabeth darling,' said Ned gently, and I flinched at the endearment. 'What on earth were you d-doing up here? I thought you were at the Manor. It's n-not like you to w-want a walk. At this time of night.'

'But I did,' said Elizabeth abruptly. 'That's exactly it. I wanted some fresh air. Then I saw Rog, and was just about to give him the fright of his life when I walked slap bang into Frankie. Simple. Ridiculous, isn't it? Sorry Frankie, sorry Edward − sorry Rog.'

'And d-did you say something about a letter, Frankie?' continued Ned earnestly.

'An . . . anonymous note,' I said reluctantly.

'Really? Saying what?' demanded Elizabeth. 'Threatening to come round and carve you up?'

'No. It . . .' I floundered helplessly. I could hardly disclose the actual contents, and she must know that. If she had written it. But if she had, she was a bloody good actress. She wasn't bothering to display sympathy or concern − that would have been too obvious. Rather, she was full of gleeful curiosity.

'Have you got it?'

'I — burned it,' I stammered. It was in the top drawer of the ugly sideboard. I almost expected Elizabeth to stalk across and find it unerringly.

'D-did the writer threaten you?' said Ned, frowning at his wife.

I pulled myself together, shook my head. 'Not really. Just suggested I'd be better going back to London. With a few non-specific comments on my morals.' I managed a laugh. 'You know the sort of thing. Anyway, I threw it on the fire.'

I turned and opened the door of the stove now, and fiercely stuffed in wood and coal.

'Quite right,' said Roger brusquely. 'Filthy things. Foul. Not worth taking a second's notice of. The people who write those things never mean their threats. Paper tigers.'

'And are you going to tell us just how you can be so sure of that, brother?'

'Hush, Elizabeth,' said Ned. 'I think we should be g-going. Frankie, are you happy to stay here — or would you r-rather have a bed with us? Or at the Manor?'

'I'm fine,' I said. 'Obviously I got into a state over nothing, and — well, there's nothing more to be said is there?'

'I'll c-come round and check all the rooms with you, if you like,' said Ned. 'No, R-roger, I'll do it. You see Elizabeth to the car. And I think perhaps you owe Frankie an apology, d-don't you?'

The sternness in his voice took me by surprise, so too did Roger's meek response. I would have expected him to turn on Ned. Instead, he took my hand and, with none of his usual swaggering bravado, kissed it gently.

'I'm very sorry, Frankie. I'm a thoughtless, selfish cad and you mustn't be frightened. Really not. Good-night.'

Then he swept his sister out of the back door, and turned back briefly. 'You won't be long will you, Ned?' he said. 'I might kill your wife otherwise.'

The door shut and Ned and I stared at one another, listening to the footsteps clattering away down the path.

'I didn't go to bed with Sebastian,' I said abruptly. 'I mean, we shared the bed physically but ... I'm sorry. It was an unspeakably cruel thing to have ...'

But Ned touched one finger to my lips. 'We've given up apologising.'

'And what did you mean, that it was *you* outside?'

Ned's square face was suffused with colour. 'I'm a f-fool, I know I am,' he said. 'Night after night I couldn't sleep for thinking about you, for w-wanting you. I used to get up and walk. And m-more often than not, I would end up passing here. As though b-being close to you would make some kind of difference. Crazy, isn't it? I even used to switch the torch off as I passed. In case it might wake you. All I succeeded in doing was scaring you to death.' He laughed harshly.

'Oh, Ned,' I said. I longed to wrap my arms round him. And he was edging away from me, locking his hands behind his back, as though to stop himself touching me. 'It's ridiculous,' I said. 'I've never felt like this before. As though I might explode – if I came anywhere near you.'

Ned nodded, smiling dejectedly.

'D-do you want me to check the rooms?'

I shook my head. 'Not much point under the circumstances, is there?'

'I r-really don't think there's anything to worry about,' he went on. 'Roger was right about that letter. P-poisonous rubbish . . .'

'It was about us, you know,' I said swiftly.

Ned nodded 'Ah, I wondered. All the more reason . . . D-don't waste another thought on it. I'm p-perfectly sure now you've nothing to be frightened of.'

Was this an admission that his wife was the writer?

'All this fuss,' I said bitterly, 'over an affair that never even was.'

'Of course it was,' said Ned passionately. 'Was and is. I s-sometimes ask myself if the physical r-restraint is worth it. What difference could the sex make?'

'A lot,' I said with feeling, and Ned smiled perfunctorily.

'B-but the real infidelity is there already.'

'Someone else said something of the sort to me recently. Do you really believe it?'

'That the emotional betrayal is more important, m-more fundamental than the physical act? Oh yes, of course I do. But whereas I *can* stop myself touching you, seeing you, I c-can't seem to do anything about the f-feelings, and I have tried. I really have tried. But I c-can't change the way I feel about you. It's like part of my soul. So I wonder, is it worth the agony? But it must be. It must be . . .'

'I wish you were staying,' I said quietly and then wished I had not, because of the pain I saw in his face.

'Go,' I said quickly, and touched his arm. 'Just my luck to fall for a saint. Ask God to issue me with a thoroughly depraved little sinner next time around, would you?'

CHAPTER TWENTY-ONE

The snow threatened for several days before it finally arrived. The sky was heavy and grey, and a cruel wind sliced up the valley from the east instead of the west, which made the chimney smoke and the garage doors moan petulantly on their hinges if I left them open.

Twice, I drove into the nearby town and filled the car with essential provisions. The first time, having woken and looked at the menacing sky, I panicked and rushed round buying frozen meat, bread and (for some obscure reason because I don't even like the stuff) canned soup. Fortunately, the snow did not come then, but the wind blew colder still, and three days later I returned to the shops. This time I bought more sensibly: fire-lighters, matches, candles, dried milk, whisky and carrier bags full of fruit and vegetables. Still, however, the snow did not fall.

There is nothing, except perhaps midday sunshine in climes far south of ours, to equal the brilliance of light reflected off snow. I find it as exhilarating as champagne. In the meantime, the light cast by the pewter sky over the blasted countryside was grimly cheerless. The river was as black and sluggish as a canal, with a murky film of ice choking its edges. By now, with my larder stocked to bursting, I was positively looking forward to the snow, feeling cheated when, morning after morning, I awoke to find the valley still green.

I suppose it was inevitable I would be caught out. It sounds absurdly trivial but, as I have observed before, the crucial events on which the course of one's life turns so often are.

I ran out of white acrylic paint. And to my amazement, in a toolbox overflowing with equipment and every sort of debris,

I could not find another tube. And this happened now, of all ironies, when I had been longing for the chance to start painting snowscapes. I was beside myself with frustration. So I pulled on my warmest jacket, scarf and boots, climbed into the car and drove into York. The round trip to the supplier who stocked the make I used took no more than two hours under normal conditions, but before I reached the outskirts of the city the snow started to fall.

The introductory flurries, those pinpoint fine crystals which blow in straight lines and dust the corners of the road like spray paint, were brief. Almost at once, big heavy feathery flakes took over, choking my windscreen wipers and blotting out the sky. By the time, on the way home, I saw the lights of the Wheatsheaf, I had already taken the decision to leave the car there in Albert's yard and walk down the hill. I would not risk my expensive baby on those hairpin bends in conditions like these. It looked to me as though snow had been falling heavily up here on the moors since the very minute I left.

Through the windows of the pub I could see a fire flickering alluringly, but I tied my scarf round my head and resisted. I felt that if I did not leave now, I might never reach the Lodge. I started walking down the hill. In one pocket, as I stuck my hands deep down for warmth, I felt the paper bag containing the tubes, and cursed.

I had walked only a little way when Roger's Range Rover came down the road and drew up beside me with a toot of greeting, its windscreen wipers manfully shovelling the snow from side to side. With heartfelt gratitude, I opened the passenger door and hauled myself up.

'Are you going down the hill?' I said. 'Thanks a –'

Then I broke off in surprise, because it was not Roger, but Ned in the driving seat. He smiled at me with such blatant, welcoming love in his eyes, I wanted to burst into tears.

'I've abandoned my car,' I said.

'Rog lent me the t-tank,' he said, putting the car into gear again and frowning as he peered between the tumbling slices of snow on the windscreen. 'I was supposed to be going to York. But I c-called in on old Mrs Wilkinson on the way and g-got delayed for ages with tea and cakes. Probably just as well. This is n-no weather for going anywhere. I'm sorry for Michael though, he was very upset.'

We began to growl cautiously down the white hill.

'Michael?'

'Michael Porrit, my colleague from St C-catherine's.'

'Ah,' I said, 'the one who – got into difficulties.'

'I was going to visit the poor chap. He's in a pretty miserable state. Tranquillized up to the eyebrows. I rang him from Betty Wilkinson's to say I'd try and get over next week. I think he understood. There's snow down there too.'

'I've just come from York,' I said. 'Not as bad as here though.'

I caught my breath as the wheels skidded slightly on a bend. Ned steered out of it smoothly, and whispered, 'Have to p-put your trust in the Lord.'

I laughed. 'Good thing you're driving then.'

The snow whirled towards us in a white frenzy.

'I'm glad I'm not out in it,' I said, 'but I'm sorry to bring you out of your way.'

'I w-was coming down Lamp Hill anyway. The long road, down Thornbeck Bank, strangely t-tends to fill with snow quicker than this. Must be p-prevailing winds or something. I'll c-cut along the lane then, if I can, back to the Manor.'

But when we drew up, without mishap, outside the Lodge, the carpet of white in the Lamp Lane had hidden all the treacherous potholes and ruts and was already drifting into a beautiful but ominous curve high against one hedge.

'Better leave the motor here,' said Ned. 'S-silly to risk it for the sake of a mile. Okay if I put it in the garage?'

'Fine,' I said, and we battled as giant flakes fluttered into our eyes and mouths to haul the doors shut and bolt them.

'I'll just telephone Rog, if I m-may,' said Ned. 'Tell him I'm not stuck in a snowdrift.'

'Tea?' I said as we walked into the kitchen, stamping the snow from our boots, shaking wet hair. 'Or maybe if you're awash with tea from your parishioner, something stronger?' I picked up a whisky bottle and Ned grinned.

Of course, I was breathlessly thrilled to have Ned here, all to myself, for as long as he could legitimately delay setting off to walk. I hoped he might feel able to wait until the present blizzard abated. Perhaps even until the late afternoon.

I poured very large whiskies, trusting it would take a very long time to drink them. I stoked the fire up high, and prodded and riddled it into furious warmth, to make it all the harder for him to quit. I deliberately hung his coat and scarf in a cold corner of the kitchen, vaguely imagining that when it came time to leave, I could steal a few more minutes by drying them in front of the fire. And yet, despite the teeming hopes and the absurd delaying ploys, what actually happened next took me utterly by surprise. I could never even have invented, let alone brought about, such a miraculous conspiracy of events.

Even now, getting on for a year later, I can still remember every tiny detail of the scene in the bright colour and over-intense clarity of a Pre-Raphaelite painting.

Our wet coats and boots are stacked dripping in a cold, dark corner of the kitchen. Ned has dropped into the armchair by the fire flexing blue stockinged feet in front of the flames. He lazily reaches to pick up the telephone and dials the Manor. He's woolly and cuddly in a soft pullover which almost but not quite hides the white collar round his neck. There are drops of water trembling in his curls, and his face is still flushed from the cold outside.

'Roger, hello, it's N-ned,' he says, and at that moment covers the mouthpiece with one large hand as he whispers his thanks to me. I am handing him his Scotch.

'Ned, thank God you've got there safely . . .' I can hear Roger's voice crackling down the line perfectly clearly. 'Look, is there somewhere you can put up? You really mustn't attempt the journey back, it's snowing like the blazes. Real blizzard. What's it like where you are?'

'M-much the same . . .' says Ned faintly.

I am standing beside him like a statue. I feel if I breathe, or utter a single word, the enchantment will break . . .

'Ned, are you all right, old man?'

I dare not look at Ned. I cannot bear the suspense of waiting for his answer.

'M-me?' he says, and then suddenly, 'Fine. I'm absolutely f-fine. Yes, I'll f-find somewhere to put up, not to worry. There are one or t-two things I want to look up in the University library anyway. See you t-tomorrow . . .'

'If you're lucky,' says Roger. 'I wouldn't be surprised if this had set in for a while. I'll ring Bess for you. She's welcome to come and sleep over here if she doesn't want to be alone in the house. Take care, old fellow.'

And the phone line goes dead.

Still holding my whisky, still not looking at Ned, I manage to say in a strangled whisper, 'Not if you don't want to. I mean, I won't be the one who makes you do something . . . you'll regret. You'd hate me . . .' And silently my body and soul are screaming, *take me, take me now!*, but I force myself to remain frozen, exactly where I am, in the middle of the hearth-rug.

'No!' exclaims Ned violently, and my heart stops beating. 'That was abject m-moral cowardice on my p-part. I realized it then. P-pretending that it was all your responsibility, that I c-couldn't resist if you made the f-first move. Shovelling the b-blame on to you. Rubbish.' He's talking faster and more breathlessly by the minute. 'I know exactly what I'm doing, and it's my responsibility and if it's wrong – well, it's g-going to be the m-most marvellous sin I've ever committed in my life.'

And all at once, he's standing in front of me, taking the glass out of my nerveless hand and putting it on the mantelpiece, and wrapping his arms round me very tightly.

'Oh, my love,' he's saying softly, as he kisses me. And he doesn't sound sad this time. He sounds wonderfully ecstatically happy.

We made love in front of the fire.

According to the text books, the first time is never supposed to be much good. Perhaps the people who write text books had never wanted anyone as fiercely and all consumingly as Ned and I wanted each other. But of course all lovers, arrogantly, believe that don't they? *It has never been like this in the world before . . .*

181

It never had for me.

Even in the frantic urgency of desire, we somehow managed to shed our clothes without too much trouble. In fact, I ended up lying on a tangled bed of them. Ned was kneeling and his penis gleamed dully in the firelight like carved marble. I touched it wonderingly with my tongue, and he shuddered and pushed me gently away. Pressed my shoulders back to the floor.

I pulled him down with me. My arms round him were thin and white against his golden solid flesh. His curls were still damp with melted snowflakes as he bent to take my nipple in his mouth. I pressed myself against him, already frantic to feel him inside me.

Dear Ned, sweet, loving, responsible Ned: even as I wound my legs round him, arching my body to meet his, squirming with lust, he hesitated long enough to ask if he could go ahead, if I was sure, if I was all right.

'Yes,' I cried, pulling his heavy body down on to mine, 'yes, yes, yes – oh please, come inside me now, please . . .' And when, so quickly, so ecstatically, that first burst of passion was spent, I cried. Wept uncontrollably for sheer happiness. Ned held me tightly against him, murmuring nothings, stroking my hair, kissing tears from my eyelids, until, inevitably, we began to make love again . . .

CHAPTER TWENTY-TWO

'I love you,' said Ned. 'I love you more than I ever thought it was p-possible to love anybody.'

We had found our way up to bed. Outside it was dark, but a magical, seemingly inexhaustible storm of white flakes still tumbled out of the night sky. Oh, the greed of human nature. Six hours ago I would have thought I could not have wished for anything more than to be granted a single night with Ned. Now I stole surreptitious glances at the snow and hoped it might bury us for a week.

'And I love you,' I said, softly and happily. 'I never knew love-making could be so . . . fucking wonderful.'

Ned laughed, pretended to cuff me. 'N-not even with all your sophisticated L-london lovers?'

'Not in a million years. And don't talk as though there was a regiment of them.'

'I won't ask how m-many,' said Ned lazily and then jumped because I sat up quickly and seized his shoulders.

'No,' I said, all at once passionately serious, 'don't. Let's not talk about people outside here at all. Not the past. Not the future.' *Not your wife* was what I was really saying and I knew Ned understood. 'As long as we're here, let's pretend there's just us. No one else . . .'

' ". . . and make one little room an everywhere".'

'Shakespeare?'

'Nope,' said Ned, tumbling me down on to his chest and burying his face in my hair, 'your s-system fails. John D-donne. Oh, Frankie, sweetheart . . .'

The weather was kind to us. Under any other circumstances I

suppose I might have said flippantly that God was kind, but it seems inappropriate here.

We were locked in our enchanted white prison for three days and nights. The snow fell intermittently, but too thick and fast for the ploughs to make headway on the local lanes. Albert telephoned from the Wheatsheaf, and I had difficulty dissuading him from despatching a rescue posse of sons down the hill with food and firewood, company and drink. I was fine, I assured him. Warm and well provisioned.

'You're *sure* you're happy?' said Albert worriedly, and I remember I glanced across at Ned on the other side of the fire who smiled back at me inquiringly. 'Perfectly, rapturously, one hundred-per-cent happy,' I said – and Albert laughed wonderingly and rang off.

Roger, when he too rang, was more easily persuaded that I needed no help. Besides, vehicle-less, with six-foot drifts from here to the Manor there was not a lot he could offer.

Ned had telephoned the Manor again on the first morning and once after that. I don't know what he said. I always stayed out of the room, pretending I wasn't aware of what he was doing. The fact that no one was in the least suspicious made it, I think, harder for him.

We tuned to the local radio station which was enjoying its own kind of heaven in the excitement of day-long emergency snow broadcasting. We knew when the problems would arise. The main roads out of York were being kept reasonably clear anyway, although motorists were being advised not to attempt any journey which was not strictly necessary. What we were dreading hearing was that the minor roads were becoming passable . . .

But we pretended not to care and tried to hide from each other the anxiety triggered with monotonous frequency by the strident traffic news jingle employed on Radio Dales, 'three-four-oh on the medium wa-ave'.

I abandoned all my serious work in order to paint a picture of Ned's magnificent body sprawled naked in front of the fire. I began the picture as he slept, exhausted after a particularly abandoned coupling. When he woke, and saw what I was up to, he was appalled – he had the modest man's horror of being painted at all, let alone in the nude – but I induced him to remain where he was. I seem to remember I threatened to publish the unfinished sketch in his parish magazine if he did not lie still.

Although for the first day we were too absorbed in one another to regard food as anything other than an unwelcome irrelevance, by the next morning we were both ravenous. Ned took charge in the kitchen. I can cook as well as the average working woman, but I have never been particularly domesticated. The shared house in Limberton Gardens, West Hampstead did not encourage culinary adventures. Even now I will tend to entertain in a restaurant rather than at home.

Ned, however, took a touching delight in the minutiae of cooking. Although he did very little at home, he said, because Elizabeth thought it was unmanly, became irritated . . . But then he broke off, because under our agreement the rest of the world, temporarily, did not exist. This half-confidence, however, ensured that I was even more than naturally content to permit Mr Bear to potter round the kitchen in my too-small apron, humming out of tune and creating extravagant sinkfuls of washing-up.

We also drank my best wines with reckless delight.

'Eat, d-drink and be m-merry,' said Ned, 'for t-tomorrow we thaw . . .'

He trickled icy, sweet Muscat de Beaumes de Venise on the warm skin of my breast as I dozed half-naked in front of the fire. I rolled upright, yelped at the coldness, called him a sadist. For a puzzling instant he seemed to flinch, but I thought I must have imagined it because almost at once he was smiling mischievously. 'I'll lick it off,' he offered.

He persuaded romantic Porter and Gershwin tunes out of the creaking, clanking piano with loving care. We talked frantically. All the intimate trivia of our lives which had once been carefully excluded from our conversations, had to be scrambled through now in the precious time we had together. Except, of course, anything to do with Elizabeth. Or Sebastian. Or any other partner come to that. But there were so many other gaps.

'Do you mind,' I asked one night towards the end of supper, 'that I'm not a church-goer – not a Christian?'

Ned stopped peeling an orange to look at me. 'You're not an atheist,' he said.

'How do you know? We've never talked about it.'

'Atheists have to believe p-positively in nothing. That there is no supreme being of any sort. Nothing whatsoever. It's quite a difficult position to maintain, intellectually.'

'Think I'm not up to it, eh?'

He smiled, shook his head. 'There's too much of the – well, almost the m-mystic about you. Too strong a sense of spirituality.'

'There is?'

He shrugged. 'You yourself described your t-talents as a God-given knack to me once.'

'Turn of phrase . . .'

'Maybe, but you do believe there's something there. That all intelligent life doesn't begin and end inside these feeble human containers.'

'Yes, I suppose I do . . .'

'Well then.'

'That's hardly the same as being a card-carrying member of the God Squad.'

Ned grinned. 'What a d-delightful vocabulary you have, love.'

'I – thought you might try to convert me. Save this soul for Jesus.'

'I'm afraid I've never been t-terribly good at the m-muscular brand of Christianity. Bashing people over the head with bibles. You see, God is there whether one likes it or not. A chaplain I admired very much described his approach as leaving a wide open door. When people are ready to find their way in, they will. One can only help, not coerce.'

I had lit a trio of candles on the table, and Ned's face in their wavering light, shone with gentle earnestness.

'You're so *good*,' I said suddenly.

'No,' he exclaimed, horrified. 'N-no, I'm not. Don't make the mistake of thinking that. Hush!'

And he fed me with orange segments to silence me.

I think, by the end of our third day, we were so entrenched in

186

our pleasures, so secure in one another, we almost began to believe in our dream world, our four walls which were everything. On the third night, when we tumbled back to bed after watching an involved film on the television, we even fell comfortably asleep in a jigsaw of interlocked limbs without making love.

I woke to the sound of dripping.

The room was entirely black, except for the green dial of my alarm clock. It was half past four. I lay still, listening. The water was dripping from the guttering to the outside sill of my bedroom window. I even suspected I could detect a new warmth, a mugginess in the air inside the bedroom.

While we slept, the thaw had silently crept up and encircled us.

Ned did not speak for some time. I only knew he was awake because his hand gripped mine. 'I love you,' he said at last.

'I know,' I answered. 'And I love you. But — we can't pretend any longer. The snow's deserting us.'

Still gripping my hand, he lifted it to his lips and kissed it.

'What are you going to do?' I asked. 'About Elizabeth?'

'I d-don't know.'

'Really don't know — or can't bring yourself to tell me.'

Then I felt ashamed because Ned replied simply, 'I would tell you anything, Frankie. I couldn't *not* tell you anything.'

'I'm sorry,' I whispered.

It's an odd sensation, talking in absolute darkness. In a way it's liberating. It becomes easier to say things which would be impossible if you could see the pain they inflicted on the hearer.

'Is divorce allowed in the Church of England?' I demanded. 'I mean, for priests? I'm sorry to sound so ignorant — but I've never had to think about it before. Would you be chucked out?'

'The Church obviously b-believes, in principle, that marriage is for life. But no, priests do divorce, and some remarry and stay within the Church. Not all priests can accept it. The High-Church lot, the Anglo-Catholics, n-naturally tend to feel rather differently.'

187

'And what about you? Where does the Reverend Cowper stand?'

'I've always accepted that in certain c-cases – it must be the only course.'

'And in your own case?'

'G-god knows,' said Ned. 'Or I hope he does. B-because I don't.'

My alarm clock, with the luminous dial, is old-fashioned enough to tick. I could hear it then, interspersed in sad syncopation with the dripping outside the window.

'I think you'd better tell me about Elizabeth. About why you don't make love . . .'

'How did you know that?'

'She was broadcasting it to the world at Christmas. It was awful. Half of me was appalled just to be hearing something so personal, so private about you. The other half was cheering fiercely because I couldn't bear to think of you making love to another woman.'

'I haven't made love to Elizabeth since . . . I can't remember when the last abysmal effort was.'

'But you must have done at first? When you first got married?'

There was a silence. 'In a way,' said Ned.

'Tell me,' I said. 'Tell me how you got into this mess . . .'

'I've known Elizabeth since I was a schoolboy,' said Ned, 'when my parents used to bring me to stay here. Here,' he added, laughing softly, 'in this very b-bed. My parents took the other, smaller room because by that time they already preferred twin beds. My father suffered from gout.

'Elizabeth's seven years younger than me, of course, and I d-don't suppose I noticed her very much in the early years. She was even worse at c-cricket than Roger, and that was about the only thing I was interested in then. Besides, strangely, she wasn't a particularly attractive child. She was r-rather plump, and horribly b-bad-tempered. Always running to her father. I thought she was a pain in the neck.'

He gave a faint cough of laughter. A laugh of embarrassment, not amusement, dry and bitter.

'Then there was her c-coming out dance. Roger had insisted on inviting me, although by then the old man and I d-didn't get on . . .'

'Suzy told me that. Because he didn't like clergymen.'

'Oh, the row between Uncle John and me started years b-before I took to the dog collar. He t-took against me while Roger and I were still at school.' Ned released my hand. I felt him shift in the darkness beside me, and prop a pillow between his shoulders and the creaking headboard of the bed.

'You must understand Uncle John didn't like anyone who stood up to him. And he wasn't the traditional b-bully who caves in to a show of strength. He d-despised you if you knuckled under – and he bloody well hated you if you opposed him. And I d-did. I was here for the summer vac. We'd barely unpacked when he started in on Roger for being a failure, c-complete wash-out, that sort of thing. I t-told him he was unfair to Roger. Rog had done b-brilliantly well in an essay prize, and all Uncle John could talk about was b-bloody cricket. Because he used to play it. Rog lost his temper and swore, and John threatened to beat him. Elizabeth was only a kid at the time. It was soon after Margaret had run off, I think. Anyway, I stuck up for Roger, p-priggishly I dare say, and the old man ordered me out of the house and never said another civil word to me.'

'You told me, when I asked, that he was a monster.'

'Oh, he was. He was a cruel, foul-mouthed bigot who . . . But I'm going off at tangents.' His hand found mine again in the darkness, and closed round it. 'Anyway, the p-point is Roger and I stayed friends just as we always had been. He was a good-hearted chap – to the people he liked – and considering that until then his beastly father had always held me up to him as an example of what Rog ought to be, it was p-pretty remarkable he managed to stick with liking me. But he did. And I wasn't sorry when Roger got into Oxford too. Our ways inevitably parted a bit after that. I decided – well, I'd always known really – that I wanted to go in for the church . . .'

'Did Roger try and dissuade you?'

'Absolutely not. As a matter of fact, Roger was toying with

189

Catholicism at the time. Wild talk about becoming a priest but n-naturally one never expected it to last. Oxford has that effect on some people. Anyway, where was I living by the time of Elizabeth's d-dance? After Oxford the people who, as it were, vet one's vocation had told me to take myself off into the world for a while . . .'

'When you became a farmer?'

'That's right. And then on to theological college. Oxford again. Yes, and it was there I got a letter from Roger absolutely insisting I must come up for Bess's party. I r-rang him. Reminded him of the terms on which his father and I had parted, but he begged me. Said he was as m-miserable as hell and there would be hundreds of guests there I could get lost among.

'I wasn't very difficult to persuade, I dare say. I love this part of the world, always have. It was during the fishing season too – so up I came. And there was Elizabeth. Looking like a picture from a fairy story. Oh, I'm sorry, darling.'

'Don't apologize. I can imagine all too clearly. She's one of the most exquisite women I've ever seen.'

'And I was amazed. Among all these good looking young men, she s-singled me out. T-told me why too. B-because I'd stood up to her father years before. By this time, I could hardly even remember the scene. But Elizabeth t-treated me like a hero. Then old John himself s-sought me out and started having a go at the cloth, telling me what he thought of parsons and – well, it all ended in a bit of a mess. I left quietly so as not to spoil Bess's party.'

'And did you never see her then, until her father's funeral?'

'You know about that, do you? No – in a word. Oh, Rog was always talking about fixing a get-together in London, but I was busy at college. Then I got my first curacy on the outskirts of Birmingham and then, as you say, the old man died and Roger pleaded with me to come up and take the service. And there was Elizabeth, a little waif in black. Weeping buckets. I couldn't quite understand it because she spoke t-terribly harshly about her father, swore she hated him and all that kind of thing which, knowing her father, didn't shock me as much as it might have done. He hadn't left her any m-money either which didn't help — just the house. Roger p-put that right in the end, bless him. All the same, she was clearly terribly distressed at her father's death.'

'When did you first know . . . you'd fallen in love with her?'

'I suppose, in a way, I had been ever since her p-party. I was amazed, as a matter of fact, that she hadn't been snapped up in the years in between. Although Roger said that the old man scared off suitors like a farmer keeping rabbits off his lettuces. I found myself feeling actually grateful to Uncle John. *Christ!*

He shuddered violently. I continued to hold his hand in the dark room and waited.

'Roger was the matchmaker, really. When I look back he seemed to bowl the r-romance along for us — although neither of us was unwilling. Bess seemed to regard me as some sort of hero. And I, lonely as hell in my first curacy, well, I was besotted.'

'Did you fuck before you got married?'

'No. Oh, I wasn't some k-kind of puritan. I was ready to. But Elizabeth seemed so innocent, so fragile, so frightened. It made it easier for me to behave myself. To wait for the wedding night.'

'The real thing,' I said with a brittle laugh, 'a honeymoon, like in all the music hall jokes. I don't think I know a single person whose first experience of sex was genuinely on their wedding night. At least — were you a virgin?'

'N-not entirely . . .'

I laughed, genuinely now, at the embarrassment with which he said this. 'How not entirely?'

'I'd had one or two flings during my first round at Oxford. And then there was a g-girl on the farm I was potty about, and . . .'

'All right, all right . . . You weren't a virgin, but Elizabeth obviously was.'

'And naturally I thought that was the problem. When — nothing happened. Oh, we managed to make love. But it meant nothing to her, I could tell. She just lay there. Winced a bit at first — and then blankness — like a doll.'

The agony in his voice hurt me. I held his hand even tighter.

'I tried everything, of course. Champagne, perfume, romantic music, oh God, I can't remember what else. You can imagine. I began to dread going to b-bed — because I wanted her so much, but I couldn't bear seeing the look of resignation come into her eyes. And I would hate myself afterwards and . . .'

I waited for a moment and then said, 'And she didn't like Birmingham either.'

'No,' said Ned, more easily, 'hated it. And then St Peter's here fell vacant, and Roger pleaded with me, and Bess wanted to live in the D-dower House. Well, who could blame her? So back we came. I thought things might improve.'

'And did they?'

'I discovered the problem,' said Ned. He was speaking so quietly I could barely hear him. 'The night we arrived we had the most almighty row. I had drunk too much with Roger — we were staying in the Manor for the first few weeks anyway — and suddenly I'd had enough. I shouted at Bess. Said terrible things, I'd never dreamed of saying before. What a failure she was to me as a wife — as a lover, as anything . . . She ran out of the room.'

He was gripping my hand tightly now. So tight it was hurting me but I didn't move.

'And all at once she came back into our bedroom. She was wearing a thin slip of a nightdress, I remember, and she had her hand behind her back. And she was smiling — and I couldn't believe this, because a minute earlier I'd been shouting my drunken head off at her. But she just walked towards me smiling — and then she held out her hand.

'She was offering me a whip.'

CHAPTER TWENTY-THREE

'She – actually wanted you to use it on her?'

'She was so full of expectation. So happy . . .'

Beside me in the bed I could no longer feel the warmth of Ned's body, although our fingers were still clasped together. I felt isolated and cold.

'Did you?'

'It completely d-disarmed me. I'd been in the most foul towering rage, but when I saw this l-little waif smiling at m-me and holding out a riding crop, saying "I've been n-n-naughty . . ." I collapsed. And then she was furious. I wanted to hold her, to comfort her – but she swore at me, telling me I was a enunch, a . . . Oh God, you can imagine. Terrible things. And I was drunk enough still to be provoked. It ended up with me chucking her on to the bed and r-raping her. Raping my own wife . . .'

'And – that was what she wanted.'

There was no answer, but I could sense him nodding convulsively.

'It was the f-first time she'd ever enjoyed it. She screamed at m-me like a wildcat and then curled up next to me like a little kitten. And the next morning she was all sweetness and light, and asked me where her p-present was.'

'Present?'

'I didn't understand either. "Pressie?" she said, looking like a little girl on the morning of her birthday. F-for one dreadful moment I thought I'd forgotten it. But this was January and her b-birthday's in June.

'That morning I'd have given her the earth and the stars if I could – b-but I warned her I couldn't afford very much. We

193

went into town. I forget what we bought. And that night I rushed to b-bed, expecting a s-sort of second honeymoon, I suppose, and it was just like before. M-making love to a robot.'

He sighed heavily. 'Darling, I'm sorry. I never wanted to subject you to a full blown account of my m-miserable marriage. But I've g-got to make you understand.'

There was another strained pause. In the end it was me who broke it.

'Was it something to do with her father?'

'Dear Lord – is it so very obvious?'

'I don't know, but from different things people have said . . . Things that you've said . . .'

'It wasn't obvious to me. I didn't know what was wrong. Me? Her? I was in agonies over what to do. I even thought about writing to one of those p-problem pages. You can't, simply can't, consult the old f-family doctor about something like this. Jack Kingdom virtually brought Bess into this world.'

He sighed. 'And then, a week or so later, it all happened again. I was under a lot of stress with a new parish – first p-parish of my own – and Elizabeth behaved appallingly to some of the old ladies in the church hall. N-no question, it had never occurred to Elizabeth that being m-married to a priest is, well, doing part of his job too. And I like a fool had never even thought to t-talk about it to her. After all, she'd been brought up with two livings on the estate and – anyway, that day I shouted at her again. Told her she must think of *me* – and she deliberately stirred me up. I forget what she said. That she wasn't being p-paid to pour tea for evil-minded old crones. And . . . well, we ended up in bed. And as she s-screamed I suddenly realized she was calling not my name but "Papa".'

'Oh, Jesus . . .'

'It had all begun with him beating her. He was a cruel bastard. He hit anything that d-didn't conform to his ideas – his animals, his children, and his wife. That's why Margaret went. And, I suppose, some time after that – I don't really know when – the sessions with Elizabeth b-began to take on a different complexion. He – never physically penetrated her. I

194

know, because she was a virgin when we married. I think he would have d-denied ferociously that he had ever m-molested his child. In so far as his twisted heart was c-capable of love, he loved Bess. He would probably claim he chastised her l-like a good parent – then comforted her afterwards. He would rub on cold cream and . . . Oh God, you c-can guess.'

His voice had dwindled away to an agonised whisper. The ticking of the alarm clock seemed noisy and penetrating as a drum beat.

'He was always roaring d-drunk when it happened though, so he m-must have needed some anaesthetic for his miserable conscience. It c-couldn't happen often, either, because Bess was away at school, and they had to be careful of Roger or anyone else finding them . . .'

'They?'

'Oh Bess, p-poor child, colluded in it. Because the following morning she could ask her father for anything she wanted. Present time.'

I wanted to roll towards him, put my arms round him, bury all his pain and anguish for him, but I stopped myself.

'Once I'd learned all this f-from her – I was horrified, of course, but I was also elated. I thought I'd found the problem. And there's a d-dreadful naïvety of thinking that once a problem has been identified, it can automatically be solved. After all, I w-wasn't some innocent young virgin. Bess could see therapists, of course, and I would p-play along with her a bit. Sort of give and take – and it would all sort itself out.'

'But it obviously didn't?'

'It's so arrogant to think – and I suppose everybody tends to – that because you happen to like sex one particular way, that's the only way. The normal way. Oh, I tried to be tough with Bess. To order her into bed . . .' He gave a bitter laugh, 'God, doesn't sex sound ludicrous when you c-come to describe it? Anyway, it didn't work, of course. I was m-missing the point. It wasn't play-acting Bess wanted. She wanted – she needed – to be hurt. And I couldn't do it. I couldn't . . .'

He was crying now, and I gathered him into my arms, holding him tightly, soothing him, rocking him gently from side to side, pressing kisses into his hair.

'I was frightened she'd break. Like a doll. It was unspeakable. You c-can't imagine . . .'

'Yes I can,' I said softly. I could imagine only too easily. 'Poor, poor darling . . .'

'Obviously, I was a d-dreadful disappointment to her,' he said after a moment. 'Because I'd once told her father to go to hell, she thought I was — like him. And she had to accept I wasn't. That's when we got into this cycle of clinics and therapists. I used to be so hopeful at one time. Now I'm not. But if the shrinks think it does her g-good, who am I to argue? It's her money. She pays the fees. I suppose I'm g-glad to have her out of the house. And Bess actually seems to enjoy it. I think she l-likes rehashing every frightful detail of her child-hood . . .'

'*Enjoys* it?'

'At least she knew her father loved her — that's what she used to say to me. When we were still t-talking. About — all this.'

'You don't talk about it, now?'

I felt him shaking his head. His curls brushed against my chin. 'It's easier now, really. Things have settled down. The w-worst times were early on. When she still — had hopes of me. She did terrible things, just to try and provoke me. Stupid, p-petty hurtful things like, oh, I came home once and found she'd sold my piano. It had just gone. The p-piano I'd had since I was a boy — and, of course, I roared at her, someone overheard and there were tongues buzzing all over the neigh-bourhood. We made some story about her needing quiet. Her nerves. I doubt if anyone believed it.

'Then the next day she would go out and buy *me* a present. It was all rows and presents: a case of wine, fancy bits of clothes. Terribly expensive ties or socks . . .'

'She has very good taste,' I said, smiling wryly into the dark-ness.

'I c-couldn't reciprocate, of course. Least of all with the only thing she really wanted . . . And still, she can't resist occasional-ly trying. She does something absolutely outrageous . . .'

'Like shooting at the window?' I said wonderingly. 'Behind us?'

'Absolutely. Yes, exactly. Sometimes I feel I d-daren't let her out of my sight. Although ironically the only time she'll get up to anything is when I *can* see. I find myself begging her, pleading with her – like when she was going hunting – to behave, not to make us the talk of the neighbourhood . . . God, I'm sorry. You don't need all this.'

He took my hand and kissed it gently. 'She knows now I would never hit her. Never raise a finger to her. But she seems to n-need to irritate me enough for me to lose my temper with her. It's as though that's the only form of affection she recognizes. B-being shouted at . . .'

I nearly spoke – then checked myself. I had been about to say 'poor Elizabeth . . .' But I stopped myself, angrily. I didn't want to pity her. It was much easier to hate her.

'Thank God we're here in Thornbeck,' said Ned. 'The p-people might be intolerant of some people's failings, but they're t-terribly kind to Bess. She can behave appallingly but they seem prepared to make endless allowances for her. I can't imagine that happening anywhere else. Not to the vicar's wife.' He sighed. 'I only worry that, as she gets older, it can't continue. To so many of the older parishioners she's still the Squire's pretty d-daughter. Not much more than a child. They smile at her now and say she's a bit wild, bit of a madcap, but what about when she becomes middle-aged?'

'Does Roger know – about her problems.'

'No – oh, a bit and I think he suspects more. He had the same parent, after all. I think that's why he c-can be un-sympathetic to her. He argues he c-came through it, so why shouldn't she? They used to get on better actually. It's only in the last three or four years things have become very strained.'

'But you do think she loves you?'

'Why else is she still with m-me? She could have left me any time in the last seven years. She has much more money than me. I told her once, when things were very b-bad, she must divorce me if she wanted to. That I would f-find another parish, of course. Leave her here in her house. But she shook her head and wouldn't say another word. I f-felt I might have hurt her very much. I never said it again.'

'And . . . you don't feel you could leave her?'

'C-could you, Frankie? Leave someone who needed you? Someone as d-damaged and vulnerable as Elizabeth. Even if you actually hated them? And I d-don't hate Bess. I just p-pity her . . . How could I justify leaving her? How could I defend it?'

The vicar, dumping his poor crazy wife for a floozy from London. He'd be an outcast. A pariah.

Please, I urged silently, don't ask me. Don't make me say it. But I knew he had to.

'Would you desert her, F-frankie?'

The silence stretched and yawned between us in a great black chasm. Even though I could feel Ned within my arms, the distance between us was opening up with harrowing speed.

'No,' I said finally, 'I don't suppose I would.'

We lay without speaking until wavy lines of grey began to define the silhouette of the curtains. I said I would go and make tea. Ned released me at once. We had lain entwined for more than an hour, awake but unmoving. All that time I hoped Ned's body might stir into life again, that he would turn to me and start making love to me. Maybe he hoped for the same from me. I think he probably did. But we lay still. Perhaps, tacitly, we both acknowledged that the time for love-making was gone.

At length when I kicked away the covers and got up, Ned did not remain but followed me downstairs. We drank our tea huddled round the chilly remains of the previous night's fire.

It was like a cruel parody of our first afternoon in front of the fire three days earlier. Now, instead of shedding our clothes, we put them on. Instead of embracing, we avoided touching. We even avoided looking at one another.

We kept the curtains drawn. Outside, although there was a new wetness and the trees were once again black instead of silvered, the landscape was still entirely white. So much snow could not vanish quickly. The noise of a vehicle revving on the hill was commonplace enough for me to forget we had not heard that sound for three days. Ned, however, parted the curtains an inch to look.

'Clearing Lamp Hill,' he said. 'I thought they would. George Danby will be able to get d-down soon.'

'And you'll be able to drive up.'

He nodded.

'Shall we see one another . . . again?'

Ned shrugged. 'What d-do you think? I can't bear, can't possibly bear to think of not seeing you. It would be t-tearing the heart out of me. But I can't bear either, to think of us becoming — shady and sordid. Having to hide you. Having to lie. I w-want to hold you up to the world as mine. Not sneak into your b-bed like a rat. Always afraid some parishioner is going to notice my car p-parked here. Or ask why I walk so often down the lane these days . . .'

I thought of Gerald. Phone calls at 8.30 am or 6.15 pm. Sex neatly packaged with a bath (he kept his own brand of soap in my bathroom) inside the regulation three and a half hours it would have taken him to wine and dine a client. Never being able to telephone him at all outside office hours. Only being able to make strained, innocent conversation within office hours, in case his secretary picked up the extension.

'No,' I said slowly, 'extramarital sex can be a pretty foul business. Or do you prefer to call it adultery?'

'I d-don't call it any of those things,' he said passionately, his face creasing in distress. 'I call it love . . .'

And that breached the gulf between us, because I flung myself into his arms, and we clung to one another fiercely, as though defying anything to separate us. A stray fragment of the marriage ceremony was repeating in my head like a malign jingle . . . *let no man cast asunder. Those whom God has joined, let no man cast asunder, cast asunder* . . . I raged at this God for having joined Ned to someone else, for casting us asunder, and clutched Ned even more desperately.

'I'll have to go,' he said at last, raining soft kisses across my face, as if he was trying to memorise the shape.

I nodded, holding him tightly still.

'Have to d-dig the garage open,' he whispered.

'You can't. You can't be seen here. I'll have to do it.'

He gave an exclamation of disgust — and despair.

'Who knows?' I said with false brightness. 'She might leave you one day . . .'

Ned only shook his head with a kind of bitter resignation. 'I think – if you d-don't mind – I might arrange to go away for a few days. There's a retreat house up in Northumberland, run by monks. I think I need to . . .'

'Do penance?' I said. I couldn't help the brittleness. Without that I would have been wailing as ungovernably as a baby.

'How can I d-do penance? Penitence means regretting what I've done. How can I regret the happiest three days of my life? I'll never be able to regret it until the d-day I die.'

I hugged him tightly.

'Come to see me before you go. I couldn't bear us to part – melodramatically. Swearing we'll never speak to one another again. When you know you're going . . .'

'And what about you? Will you be all right?'

'Of course.' Resolutely, I pulled myself away from him and smiled. 'At least, I shall cry myself to sleep every night but suffering's supposed to be good for the artist and . . .'

'You won't be frightened on your own?'

I touched his cheek fondly. 'Ned – I've been living here alone for two and a half months.'

'But I know you were frightened by that stupid letter, my p-poor darling . . .'

I had forgotten all about the letter.

'Not any more,' I said. 'After all, surely it was only Elizabeth who wrote it. Do you want to see it? I realize now she isn't . . .'

'N-no,' said Ned. 'I d-don't think it was written by her. Not Elizabeth. But there's no cause for worry. I p-promise.'

I thought he was defending his wife – worse, I thought he was lying to me to defend her. How else could he be so certain there was nothing to fear from the writer of the letter?

I shovelled the snow from in front of the garage with vicious energy. And, as I watched the car twist and accelerate in grey clouds of exhaust smoke up the snowy hill, misery at losing him was laced with a sour aftertaste of jealousy.

CHAPTER TWENTY-FOUR

The snow lasted for a long time, strangely. There were still pockets of white, with snowdrops and aconites poking through, even by the time I left Yorkshire.

Although little more fell in the days that followed, that first brief thaw had been a freak. It unleashed the roads but by the afternoon the white landscape was freezing solidly again. I climbed up to the Wheatsheaf at lunchtime to retrieve my car, and called in to thank Albert for having cleared a path to it.

I suppose I might have been inclined to douse my miseries with alcohol anyway, but what made the need imperative was the arrival in the bar, immediately after my own, of Elizabeth Cowper.

I was quite irrationally amazed to encounter her. It was as though, in the course of that long conversation in the dark early hours, she had become fictionalized in my head. A character to be dissected, understood, pitied even, although her effect on my own life remained tangible enough. But it was a profound shock when the flesh and blood woman walked into the bar, stamping the snow from her boots, shaking out her headscarf – and greeted me as casually as though nothing had happened. In fact, the first thing she did was to apologize.

'I was rather rude to you at Christmas, wasn't I?' she said, smiling charmingly. 'My father always used to say I had a wicked temper. You must forgive me. Put it down to drink. And me completely misreading – certain situations. Anyway, it was all my pig of a brother's fault. I'm surprised Roger and I haven't murdered each other in the last three days, cooped up in the bloody snow Still,' and she gave a most extraordinary, secretive smile, 'I don't think the time was entirely wasted. Quite the contrary, in fact. How on earth did you manage down at the Lodge?'

I felt faint. 'Fine,' I said. 'Stoked up the fire and kept warm, really . . .'

'Was your man with you?'

I downed the rest of the whisky in one mouthful. 'Sebastian left for Scotland – nearly a fortnight ago.'

'Shame,' said Elizabeth calmly. 'Best way to keep warm – or so everyone says! No drink, thanks Albert. I just wanted a couple of packets of fags. Thank God, they're clearing the roads. I can't wait to get into York, but Ned's insisting I take the Range Rover unless the snow melts quicker, and bloody Roger won't lend it to me until next week. Nice to see you, Frankie. You really must come round some time. Bye.'

Albert poured another whisky for me without my asking.

'I don't know what's got into her ladyship,' he said thoughtfully. 'She reminds me of a cat outside a mousehole.'

I finished my painting of Ned. It wasn't quite life-sized, but it was pretty damned enormous. It could never be exhibited, of course. Even in far-off London, there was always the chance someone who knew him might see it, and he was perfectly recognizable. Moreover, the whole scene reeked of sex. I amused myself by visualizing him hung in a gallery. With a simple, enigmatic, rather modern title like VICAR I.

It was the only picture I was unequivocally convinced was good. I would never have considered selling it anyway. If I could not live with the real thing, I was not going to be deprived of living with his image. In the meantime, however, as soon as the bulk of the work was done, I hid the board away behind my giant blue folder. Even so, the feet stuck out at one end. Not only was I wary of anyone else catching sight of the picture which would be disastrous enough – Mr Danby had nearly surprised me working at it one morning – but I could hardly bear to look at it myself. I was irritatingly inclined to burst into tears at the least little thing. In fact, I began to wonder whether I was succumbing to the prevalent flu bug because I felt miserably wan and bilious.

Resting was impossible, however. That only expanded the

opportunities for thinking. I painted on. I was totally un-prepared for Gerald's arrival.

It was about ten days after the main snowfalls. I looked out of the window to discover who was beating such an imperious tattoo on the front door — and saw the unmistakable snub-nose of a dark green Porsche. Gerald was standing on the doorstep on tiptoe, trying vainly to protect his glossy loafers from the tide of slush. When I knocked on the window, pointing him round to the back of the house, shouting that this door could not be opened, he gazed at the sodden path in horror.

He gazed at me in something close to horror too. I was dressed in the ugliest and best-beloved of my painting clothes. A sagging black sweater knitted on telegraph poles from a thick velvety wool which absorbed splashes of paint with generous discretion. Leggings so baggy they were comforting as pyjamas. My hair was unwashed and I couldn't even remember where my make-up bag was.

'But I told you I was coming,' he said, following me into the sitting-room and looking distastefully round at the chaos. 'Dates, times, I confirmed everything.'

'I forgot,' I said. 'I intended to check it all when you rang again. But you didn't ring . . .'

'I've been half way round the world since Christmas, babe. I told you I couldn't telephone. Jesus, what a place to find . . .'

'Beautiful though, isn't it?'

Gerald peered out of the window. He did not look impressed. I suppose no landscape looks its best when stranded in the piebald limbo between snow and thaw, when the drifts are spattered with black and the tall grass is beginning to point scraggily through half-melted holes.

'Tell you what,' he said suddenly. 'How about you pack a bag and we go and book a big and wonderful hotel suite in Scarborough for the night? How far is it — twenty, thirty miles? No . . .' he said, holding up one finger. 'No objections. My treat. Bubbles all the way. I've got something to celebrate. I'm going to be a father again . . .'

I gaped at him. Before I could find words the telephone rang and I picked it up.

'Frankie?'

'Ned! Oh, Ned . . .'

Ned had managed to telephone me just once in the last ten days. When Elizabeth was out riding. But even when she was out there was Beverley. And the daily woman, and his constant stream of parish meetings . . .

'L-look, I just wanted to check you were there. I'm driving up to Northumberland this afternoon. Elizabeth's gone to York. I thought I could come d-down quickly . . .'

'Now?'

'Is s-something the matter? You're not alone?'

'No. Look, could you make it in, say, a couple of hours?'

Gerald looked up at me and frowned.

'Oh, d-darling, I've got to leave by then. They're expecting me by six. I just had an hour free now.'

'Never mind,' I said, 'I'm − sure I'll see you when you get back. How long are you going for?'

'Only a few days. I d-don't think I should telephone you from there.'

'Hardly. Negate the object of the exercise really, wouldn't it? Well − take best care.'

Iloveyouiloveyouiloveyouiloveyou, I was thinking fiercely, but I could not say it with Gerald in the room. Not for Gerald's sake − I didn't give a stuff about hurting him. It was for my own. I didn't want Gerald to know about Ned. Gerald would soil everything. He would automatically reduce the shining and precious bond between Ned and me to another grubby little extramarital coupling like his and mine had been.

'I love you,' said Ned softly.

'− You too,' I whispered, even more quietly and put the phone down.

'What was all that about?' said Gerald. He was perched delicately, one buttock barely touching the corner of my table, afraid of blemishing his pale beige trousers. He was dressed as in magazine photographs of The Country Weekend: slacks which would offer no resistance to the feeblest bramble, a too-thin pullover, and a heavy tweed and leather jacket which was clearly too expensive to be exposed to any weather other than the most clement.

'A friend,' I said.

'Well? Are you packing?'

'No,' I said. 'And do you know what I think you ought to do with the money that hotel suite would have cost you?'

'Babe?'

'I think you should spend it on your poor bloody wife.'

'Ah, *that's* it,' said Gerald, smiling and shaking his head. 'Sorry, I never thought it would affect you like that. Of course you feel a bit shocked that Helen is preggers again. But you should know by now that you and she play entirely different rôles in my life —'

'Dead right,' I said, interrupting without compunction. 'And mine has just ended. In fact it ended months ago, and I didn't even notice.'

'*Frances?* What the hell's got into you?'

'Sense. And seeing other people behave like decent caring human beings, instead of self-obsessed, single-minded, egotistical grasping bastards.'

'You can't be talking about me?'

'I couldn't be talking about anyone else. I haven't done many truly wicked things in my life, I don't think. But permitting you to indulge in your sleazy games, to lavish money and time on me while your wife battled with babies and the house and loneliness ... All I can say is that I'm deeply, deeply ashamed. It'd serve you right if she left you, Gerald. If she has any sense she probably will.'

'I think the isolation has affected your brain, Frances,' said Gerald stiffly. 'Shall we go?'

'We?' I shrieked. 'We? Don't you understand, there is no *we*? You're going. I'm staying.'

If I hadn't been so angry, the dismay on Gerald's handsome sun-tanned face would have made me laugh.

'What am I to do? I've arranged everything so that no one knows where I am. I can't join the crew in Newcastle. I can't go home ...'

'Try a little solitary soul-searching,' I said. 'Join the club.'

Gerald did leave eventually. I could hardly refuse him a hot drink. The man had driven from London. As soon as he

205

walked out of the kitchen door, however – I didn't even wait for the car to roar away – I telephoned Ned. And Elizabeth answered.

I floundered. Ironically, she sounded pleased to hear from me.

'I'm on my own again. Ned's left for a bloody monastery this time. What can I do you for?'

I was unprepared. I had thought of no lies. 'I, er . . .' and suddenly I was inspired. 'Ned seems to have left a scarf here.' Gerald had reminded me of it as a matter of fact. As he left he had been visibly snuffling around for evidence of Another Man. Little did he know, he had found it – but he assumed the scarf was mine and, for once, approved my taste. The label was *very* Gerald. 'He must have forgotten it that night you all came round. When I was so foolishly scared . . .'

'We were all behaving pretty foolishly that night,' said Elizabeth acidly, 'me more than most. I'll tell him when he gets –' She broke off and said wonderingly, 'Not a blue scarf?'

'Yes,' I said uncertainly. It was hanging on a hook beside the kitchen cupboard still. Where I had tucked it away on the first day of the snow.

Elizabeth gave her tinkling laugh.

'Cashmere?' she said incredulously.

'I . . . yes, I think it probably is.'

'How extraordinary,' she said, laughing as though I'd just imparted the most marvellous joke. 'How absolutely amazing. But how careless of my absurd husband. That's my scarf, as a matter of fact.'

'Really?'

Why did she make me feel so uneasy?

'I told him time and again not to borrow it. Well, this will teach him a lesson, won't it? Thank you, Frankie. Thanks so much. Sweet of you to telephone. Bye now.'

And she rang off. She had never spoken to me so affectionately. It was as though I were her dearest friend.

CHAPTER TWENTY-FIVE

I woke up the next morning *knowing* two things I could not possibly have known.

At least I could have offered no tangible evidence for either of the dismaying convictions which gripped me. I am not claiming clairvoyance. Not that I actually *dis*-believe in that kind of thing. I dare say I'm as open minded as anyone else, but only in so far as other people are concerned, not when it comes to ordinary earthbound me. I had come to terms years before with the disappointment that my own senses stopped short at the conventional five.

Nonetheless, I really did wake up with a sick sense of dread that something terrible was going to happen that day. It hardly proves clairvoyance though, because I had not the least notion at all of the nature of the events in store. The worst I feared was our affair being discovered somehow or other by Elizabeth. It sounds pitiable in retrospect. And I was too preoccupied with my other fearful certainty to speculate how this might come about.

I could never, never have anticipated what actually did occur. I've asked myself a hundred times since — if I had anticipated it, could I have done anything about it? Of course, other people have asked me too: policemen, lawyers, the coroner — could I have done anything to avert the tragedy? But questions of that nature are meaningless. All they offer is anguish, never reassurance. Because with the wisdom of hindsight it is easy to persuade oneself that almost anything could have been averted.

Anyway, I was unsurprised when Elizabeth Cowper appeared outside my kitchen door. Dismayed, yes, but it was as though I had been frittering away the morning with trivial household chores, diversions for restless hands and mind – simply because I had been waiting for her. The blue scarf hanging from a hook in the corner had been shouting my folly at me ever since I put the telephone down the previous day.

Of all prosaic activities, I was heating a cup of milk when she arrived. It was just after noon. I had been unable to eat breakfast, or indeed supper the previous night, and was beginning to fuss over my lack of energy. This morning I had felt so listless I could barely summon the will to get out of bed. Only Victorian maidens, I told myself irritatedly, pined away of broken hearts. I remember I was dithering over whether or not to add a spoonful of honey to the pan. The nursery smell drifting up from the warm liquid was revolting.

'May I come in?' called Elizabeth, and then with a giggle, '"Or I'll huff and I'll puff and I'll blow your house down . . ."' No one could look less like a wolf than Elizabeth Cowper. Vulnerable as a baby chicken in a downy yellow mohair pullover, she beamed as she walked in, shaking her fingers through windblown black hair and apologising for the mud on her wellingtons.

'Had to walk,' she added breathlessly. 'Ned's taken our car off north, and Roger – well, I don't think Roger was in any mood to lend me cars when we parted. Ah yes, that's the scarf.'

She picked it off the hook and hung it round her neck. Then she pulled a face at the combination of colours and took it off again. She seated herself comfortably on one of the kitchen chairs and looked up at me, bright-eyed and mischievous.

'*I know, you know . . .*' she droned with sonorous, doom-laden theatricality, and then giggled.

'Know what?'

'Don't be stupid, Frankie. You and Ned. He was here, wasn't he? During the snow.' She shook her head, apparently marvelling at the idea.

'Is it me you should be talking to about this?' I said quickly. 'Surely, this is a matter for you and Ned . . .'

She burst into laughter. Real, genuinely amused laughter. 'Do you honestly think I should go to St Aiden's and confront the poor fool with my grounds for divorce under the interested eyes of the monks?'

Behind me the milk boiled over.

'How wonderfully poetic,' said Elizabeth. 'Is it in *Cold Comfort Farm* that the porridge boils over every time there's a crisis? You might have been timing it for me.'

'I don't know what to say.'

'Oh, come on. You might start with, "Sorry for borrowing your husband." Or something along those lines. And then I would reply magnanimously, "Not at all, my dear, feel free. He's been bugger-all use to me . . ."'

I turned to wipe up the scorched mess of milk. Outside the sky was darkening.

'That's quite poetic too, isn't it?' said Elizabeth, glancing out of the window. 'Storm clouds lowering. I hope it doesn't turn to rain yet, though. I've walked down here without a coat. Do you mind if I smoke?'

I dumped pan and cloth in the sink, and lowered myself into the chair opposite hers.

'It's all over, you know,' I said, abandoning a half-formed cowardly scheme of refusing to admit anything. Of leaving the battle to be fought between husband and wife. 'He won't leave you. But, Ned himself can tell you . . .'

'Won't leave me?' and she gave an exclamation of contempt. 'Well, *do* go on . . .'

'What do you want me to say? There isn't a great deal I can add, except I'm sorry. And I can't even say that and mean it entirely wholeheartedly.'

'Good. Honesty. Keep going.'

'Keep going? I can't . . . This is completely mad. Sitting down at my kitchen table to talk about – such a thing. With you. It's soap opera – not real life.'

'Isn't it just? You're absolutely right. But, forgive me, you ought to be better dressed for a soap. I'm sorry, was I interrupting you working?' She glanced around the kitchen. 'Do you know I could see Edward being quite happy in a twee little cottage like this. I'd never thought about it before, but I dare say he'd be happy as a sandboy, pottering round the kitchen and the garden. As long as there was room for his damned piano. He hates my beautiful Dower House, you know . . .'

'Does he? No, I didn't.'

'You mean you didn't lie in bed talking about me?' For the first time there was an acid edge to her voice. Her cigarette was poised in her fingers, unlit. She waved it towards me enquiringly.

'Please, do smoke,' I said faintly — astonished that the ordinary rituals of courtesy still held sway under these extraordinary circumstances. It would seem more understandable for her to be wanting to stub her cigarette out on me, than to be waiting, uncomplainingly, for my permission to light it. 'There's an ashtray somewhere in here. I found it for Suzy . . .'

'Ah, Suzanna,' exclaimed Elizabeth. 'Suzy knew, didn't she?'

'I don't know,' I said. 'For heaven's sake, there wasn't anything she could have known. Not when she was up here. I certainly didn't tell her anything.'

'Oh, Suzy's clairvoyant when it comes to juicy gossip. She can divine it before it happens . . . I wondered why she was looking so pleased with herself. Mean cow.'

'She — didn't tell you?'

Elizabeth shook her head. 'She was cross with me. She'll get over it.'

'So how did you know?'

'My dear — the most extraordinary coincidence . . .' She could have been telling me about a new dress shop. The surreality of the conversation was making my head spin. 'I — just happened to be visiting Michael Porrit, you know the old queen from St Catherine's? He's staying in York.'

'So I gathered . . .'

She laughed merrily again. 'Well, of course you would, wouldn't you? Anyway, quite by chance he mentioned that he hadn't seen Ned at all in weeks. And I said, that's odd, because Ned was in York for three days, stranded by the snow. Well, the old boy was fearfully upset. "But he rang me," he said, "to say he couldn't get out of the valley . . ." Nearly in tears Michael was. So I told him I'd probably made a mistake, and that Ned had been stranded somewhere else. I could tell he didn't believe me. But you know . . .' She paused to take a drag from her cigarette, 'I still didn't suspect a thing. I automatically

210

assumed Ned had been in York all right, but hadn't been able to face visiting Michael because he got too enthralled in his libraries or whatever. I didn't blame him. Michael Porrit is the biggest bore for miles around, and now he can't stop bursting into tears every other word. Frightful . . .'

She smoked like a novice, I noticed, pursing her lips too tight and shifting the position of the cigarette between her fingers, uncertainly.

'Anyway, no, I didn't suspect a thing. Until you, my dear, told me about the scarf. It so happened I had watched him tie it round his neck that very day. And later I'd had plenty of cause to remember because it was damned cold walking over to the Manor and that's by far the warmest scarf I own . . .'

She squeezed the soft fleece affectionately as it lay across her lap.

'As soon as Ned returned after his . . . little absence, I taxed him about it. And he coloured up like the great bumbler he is, and told me he must have left it in his hotel. I thought it was just embarrassment at having lost my scarf. But then yesterday you rang, and I realized my husband, George Washington incarnate, had actually told a fib about the scarf. Well, then it was obvious.'

I watched and listened incredulously. Inevitably, I had imagined this scene over the past ten days. Visualized Elizabeth confronting me, screaming at me – even, for God's sake, threatening me with a gun. I had never in a million years anticipated she would be sitting in my kitchen laughing, as though at a splendid joke.

All at once, after the misery of the last ten days and the irrational terrors of the morning, I was filled with crazy, disbelieving hope. Out of nowhere, there seemed to be the unlikeliest and most perfect of outcomes promising.

It was a struggle to make myself speak composedly. 'You sound – as though you actually don't care.'

And, incredibly, she shrugged. 'Why should I care? Oh, one feels a certain pique, when one's husband finds consolation in another bed. In fact, I might have been absolutely bloody furious. But under the circumstances, well, it couldn't be more fortuitous.'

I hardly dared frame the question. 'So, you wouldn't . . . You might even – be prepared to divorce him?'

'The Lord Chancellor himself couldn't stop me. I must say I'm rather surprised in you, though.'

'What do you mean?'

'I can only suppose from that anxious question that you're actually planning to marry him. And, really, I wouldn't have thought you were any more of a vicar's wife than me. It's a dead bore, my dear, I warn you.'

I flushed. It seemed indecent to be discussing the desirability of my marrying Ned with his wife.

'If you really feel like this,' I said, 'why haven't you left Ned before?'

'Ah,' said Elizabeth, stubbing out her cigarette, 'I had my reasons . . .' And then she fell to studying the blue scarf, counting the woollen tassels between her fingers.

I couldn't do anything. Mesmerised as a mouse between the paws of a cat. A scraggy street-smart rat maybe, confronted only with a purring fluffy kitten half my size, but I was still unable to act. I could only react.

'Roger,' she said suddenly, looking up. 'It was all Roger's fault. He wouldn't let me leave Ned.'

Was she telling the truth? There had been that kind of speculative hesitancy in her voice which suggests a story being spun even as it is relayed.

'How could he stop you?'

'By cutting off my allowance, of course,' she spoke with quick certainty now. 'All Daddy left me directly was the Dower House, you know. Roger gives me enough to ensure I can live in it − and just about survive. From the first, when I realised my marriage might have been something of a mistake, he made it quite clear. If I walked out on Ned, that was it.'

'You stayed with Ned − for money?'

'Don't be priggish. How else was I supposed to live? I'm not good at anything worth doing, and I'd rather not end up serving bacon in the Co-op, thank you.'

'You could have married someone else . . .'

For the first and only time, I glimpsed distress behind the perfect china doll features.

'I don't think I have much talent for marriage. Anyway,' she looked up defiantly, 'you've made it easy for me now. I told

Roger about your little honeymoon in the snow and he was furious. My God, I don't think even *I* have ever seen my brother so angry. He could hardly object to my leaving Ned now — as I told him.' She added with frankly malicious pleasure, 'I should keep out of Roger's way if I were you for the next few days.'

She stood up and walked to the window to survey the weather. 'Mind you, he was one step ahead of me. He *had* suspected there might be a bit of hanky-panky going on. Probably Suzy tipped him off. Clever old Suzy. Several steps ahead of me.'

I stared at her serene, smiling face incredulously.

'But you . . . You *really* didn't suspect anything?'

'Why should I? I thought Ned was in serious training for canonization.'

'But the letter?' I protested. 'My car keys?'

She turned to look at me, her face betraying only polite enquiry.

'I don't understand . . .' I said.

'I may have been rather rude to you,' she said. 'I've apologized once already. I was naïve enough to think you were actually aiming to marry my brother. And, I didn't think that was a good idea. Oh hell, is that rain?'

I joined her at the window. 'Sleet . . .'

'I'm borrowing Roger's tank this afternoon whatever he says. I want to go and see my solicitor.' She smiled with satisfaction. 'Maybe one more cigarette while I see if the weather clears up, then I'll leave you to your painting. How long will you stay? Do you want to escape while the going's good?'

'I'm sorry, I don't think I quite follow you . . .'

She sat down again, lit a cigarette. 'Before the scandal rocks our narrow little world.'

'You mean, your leaving Ned? Will that be such a scandal?'

'It will be when news leaks out I'm suing him for adultery. Lucky old you. I've always thought it must be rather glamourous to be cited as co-respondent.'

'Adultery? What on earth for? You don't have to prove wrongs in a marriage breakdown these days, you know. If both partners are in agreement, surely all you have to do is separate for a certain length of time and . . .?

'I know all that. But no one's going to deprive me of my fun.'

'Fun? You'd consider it fun?'

'I think it might get quite widely reported. In the national press even. The tabloids seem to have an inexhaustible appetite for the sins of the clergy. It'd be a wonderful joke if I got my picture in the *Sun*, wouldn't it?'

'But what about Ned?'

'Ah yes, poor old Ned. He'll hate every minute of it, of course. But it serves him right. He won't deny it, will he? Dear truthful Ned . . .'

'I can't understand why you want to subject him to all that. Me, maybe − anyway it doesn't matter to me. But him?'

'I'm sick of everyone pitying saintly, sweet-natured Reverend Cowper, burdened with his foul-tempered, crazy wife. This area is *my* home, not Ned's. I think I deserve the balance of sympathy swinging back to me a bit. And I intend to get it. I shall play the wronged wife to the hilt. A little black suit, with a Bette Davis veil. And it will drive my brother insane with rage . . .'

She giggled as she stubbed out her cigarette and stood up. 'Don't take it personally. I've nothing against you. For what it's worth, I wish you every happiness. I say, it's still raining. Can I borrow your mac?'

CHAPTER TWENTY-SIX

Even now, I can't paint that particular shade of blue. I wonder whether I ever will. Whenever my palette knife begins to blend anything even close to that subtle tint – a soft sky colour, a little darker than Wedgwood – I begin to shake. I can't help it. I'm automatically seeing the blue splashed and saturated with glorious shining sticky scarlet.

Elizabeth Cowper wound the scarf over her head, carefully tucking in stray strands of hair, and shrugged herself into my mackintosh, which was absurdly big on her tiny frame. This made her laugh even more merrily.

It's unreal, I kept thinking. This woman has accused me of sleeping with her husband, she intends to cite me as co-respondent in the divorce, and she's laughing and walking off in my ancient mac as though we're the best of friends.

I suppose I said goodbye – all the usual things. I could barely make sense of my thoughts. Ned would be free. But the scandal. Oh God, Elizabeth didn't guess the half of the potential scandal . . .

I remember, as soon as the door closed I jumped to my feet and ran through to the sitting-room. Directory Enquiries. I was going to telephone Ned at this monastery place. He ought to be here, not examining his conscience in glorious isolation. I think I registered the sound of a car engine, but I was too intent on racking my brains for the name of the monastery to pay attention. Then I heard the shot.

It wasn't terribly loud but it was shockingly final. Just one shot. For a moment I couldn't bring myself to stand up. Like a child putting her hands over her face. Pretending that, because she can't see, nothing has happened.

I made myself walk to the window overlooking the road. Elizabeth was lying in the path. And her head, swathed in the blue cashmere scarf, was almost entirely blown away. Her tiny pearly-nailed hand was splayed like a little starfish on the muddy flowerbed, shockingly unblemished. Beside her was a clump of shining yellow aconites. I heard a click. Roger, standing by the Range Rover, was reloading his gun. He had not seen me.

I jumped away from the window. I had begun to retch violently, but in that instant terror took over from every other emotion, literally paralysed every muscle.

He's going to kill me! The words screamed in my head. Even though the physical world seemed to have slowed to the clumsy lumbering of underwater ballet, my brain was hurtling along. *Roger's going to kill me.* I realized then with terrifying clarity that he had intended to kill *me* just now, when he shot her. Elizabeth as good as warned me herself. Told me to avoid him. Then she walked out of *my* house, in *my* coat, her head wrapped in a scarf. Her head, oh, dear God . . .' The horror of that image shocked me back into action.

I could hear Roger's footsteps on the path.

'Frankie?' he was calling. 'Frankie . . .?'

The telephone was no good. By the time I picked up the receiver he would be looking through the window. Poking his gun through the window. I ran like a mad thing through the room, sending a chair flying, to the stairs. Bolted the door on the staircase behind me. Then pressed myself against the wall listening. Silence. Then a bang – the kitchen door slamming back against the edge of the sink.

'Frankie. Oh God, where are you?'

He was inside the house. I hadn't locked the door after Elizabeth. How long could I last out up here, I wondered? Roger was a strong man. He could probably break down the staircase door without too much trouble. What were the chances of anyone passing along the lane in the meantime? Non-existent. Could I climb out of the window? Get to my car before he heard me? Even as these ideas pelted through my head, I rejected them angrily. The stuff of motion pictures, not real life.

'Oh, Frankie, for Christ's sake. You must be here somewhere . . .'

Then I heard him rattling the door at the foot of the stairs. 'Are you up there? What are you doing? I want to talk to you, Frankie . . .'

'Please . . .' I began. My voice sounded foreign to me, like the voice of a very old woman. Shrill and quavering. I couldn't lower it, couldn't control it. 'Please, Roger, don't . . .'

'You *are* there. Don't what?'

'Don't . . . kill me.'

'Kill you, Frankie? Why in God's name would I kill *you*?'

He was rattling the door again.

'Because of us – me and Ned.'

The rattling stopped. Roger gave a bitter cry of pain.

'Kill you for loving Ned?' he shouted. 'How could I blame anyone for that?' Suddenly I could hear the tears in his voice. 'I've loved Ned all my life.'

He was standing by the sink when I opened the door. 'Look,' he said with a tremulous smile. 'No gun. Over in the corner.'

'But you loaded it again.'

'Of course I loaded it – don't be a fool. Do me a favour. Give me a brandy, a big one. If you've got it – whisky, anything otherwise. Last request. Those of us about to die . . .'

'Die?'

'For pity's sake, woman . . . I need a drink. So do you by the look of you.' He picked up the chair I had knocked over and made me sit down. 'In here?' he said, opening the top cupboard.

I nodded.

The smell of the brandy made me retch. Roger downed his and immediately refilled his glass.

'Suicides always leave letters,' he said. 'I tried and I couldn't. I'm telling you instead . . .'

'Roger, it's not suicide. You shot Elizabeth,' I said stupidly. 'Killed her . . .'

'Of course, I shot her. She deserved it. She asked for it.'

'Oh Jesus,' I said softly. 'Sweet Jesus . . .' My voice was

rising – I heard it as though it was coming from another person entirely, and I could feel a tidal wave of tears bubbling up inside me. It was as though someone else was controlling my mouth, my limbs – as though my body had nothing to do with me. Different objects in the room were oozing in and out of focus, disconnected as stray pieces in a jigsaw . . .

'No,' said Roger harshly, and shoved the glass of whisky roughly against my mouth. 'You mustn't lose control, mustn't Frankie. I need to talk to you.'

I retched again, but swallowed the spirit and the kitchen slowly settled back into focus. 'I'm all right,' I said. 'Tell me . . . tell me why you've . . .' but even now, I could not complete the sentence, putting into words what he had done. I looked at my hands. I was surprised to see that they weren't shaking. The trembling was all inside.

'I've always loved Ned,' said Roger. 'Ever since I was a boy. Long before I knew there was – anything wrong in that . . .'

'Roger? Are – are you telling me . . .' In the nerveless, unreal limbo which follows shock, nothing can surprise – I was just sure that my numbed brain must have misheard, misunderstood in some way. 'You can't mean that you're . . .'

'Queer? Or, to use your term, gay?' He spat the word at me. 'Bloody stupid euphemism. Try telling me what's gay about it. It's misery, sheer unadulterated misery. No, don't argue. I don't want to hear any liberal claptrap. Just *listen* . . .'

He was still leaning against the sink. Sitting at the kitchen table, I was between him and the gun. He glanced at it now, propped up in the corner and it seemed to reassure him.

'My father was a fiend. He despised me, hated the sight of me – and he was a sadist. He used his whip on anything that moved and he enjoyed it. My mother ran off with her gigolo when I was thirteen. I'm not offering mealy-mouthed excuses, I'm just telling you the facts. If I'd been brought up on a council estate, bloody social workers would have had a field day with me. But I am *not* asking for sympathy . . .

'In the whole of my rotten childhood, Ned was the only person who was ever really nice to me. Oh, school was all right. I was the only boy there who cried at the end of term, not the beginning. Some of the people round here were all

218

right too. But they were all scared stiff of the old man. Not Ned. He actually stuck up for me . . .'

'But your sister – she suffered too, didn't she?'

'Bess was thick as thieves with Father. She could twist him round her finger. Don't interrupt, Frankie. I want to tell you now. Get it over and done with. Anyway I – I loved Ned. I always did. So yes, of course, I moved heaven and earth to get him here. I knew he would never . . . but, I didn't care. I just wanted him here, close to me. Permanently. It was the answer to my prayers when Bess fell for him. I had a terrible job shovelling the incumbent vicar of St Peter's into early retirement, but I managed it.'

He glanced at me sourly. 'Know what the locals said at the time? "Chip off the old block. High-handed as his father." They said it admiringly too. Christ.' He drained his glass.

'And after all that, two months later, Bess comes up and tells me she doesn't like being married after all. That it wasn't all it was cracked up to be. I'm surprised I didn't strangle her then . . .'

'Can you really blame her, Roger? Marriages break up all the time, and with your sister's problems –'

'Shut up, Frankie. This is my story. My sister was a selfish, neurotic bitch. And I knew if the marriage foundered, Ned would be off, at once. I might never seen him again. So I offered Bess an allowance. Christ, she was the luckiest woman on earth. How can you argue? She was actually being paid just to stay with a man like Ned . . .'

He smiled faintly. 'It's ruined me in the end. More or less anyway. Even with the money from my mother's family – Ned won't get much.'

'Ned?'

'I'm leaving everything to him. Besides, he's next of kin, or as near as makes no difference. I only wish there was more. But the taxman will mop up most of what's left. The divorce cost me a packet, of course . . .'

'Why did you get married, Roger, if you knew you were . . .' I stopped myself saying gay, '. . . not interested in women?'

'Precisely because I *was* homosexual, of course. To hide it – I was doing my damnedest to fight it. But I couldn't I would look at Caro, waiting in bed for me, and feel sick.' He held up his glass. This was the only way I could face it – and look at me now ...' The light glimmered in the bronze liquid as his hand trembled, and he slammed the glass down on the draining board.

'But all the other women?'

'What other women? People have always been ready to believe stories about me just because the old man was such a satyr. I encouraged them, that's all.'

'And ... me?'

'Ah, you, Frankie. I wanted to try again. Desperately and ...' he laughed bitterly, '... you looked so much like a boy. You didn't have Caro's horrible flabby curves. I thought maybe this time ... Can I have more brandy?'

I poured more into his glass. Outside the sleet thickened into a blizzard of splintered ice. Outside, Elizabeth Cowper's body was splayed dead on the path.

'Pursuing you began as a joke really. It was for you too, wasn't it? And for me it all added to the smoke screen. Randy old Roger. But you were such fun, so ... Well, I'd actually summoned up the courage to tell you. Everything. You remember that night when you – poor child – were frightened, because you saw me outside?'

I nodded.

'I thought – after everything you'd said about open relationships, about gay men, if you must use that word, I thought maybe you would understand ...' He took another swig of brandy and turned to stare out of the window.

'I was going to suggest a kind of marriage where each of us went our own way. I even thought you might accept just so you could stay near Ned too, if what Suzy had hinted was true.' He glanced over his shoulder at me, grimacing. 'Ludicrous, I know. As if being neighbours is some kind of substitute for ... That kind of half loaf is worse than no bread at all. I should bloody know. Anyway, I walked down here – and then didn't have the courage to come in. All I succeeded in doing was scaring you to death. I'm sorry about that letter too. It was cheap ...'

'The anonymous letter? *You* wrote that?'

Roger turned back to face me. 'When Suzy told me she thought there was something going on between you and Ned, I was angry. Jealous I suppose – but really I was terrified that if Ned fell for you he would leave. As soon as I thought about it sanely, I realized Ned wasn't the type to walk out on his marriage. If he had been, he'd have done it long since with Elizabeth's behaviour. But it was too late by then. I'd sent the filthy thing. I think Ned guessed. There was a rather messy episode at school he probably remembered – and he made me apologise to you. He sounded . . .'

'My car keys,' I said suddenly. 'Not you as well?'

Roger looked up blank-faced, then nodded impatiently.

'Oh, that was nothing. A stupid drunken party trick. I'd have told you if you'd asked. I just wanted to keep you there for another drink. And Ned, of course. But you went sneaking off together on foot . . .'

'I thought all that was Elizabeth's doing. The letter, the missing keys . . .'

'And Bess thought you'd hidden your own keys. Can you imagine it? She thought it was an excuse to stay overnight. She suspected you really did have designs on me, or rather, on the Manor. She at least knew me well enough to see I meant it when I said I wanted to marry you. Everybody else laughed – but she was petrified you might say yes, and spoil all her plans. God, she's a bitch – was a bitch . . . She intended to ruin Ned, did you know that? Drag the whole thing through the divorce courts with maximum publicity.' His eyes were clouded with alcohol now, although his speech was unslurred.

'Is that why you did it?' I said. 'Killed her just because she was going to kick up a bit of scandal about Ned? Surely you don't think he could have wanted . . . Oh, my God.'

Roger sneered at me. 'You don't understand,' he said. 'You just don't understand my sister at all, do you? She has spent the last seven years making Ned's life a living hell. She humiliated him, took advantage of him. Everything he liked, she tried to take away from him.' He was talking faster and faster. 'His career, his piano, his respect in the neighbourhood . . .'

'But Roger – Ned told me. After everything Elizabeth had been through as a child . . .'

221

'Everything?' shouted Roger. 'We had the same father, you know. We both got beaten. Bess just got some affection afterwards. Which was more than I bloody did. Father never did her any real physical harm. So it gave her a few funny ideas about sex – I've got a few funny ideas about sex too, and they've got nothing to do with my father. Sex isn't the whole of life. It doesn't excuse what she did. My sister was a spoilt child who grew into a spoilt adult – but she was not mad. She knew exactly what she was doing. No one ever understood her own problems better than my sister. She spent thousands of pounds of my money charting them in intimate detail.'

He glared at me blearily, willing me to agree.

'And did she ever make one single move towards Ned? Ever make one tiny effort to make his life easier? He, poor innocent fool, didn't believe in anyone being plain bad. She must be mentally disturbed, he said. He went on believing kindness would cure everything. I tried to tell him. A million times. He would never listen.'

Roger leaned towards me, seized my hand, gripped it painfully. 'Remember the family motto? My sister knew full well there was a better way she should take. She bloody well deliberately chose not to. She used Ned like a whipping boy.'

'But Roger – it's not, it can't be, a reason to *kill* . . .'

'I didn't kill her because of that – although I'd argue it was every reason to kill her. She deserved to be put down, like a vicious dog. No, I had to kill her because she was going to expose me. My sister had turned her hand to blackmail. That selfsame night, when I was pacing up and down outside here, plucking up courage to come and confess all to you, do you know what Elizabeth was doing. Do you?'

He stared at me, waiting insistently for a response before continuing. I shook my head.

'She was following me. Looking for evidence. She must have been absolutely furious to discover you were the only person I was going out to meet. She was unlucky. I do use the back lane when I want to slip out of the village discreetly. Just like the old man used to, and probably twenty generations of Vaiseys have. But not on foot. In the Range Rover. That's why I bought the bloody tank in the first place. Who the hell she thought I might be *walking* out to meet is anybody's guess. One of the local farmers? Stupid bitch . . .'

He released my hand to take another swig of brandy.

'And then there was the snow. And, like the good brother I occasionally tried to be, I brought my sister over to the Manor. To share my fires, and my booze. She rewarded me by searching my room, where she found a small, but significant sheaf of press cuttings . . .'

Roger smiled brilliantly, rocked to and fro on his chair.

'Then she borrowed my motor – mark that – *my* Range Rover, and drove to York. There she searched out Michael Porrit and bullied the half-doped old fool into admitting that yes, he had recognized the man escaping through the window of that goddamned piss house. How the fuck was I to guess that the vicar from one of my own livings would be in the next stall, in that nest of desperate queens?

'Whereupon, my sister came to me and said that unless I let her divorce Ned – and doubled her allowance – she would expose me to the world.'

Roger drained his glass and stood up.

'That's why I shot her.'

CHAPTER TWENTY-SEVEN

. . . *And so, my darling Ned, I don't think there's anything more I can add.*

You could have overpowered him, stopped him. I couldn't. It was awful, terrible. I know he was a murderer — I think by the end he was mad. I certainly told the police he was mad. I shall tell the coroner the same. Maybe they won't say it was suicide then. Maybe they'll say something about the balance of his mind being disturbed. But I couldn't stop him. I'm not even sure I would have wanted to.

He kissed me goodbye. And said to give his love — all his love — to you.

My poor Ned. What appalling tragedies you've had to face. I wish I could think of something to write to comfort you. And I know it must seem that my desertion is the final blow, cruel beyond words. But it's the only possible course, you must see that. We couldn't be together, not now, not with all these horrible journalists crawling everywhere. They've already tracked me down here. I've taken the phone off the hook.

Even after the whole thing eventually blows over, if I came back to Thornbeck and we spent so much as an hour together, the whole village would know, wouldn't they? You said yourself there's no escaping the watchful eyes. Things are ghastly enough already without the affair between you and me entering the public domain.

So I've come back to London. I couldn't have stayed another night, not alone. The police actually saw me across the Pennines to my mother's yesterday. Now I'm home in Clapham. I shall have to come north again for the inquest, of course, I've already been told that. Chief witness. I know you'll be there.

Let's not meet . . .

I had to stop writing temporarily. A tear had splashed on the first line of this new page and swirled into a betraying inky puddle. I took a fresh sheet and picked up again.

I suggest it's better we don't meet.
Elizabeth actually said to me that I seemed no more cut out to be a vicar's wife than she was. I'm awfully afraid she was right. You've got to piece your life together again, somehow. Now, at just the time when I realize you might need me most desperately, I absolutely cannot be with you. The potential for scandal is just too horrendous, isn't it? And then later, when the need will be less, I'm afraid you might actually be better off without me.

Would he believe this? Accept it? Exit Frankie Cleverdon, asking the bear not to pursue her . . .

So please, let's just part friends. I almost didn't put my address at the top of this letter — but that would be silly because you could find it out easily enough. I just ask you not to try and see me, not to telephone. If we are going to part, better to do it now than to create fresh bleeding wounds later.
I shall have my work cut out picking up the threads here again — and finishing the pictures for the exhibition.
I shall never forget you . . .

But I couldn't write any more. The tears were cascading down my face in a hot choking waterfall. I scrawled my name. Stuck the sheaf of paper in an envelope and ran outside to post it before I weakened.

For once I was choosing the better way. And it may have been a far, far better thing I was doing now etcetera, etcetera — but that was bugger-all consolation.

I wept until, eventually, I fell asleep murmuring words I thought I had forgotten years ago. I was asking God (if he existed) to help me through this God-awful mess.

OCTOBER

I stared down at the road, breathing deeply to calm myself. It was discouragingly ineffective. All it succeeded in doing was making my head spin. Another 137 bus. I made a pact with myself. I would wait for two more buses to pass, then I would ring for a taxi and to hell with Sebastian.

The flat was unrecognizably tidy. In the last two months I had discovered unplumbed housewifely talents. Even the door handles which had languished unseen for years under a coating of muddy green were now discovered to be art nouveau masterpieces of curling shiny brass.

My flat had always smelled of paint – the rich lustrous odour of linseed oil, the tang of turpentine, the plastic-bucket whiff of acrylic. Now these familiar smells were overlaid with the more commonplace stink of vinyl emulsion and gloss. I hoped anxiously the smell would have dispersed before I returned. Before *we* returned. I would ask Sebastian to open the windows daily to air the second bedroom.

My suitcase was in the hall. It had been waiting there for nearly a week, packed with all the recommended paraphernalia. This morning, I had added only one item. Ned's letter to me. This, superstitiously, I had kept close by me ever since it arrived so many months ago. Only today, when the navy-blue bag in the hall suddenly stopped looking like an over-careful precaution (superfluous as a leaflet on nuclear household-defence) and began to assume an air of self-importance, did I take the letter from the drawer beside my bed and pack it along with the new nightdresses.

Even that was unnecessary really, because I could, if required, have recited the contents, more or less verbatim.

Maybe not the earlier pages. These dealt with facts rather than feelings: the tying up of the estate, the after-effects of the double tragedy in the village. Much of it I had known by the time Ned wrote, except for one thing. I was amazed to read that Ned had taken for granted, since schooldays virtually, that Roger was at least bi-sexual if not homosexual. After all, he had even warned me not to take Roger's pursuit too seriously. Now, he blamed himself bitterly for not having confronted his brother-in-law with the truth.

> . . . But he was so terribly ashamed, I sensed it would distress him immeasurably to learn that I knew. For years he had gone to such absurd lengths to hide his secret that it seemed cruel to confront him. I can only reproach myself now for a shortsightedness which begins to look unpleasantly like cowardice. But I never recognized the depth of his attachment to me. I can't believe my own obtuseness. The only feeble excuse I can offer is that I don't suppose I expect to inspire great love. The guilt — for not seeing or guessing — is almost unbearable.
>
> I lie awake asking myself what I could have done; how I could have averted this horrible waste of life. You tell me the same questions trouble you but, my dearest darling, truly you had no responsibility for this tragedy. Our love was incidental to the battle between brother and sister. I, on the other hand, as husband to one, friend to the other, seemed to have failed on all sides.

I wasn't surprised that Ned refused to benefit from his tragic inheritance. I was filled with admiration for his plans, however. The Dower House he put on the market immediately, and intended to follow that with the lands which comprised the Thornbeck Estate as soon as legally possible. The Manor he did not intend to sell, however. He was planning, if enough money was realized, to establish a charitable trust. To turn the house into a kind of therapy centre. A place of refuge and professional help for disturbed and 'at risk' families, *in the desperate hope that the Vaiseys' tragedy might, in the end, help avert another.*

The only part of the Estate he was not planning to sell was, I read with tears stinging my eyes, Lamp Lodge.

. . . It has brought so much happiness to me, with you, of course, my darling, but even as a child I was fond of the place. It would be foolish to let the present tragedy taint that, a tragedy which has no real connection with the Lodge. I shall look for another parish, but couldn't bear to lose this last small link with the past. I've no idea where I will end up.

I can't put into words the agony of not seeing you — of agreeing not to come and find you. But a priest I am, and must remain. Try to remain anyway. Marriage for me must, I suppose, be a triangular relationship with the Church occupying the third side. I would like to think of the Church as the base, supporting the inclination of the other two sides. I have learned that it can become the obstacle which drives them apart. And I have also learned how wrong it is for a wife to be forced into the demands of marriage to a priest — against the natural free inclinations of her spirit. We've both learned that in the bitterest possible of ways.

So I don't reproach you. Of course I don't. I can only be grateful for your honesty, and tell you again that I love you. That I will always love you. And that whatever terrible events were fomenting in the world outside, our three days together, imprisoned in the snow, are the most precious memory of my life.

The monks have agreed to take me back for a rather longer spell, once I have disentangled Roger's grotesque financial mismanagements. Never fear, I have no intention of actually joining them for good, but I'm in need of silence outside before I can begin to look for peace inside.

Yours as always,
Ned

He would not become a monk. I knew that with certainty. His was not the temperament. Moreover, after a few months back in the world, he would be gobbled up by some predatory woman. Of that I had no doubt either. He was too vulnerable, too trusting, too *lovable*, to remain alone for long. My only fear was that it might have happened already.

You see, I had no intention of letting Ned go. You have to be joking. As soon as it was practical, possible, I intended to travel up to Yorkshire, or to wherever else he might be by now, and find him. Perhaps it would be too late, perhaps I would find him and sense a change, but I would not give up without a fight.

Every night for months my recurrent painting nightmares had been replaced with a new one. In this dream, I would walk down to the Lodge — strangely it was always the Lodge, not the Dower House — looking for Ned. And a woman would open the door. The front door, which had never been opened. This stranger, would look at me with eyes as blank as a statue's and then call for her husband. And Ned would appear with a baby in his arms, and a toddler stumbling and clutching his trouser leg.

The dream was nonsensical, of course. We had only been apart since February. There would be no young Cowpers in the world yet. But I feared that woman, staring unrecognizingly at me as she stood in my house, in my doorway, beside my man. Because Ned was *mine*. And whether he had found another lover elsewhere or not, a part of him at least would always be mine.

At that moment a fierce band of pain winded me, and I collapsed into an armchair. That part of Ned was inside me now, and was unmistakably preparing to emerge.

Damn Sebastian — where was he?

This was the reason I had left Ned. This enormous bulge of life, signalling ever faster and more painfully its intention of entering the world.

The stuff about not being able to face the life of a vicar's wife was rubbish, pure fiction. I would have been ready to voyage to the end of the world as a missionary's wife if Ned wanted me to. I simply had to offer an excuse for disappearing.

How could I have told Ned I was pregnant? It wasn't his fault. Dear responsible Ned had asked if I was all right, and I had understood perfectly that what he really meant was whether it was safe to make love. Reckless, feckless me who had barely had a period in a year and, naïve as a convent schoolgirl, assumed she must therefore be infertile, had assured him it was.

As things stood now in the public view, a man had shot his sister and then himself in a cottage on his estate. A mildly titillating scandal because he owned the Manor and she was beautiful and married to a vicar – but no more. Soon forgotten. Add to that the vicar's pregnant mistress, however, outside whose cottage the shootings took place and I could have ensured Ned's notoriety in perpetuity.

But dear, loving, dutiful Ned would, I knew, have insisted on standing by me. The same rigid sense of duty which kept him married to Elizabeth for seven miserable years, would have ensured he married me as quickly as possible – even if it ruined him. As, without question, it would have done.

And what about the baby? Who would believe that the innocent child – tangible proof of our adultery – was not connected with the deaths?

A year later, in a different parish perhaps, I hoped things might be different. It was all I could hope for. I would go and look for Ned as soon as the infant could safely be left with my mother. And then I would have to see what happened. Only when – if – I could be sure he still wanted me would I tell him about the child, our child.

In the meantime, the waiting, the inaction, the increasing immobility had been torture. I had soon learned, having sent my letter of farewell to Ned, that I lacked the nobility of character required for happy martyrdom.

Sebastian had been my salvation. He had been so good to me over the long breathless summer months. I could never have anticipated the change in him, the softening, ever since he had learned I was pregnant.

'And you just knew?' he said with awe.

I nodded. 'On the day – when everything happened.'

I couldn't explain it. There was obviously no question of a period awaited and overdue. I had just woken up knowing I was pregnant as surely as I had known the bedroom curtains were blue. I've read since that some women do simply know instinctively. Some even claim they know the minute after they've made love. It took a couple of weeks with me, but the realization – pathetically in retrospect – preoccupied me far more than my formless premonition of the day's terrible events.

*

Sebastian had begun studying textbooks as though he were the father. In fact he studied so intently he might have been preparing to give birth himself. He had informed me when the foetus reached three inches long, five inches long, seven . . . He had monitored my diet with the strictness of a school matron. Over the summer, he had performed all kinds of complicated rituals to guess the sex of the child from listening to its heartbeat, to swinging a gold ring in front of my bulging belly. Then he forgot which sex was indicated by a clockwise spin, which by anticlockwise. He begged me to let him be with me for the birth. I could only be grateful, although I was honest about my feelings. Once the child was born, I warned him I intended to go and search for its father, for Ned. Sebastian had waved away such protestations as bourgeois notions of property and possession.

He was, he said, acting as my friend.

So where was my friend now? Was he at the gallery? I never doubted, even though he eschewed the formality of the private view, he would sneak in to look round as soon as he could. At least, in my present condition, he might feel it necessary to be kind to me, although I had never known anything compromise Sebastian's merciless objectivity. If indeed that's where he was. Should I ring Christopher at the gallery? Admittedly, the baby wasn't supposed to be due until Saturday, but Seb had promised not to be out of touch for more than a few hours.

When the buzzer sounded in the hall, I felt simultaneously faint with relief and furious that he expected me to let him in. I struggled out of the chair and stumbled across the room into the hall to press the intercom button.

'For God's sake, Seb!' I shouted into the receiver. 'Where the hell have you been – and where's your bloody key?'

'I'm . . . awfully sorry,' crackled a hesitant voice in my ear. 'B-but it's not, um, Seb. If you d-don't want to see me I shall –'

'Ned? *Ned,* I don't believe it . . .'

'I came down especially to see your exhibition. F-first day, but I was t-terribly upset. Someone had b-bought the painting. You know, that f-fishing one? I'd scraped t-together enough money . . . Anyway, no matter. The exhibition's a great success apparently. They're nearly all sold, you know.'

'Are they?' I said faintly, then I leaned against the wall gasping as a contraction clutched me in two. I should be timing them. How long since the last one?

'D-darling? I mean . . . I'm sorry. *Frankie* – are you all right?'

'Ned, I've got to ask you one question. Before you come up.'

'Ask whatever you l-like. But I've got to tell you one thing first. If you've settled down with this Sebastian, w-well, I'll do my best . . . But I love you, Frankie. I'm sorry. I've never stopped loving you.' He paused for a second and then rushed on. 'And there was this b-bloke wandering round your pictures this morning, looked like a tramp but he was arrogant as the art c-critic of the bloody *T-Times*. He condescended to say to his companion they were the best things you'd ever done. "B-bit sentimental," he said – I nearly hit him – "but that's only to be expected." "Why?" said the g-girl with him – Frankie, are you sure you're all right? You're making the most peculiar noises . . . "She lost her head c-completely over some man while she was up there," said the scruffy leather jacket, in what appeared to be p-pretty total disgust, "but at least it put life back into her brush. A year ago she'd copped out completely. Now, you look at that picture and see a bloke with a fishing rod. I see a f-fucking love affair. She never got over it either . . ." '

I tried to speak.

'No, don't interrupt just for a second *please*, sweetheart, because I thought, hell, if that was me he was talking about, and if you really loved me, surely we c-could make a go of it. You once gave me a lecture on how love was about t-taking as well as giving. Well I think you were right, and you may not have planned to marry into the Church but . . .'

Another shooting pain, and I gasped desperately, 'Ned!'

'. . . but I thought, hoped, you might re-c-consider and, hell, I'm rambling, aren't I? Not giving you a chance to get a word in . . .'

I could feel the sweat breaking out on my forehead. Much less than five minutes apart . . .

'By the way,' added Ned with hardly a pause, 'the chap running the gallery gave me the most p-peculiar look. As though he sort of recognized me ... No bad thing, really, because he was terribly helpful about t-telling me the quickest way to get here. What was that? Oh God, sorry, what did you want to ask me?'

'You've answered already,' I gasped. 'I'm pressing the button now, so you can come up. And Ned — I think you'd better hurry.'